◇ **THE VEILED SAGAS** ◇

WILD THINGS

For the wild part in all of us, the beast, the monster, the barbarian.

TABLE OF
CONTENTS

◆

Beyond the Veil, through space and time, is a realm undreamt of. A place with the glowing eyes of a sorceress and the quaking wails of titans, with the forgotten oaths of failed warlords and double-edged promises of cyberspace.

Breathe the dead air of the Underground, the stinking heat of Yarldom marshes and the mists of NeoAnglian shores. Lords and ladies live in twenty-first century luxury while backwater peasants die of the pox. In dire circumstances, the Exposed join this world. They come as the missing, the vanished, the forgotten... the nameless.

A realm of monsters and magic, of blades and bullets, where kings and heathens rule.

On the Wrong Side, nothing is right anymore.

These are The Veiled Sagas.

◆

THE
GOLDEN PELT

Jhonas entered the Pyanda Outpost after two months in the wilderness, windblown, dirty, and carrying a trio of deer kills on his back, just as a caravan was leaving through the gates.

A camel brayed, spraying spittle, as its rider dug his heals into its sides. The baggage piled between its humps was topped with a minuscule human rider hidden behind numerous wraps of fur and cotton. At the head of the baggage column, a mammoth wailed a long trumpeting call as its rider, a grizzled Jotunn that rocked back and forth on his seat, urged it forward.

The caravan of twelve camels and two mammoths left the outpost and rode southwards, into the rolling hills of the steppe. The leader of the convoy watched as Jhonas hurried through the gates and scoffed.

Jhonas ignored the riders as they passed. He kept his gaze ahead of him, his thick eyelashes blinking away the dust. His short black beard highlighted his handsome rugged face. He grunted and adjusted his pack. He had been trapping and hunting, but now he'd returned with his Yhasaq, carrying his cannon on his shoulder.

Pyanda Outpost was a low, squat Jotnar settlement at the edge of the steppe, south of the hills and forests of the true Siberian wilderness. Jhonas passed a huge barn that housed the mammoths, camels, and horses. The single windswept road was flanked by the inn, the smithy and garage, the grocer, and other necessities of a distant outpost. All the buildings were single-story, stocky structures of earth, wood, and metal.

Jotnar went about their daily lives, working and living the rugged lives of conflict—conflict with the elements, conflict with the Turkik or Scythian tribes to the south or the Slav kingdoms to the west, or conflict conflict among themselves. Between tribes, families, and sometimes between brothers. Now was peace time, children played, a smith worked his power hammer while the mechanic fixed a carryall.

"Hi, Jhonas," called a girl's voice.

"Greetings, Kharla," he replied, not meeting the girl's eyes.

Kharla, a young giantess, stood on the stoop of her family's diner. She handed drinks to two elders, who sat playing a dice game at a small table. The girl was certainly beautiful, a strong build, long coiled hair, dark tanned skin. She waved longingly at the hunter, hoping to catch his attention.

Jhonas hurried past towards the trading post, a large wooden structure across from the inn. The girl's desperation for a husband was as visible as mammoth tracks. Jhonas tried to take her interest as a compliment, but really he just wanted to be left alone.

He climbed the steps and entered the warm, musty structure. The walls were lined with hundreds of furs, pelts, and bones, along with a fireplace set against one wall, next to which sat several chairs layered with furs. A butcher shop was attached to one side. When the door rang, a voice called from the back. "I'll be right there!"

Ninn stepped out from the butcher shop, wiping blood from her arms with a rag. "Gods, Jhonas, you look like Hel!"

Ninn was a tall giantess with huge powerful arms, like the industrial cranes in UralHeim. She had deep blue irises that left her eyes white-less. She favoured her Hyborean side more than her Siberian. Her husband, Ail, was an expert tanner who handled the furs and skins. The wife handled the meat, and the husband, the skins. There was a joke in that somewhere.

"Your mother would have a heart attack at the sight of you!" she said.

Jhonas shrugged. *That's not what killed her,* he thought as he shouldered off his pack and placed his kills on the counter. Three prized deer, all killed with a pinprick pellet through their heart or eye. There were also a dozen foxes and sables, all trapped.

On a hunt, Jhonas carried his bolt-action cannon and a much smaller air-gun. If a deer was hit by the thumb-sized cannon cartridges, then there would be nothing left of it. The cannon was for unicorns, mammoths, and other megafauna.

Ninn began studying the kills. "There's beer in the fridge."

"Much obliged." Jhonas went around the counter and into the butchering room. Slabs of meat and other kills hung on hooks. The bloody musk in the air was suffocating. In a white ceramic ice box, Jhonas found bags of frozen meat and several bottles of Ural-Heim ale. *The Dwarg make decent beer at least.*

Only when Jhonas collapsed into the chair beside the fire did he realize how exhausted he was. He couldn't afford to feel it out in the wild. His legs and feet tingled, his back ached, and he was famished. If he could find a bed in town, he would sleep long and dreamlessly.

Ninn turned over the deer, nodding at the clean kills and substantial amount of meat. "Excellent as always. Yhasaq well accepted."

Jhonas nodded. *Yhasaq,* the tribute. Food, fur, and ivory, the three things expected from all Jotunn hunters. It once meant tribute that Siberians owed to the Hyborean government, then it meant the arrangements between tribal exchanges, until it was simply tribute brought in by hunters. Jhonas would be paid for the skins in credits that allowed him to buy food and ammunition.

"You know," said Ninn, turning over the sable pelts. "That Kharla girl has been asking about you."

Jhonas sipped his beer quietly.

"And Gruta's daughter *and* Voda's girl. I think Virdai was asking about you. Poor girl, widow before her time."

"You sound like my mother."

"Yeah," said Ninn. "And if she was alive, gods be good, she and your father would be saying the same thing. You ought to find a wife."

"I don't have time to get married," said Jhonas.

"Sure, you do! All you ever do is hunt and trap, maybe it's time to settle down. You choose to wander the wilds," she placed her huge fists on her wide hips. "Your mother would tell you to get a job leading caravans or save up enough to buy a herd, build a hall, marry a girl from a decent family. By the time you return on a convoy, you'd have a child."

Jhonas stared flatly, unamused at the prescription for his life.

"It's expected, Jhonas," said Ninn. "You're a young man. You have a good reputation. You aren't bad looking. You're strong. C'mon, whatever you're looking for out there isn't there. It's here. Settle down."

"And spend the rest of my life that way."

"Yes!"

That's exactly what I'm afraid of. Jhonas stood up, brushing himself off. His turga was stained and dirty. "I'll take my Yhasaq and be gone by morning. Give Ail my love."

Ninn frowned. "You're going to have to stop eventually, Jhonas. I don't want you dying out there or worse, coming back broken and without any options." She crossed around the counter, glaring at the young hunter. "Your mother asked me to watch over you."

Jhonas felt trapped between two bull unicorns. He starred up at Ninn. Her eyes bore into him. He didn't want to hear this. Not from Ninn, not from anyone. He was thirty-seven. He guessed the human equivalent was the early twenties. He still had plenty of good years ahead, assuming he survived the wilds unscathed. He swerved around her to gather his pack and cannon.

The door jingled, and two young Jotnar entered the warehouse. Both were several winters younger than Jhonas. Akil and Heras, a pair of impressive half-Hyboreans. Broad-chested, long legged with clean ox-skin turgas. Their blue eyes shone beneath their heavy brows.

Ninn gave a glare to Jhonas before turning to her customers.

"Greetings, Ninn!" said Heras. He nodded respectfully to Jhonas. His face was clean and tanned. "Greetings, Jhonas." Akil just grunted, the heavy Jotun looked as if he'd been carved from an ancient oak.

"What can I do for you boys?" asked Ninn.

"We would like a month's rations and five packs of bait," said Heras, bowing.

"What're you hunting?" asked Ninn.

Jhonas finished his beer and put it on the counter, his curiosity piqued.

"We just heard a rumour from some Rus traders, there's a golden lion to the north."

A smile crept across Jhonas's face. Ninn saw the look. "No. Jhonas, we aren't done."

"I am," said Jhonas, throwing on his pack and putting his cannon on his shoulder. He turned to the two other hunters. "Where did they say it was sighted?"

♦

Jhonas trekked north for two weeks. With one foot in front of the other, he crossed grasslands and rugged hill country towards the snowy northern forests, his fur-lined turga and mammoth skin cloak wrapped around him with his hood up. He was nearing the realms of eternal winter, where the gods and spirits still ruled. The snow had melted here, but soon it would be everywhere.

He circled the edge of a huge prairie, the spruce and pine forests on his left stretching on into the distance. A massive herd of reindeer grazed in the fields. Their antlers were like a field of ivory spikes and their breath formed a fog across the landscape. They paid the young Jotunn no mind. He was lost in his thoughts, haunted by Ninn's words.

He breathed the frosty air into his lungs. He had no desire to sign onto a caravan or start a family. He felt suffocated enough entering a town or outpost. Only out in the wilds could he breathe clearly.

He was free out here. He was able to be himself and alone with his thoughts. In the settlements, he felt trapped, confined to a box. Out here he only had himself to worry about. His heart ached at the very idea of settling down.

Yet… How many more years could he do this? How many more years could he survive out here? How many more years would the Yhasaq sustain him? What if he was hurt too badly to continue? Would he die alone in the wilds? Would he find his way back to a settlement, forever unable to provide for himself? Would

11

he vanish from the memories of those who knew him? Would he become a ghost of the forests?"

That last part doesn't sound so bad.

Jhonas paused, his calloused hand gripped the stock of his cannon. He looked out over the herd, meeting the eyes of a distant reindeer. His heart sank knowing how fragile his life was out here. He looked up at the huge blue sky, not a cloud visible for a million miles. Many Siberians and steppe peoples worshipped the blue sky as the highest of the gods. Jhonas's parents had been practitioners, but he never learned to be religious or spiritual.

"Maybe Ninn is right," he said to himself. *Maybe it will be time to settle down sooner than later.* If a bad hunt broke him, then he would be forced to find a new way of living. He would be forced to abandon the life of a hunter. He would be forced to build a life in a worse place than he was in right now.

The ground trembled beneath his feet. The trumpeting calls of the reindeer echoed across the plains as the field of antlers evaporated towards the east. Something burst out from the forests a mile across the slopes.

Jhonas narrowed his white-less black eyes.

A trio of steppe lions had launched themselves from the treeline. They were a blur of motion as they peeled off to catch a slow deer. The herd scattered, creating an earthquake in all directions. One of the lions had a bright golden-brown coat, speckled with black spots.

Found you.

Jhonas burst into a sprint, his long legs carrying him over the taiga plateau. The reindeer scattered around him, splitting like a river around a rock. He charged forward, seeing the lions half-a-mile out, converging on an old buck.

He swerved around the bend of a rise for a better position. He cleared the fleeing stampede. Over the next rise, he saw the golden lion had brought down the buck. It sunk its sabre-fangs deep into the reindeer's throat, silencing its braying call.

Jhonas dropped onto his stomach, reducing his profile. The hair of his mammoth cloak rippled with the grass, leaving him little more than a brown patch on the plateau. The pelt of a golden lion would be worth a fortune, more than enough to cover his Yhasaq for an entire year. It was a prize unmatched. He aimed his cannon, peering down its sight with expert precision. *One shot in the chest.* He exhaled and cocked the action.

The golden lion raised its gore-stained maw. Its ears perked up. It turned and bolted just as Jhonas pulled the trigger. The slug vanished into the distance. The thunderclap report echoed across the plains.

Fuck.

The lions fled for the cover of the forest.

Jhonas growled. *Too hasty. Should have waited for them to begin feasting.* He pursued, climbing back to his feet, each long stride carrying his massive bulk further. The lions bounded with their short wolfish tails between their legs. The distance to the forest's edge closed by the second.

Jhonas cursed and pushed harder, his legs burning. His black hair whipped behind his head. The lions crashed into the bushes and dispersed through the forest. Jhonas plunged into the tree line, black needle branches striking his face.

He dropped to a knee and aimed. *I can save most of the pelt with a shot in the flank.* It was dirty. The lion's golden-brown blur grew faint in the forest. Jhonas exhaled and fired.

The lion vanished behind a tree.

The slug bit into a pine, blowing out a section in a shower of fibres.

Jhonas cursed.

He pulled the action on the cannon and caught the hot brass in hand. The golden lion had escaped this time. He growled, grinding his teeth, and continued the long hunt.

♦

A week later, Jhonas still found nothing. He entered the snowy northern forests and the trail of the golden lion had gone cold. The wily beast had evaded Jhonas twice since the grassy plateaus. He knelt by a tree, finding a recent rupture in a pine tree, but no clues.

Instead, he found the tracks of Jotnar and humans in his travels. Clumsy fools, they left their shits and their fire pits for all to see.

Jhonas marched through the forests of Jotunheim. Black needled pines rose high above the Jotunn's head. To the south, he could often touch the tops of trees, but here he was dwarfed by the endless forests. His boots crunched in the snow. It was spring. Snow and storms still raged this time of year. The hunting season usually ran from October to February, the coldest months when creatures were forced to migrate southwards, but many predators hibernated during the darkest months.

Jhonas knelt by a patch of grass. The musk in the air told him he was finally on the right track. He paused and smiled… reaching to touch a tuft of golden fur left in a bush. *Finally.* He was within a few hours march from shelter. It had been a long trek and he craved warmth.

I just hope she's eager for guests.

His distracted mind was likely the culprit for his failure to catch the golden lion. He was still plagued by indecision over his future. *Gods, fuck you, Ninn.* She was worse than a mother, she was that aunt that tried to manage your life. He *could* court Kharla or some other maiden. Perhaps they could build a life together. He would treat a wife right, bring her Yhasaq, share in raising children, and build a good solid hall in the foothills of the Urals. Maybe it would be alright?

Then he thought about tending herds or guiding convoys through the steppe. Changing his movements from the predictability of the seasons and the elements to the whims and trends of merchants and the price of wool. Out in the wilds, in the lands of always winter, he could breathe free. He knew how to survive out here. *This is my world.* Could he trade it for the safety of a hall and a wife? Was it even safe? He met Jotnar who lost everything in bad deals and ventures. They were then forced to indenture themselves to Hyboreans, humans, and worse. They had to make serfs of themselves in their own mother country.

He breathed in the clean air, the frost tingling his lungs. He looked up at the titanic black pines. Their regal beauty as ancient and powerful as the gods themselves. As sacred as the pools and mountains.

I can't do this forever... He kept wrestling it in his mind. He was young, but he wouldn't be young forever. *Could I do this forever?* He didn't know the answer.

A smell drifted through the trees. His broad nose flared, and he could taste the metallic tang. *Blood.* He attached the bayonet, a barb of silvery steel at the tip of the barrel just in case.

He followed the scent with his cannon held low and defensively. He walked through the snow until he came to the corpse, two corpses actually. A horse and its human rider. Half-buried in snow beneath a pine tree, the bodies had cooled, but had yet to freeze.

15

A Rus trapper, he concluded based on the make of his clothing and the small pelts and bundles loaded onto the saddle. Both bodies completely eviscerated. Long claw strikes cut deep into the flesh, leaving splashes of red on the tree. The horse's belly had been opened, entrails scattered. The human was missing his head and chest.

The lion?

He knew it wasn't the lion immediately. The damage was too wild. Lions killed with a bite to the throat, slicing the windpipe. This was a frenzy of attacks. Jhonas brushed away some snow, revealing a three-toed foot print pressed into the ground. Long gouges from dagger-like claws pulled up the soil.

A snap echoed behind him.

Jhonas whipped around and was struck in the chest. He was slammed into the ground, the cannon slipping from his fingers. He groaned, touching his chest and finding three deep gashes in the front of his turga.

An ear-piercing squawk stung his ears.

Jhonas rolled away from the following attack just as a razor sharp beak slammed into the ground where his head had been.

A ten-foot-tall terror bird stood over him. It squawked again, puffing up the brown feathers that ran its long periscope neck. Its furry raptor legs ended in long black claws. A stripe of long sand-coloured feathers ran down its back from the crown of its head. It flared its vestigial wings in a mock intimidation display.

Jhonas cursed. Before he could roll away, it snapped its huge yellow beak.

He caught the attack on his forearm and felt his bone shudder from the force. He roared. The bite would have surely snapped a human in half.

The terror bird lifted one foot, claws ready to rip out his entrails while he was pinned. It was their hunting tactic. It was why the horse was eviscerated. He reacted with his years of hunting experience and rolled the instant the bird raised its leg.

They tumbled in an explosion of snow, needles, and feathers. Jhonas managed to free himself, sliding back on his heels like a skidding rhino. He saw his cannon across the clearing, on the opposite side of the recovering terror bird. He drew his small hatchet. Its meter-long ash haft ended with a small rectangular blade.

He grit his teeth, fighting through the pain in his arm.

Jhonas and the terror bird stared at each other. The wind began to howl through the trees, snow pelting Jhonas's face. A storm was coming. A springtime blizzard. He felt the hot wetness across his chest. The terror bird puffed its feathers, humming in its throat before squawking again.

Jhonas roared like a beast, spit flying from his teeth. "I am Jotunn!" He was of the wilds and the steppe. He hunted mammoths with his father, he ran with the great elk and the thunder falcons, he had battled wyrms and slayed unicorns. He would not be intimidated by some overblown winter chicken.

The two opponents charged in a blur of motion. They slammed together in a chaotic mess of feathers, snow, and howling noise before falling to the ground in a violent embrace, completely still. A long silence followed, silence only possible in a winter forest. The wind began to whistle, then blow, tugging at the black needle branches. The storm gathered to the northeast with thick grey clouds promising to bury the forest in a meter of snow. A clump of snow slid off a branch and landed with a crunch.

Jhonas groaned as he shoved off the bird's corpse. He gained a fresh gash across his right thigh and a cut over his left eye. The fracture in his arm and the gashes in his chest were the worst of it. None of it was lethal if he could find shelter soon.

His chest rose and fell with desperate gasps that puffed in front of his face. He brushed the sweaty strands of black hair out of his face. He pushed himself to his feet, feeling the pain in his chest and arm more acutely.

The axe was buried deep into the side of the bird's skull. The beast had bitten off more than it could swallow. He wrenched the bloody axe free.

Pain surged through Jhonas's arm. The wind stung his face. He felt the storm coming and he would have to hurry in order to reach his shelter. He gathered his missing belongings before pulling coil of rope and a long metal hook from his pack. *She always likes gifts.* He hooked the bird behind the wish bone and wrapped the rope around his uninjured arm.

He began trudging through the snow, towards the incoming storm, dragging the kill along with him. The snow began to fall, drifting into his face. *Gods bless me for the gift. Curse me with the price.*

◆

The door to the hall burst open, and Jhonas collapsed onto the floor, gasping like a dying fish. The wind scattered snow into the building until it was forced shut, silencing the noise. Jhonas's clothes were caked with snow, and he rolled onto his back, revealing a face frosted white with icicles.

A giantess stood over him with a look of disappointment. She was seven-and-a-half feet tall with a long turga dress and a woollen blanket over her shoulders. Her face was hard and narrow with deep brown eyes. Her black hair pulled into long braids down her back.

"By the gods," hissed Zora. "Fine. Fine. You can stay."

"Thank—you—" gasped Jhonas, his breath coming as a

jet of steam. He yanked the rope to show Zora the dead terror bird, half crusted with snow and frozen blood. "I brought you a gift."

Zora sighed, her beautiful narrow features almost smiling. "Come on, let's get you out of those clothes." She helped him up. He winced when she touched his arm. "Gods. Again?! You fucking deserve it. Stumbling around like you own the place. I hope it hurt." Jhonas was too cold and exhausted to reply.

Zora guided him to the hearth at the centre of her hall. The logs crackled and snapped, warming the immense wooden building.

Slowly, she helped peel off his mammoth cloak and his ice-crusted turga. Piece by piece, she freed him from his frozen clothes until he was completely naked and sitting by the fire, wrapped in her blanket.

"You can stay the night," said Zora, placing his clothes over a rack by the hearth, steam rising from the fabric. "The storm will clear by morning."

"So says the gods?"

"So says anyone with good sense to know what springtime in the north means."

Zora was what one would call a witch. A giantess with a deep connection with the wilds, the spirits, the gods, and the natural world. She was a healer, a guide, and a priestess to the old ways. She was no sorcerer, but she knew the deeper magics of the world.

Jhonas had known her all his life. Though she was over twenty years his senior, they always had a rugged mutual understanding. The kind of relationship you develop when you see each other maybe twice a year with no one around for a hundred miles.

The hall was a long single structure with the hearth in the centre, tripods and various cauldrons hanging over the fire. The stone floors were covered in animal skins and the walls were lined with crowded shelves. Dominating the room was the massive skull of a long dead mammoth. Its long-curved tusks filled up the rafters. Its dead eyes watched Jhonas.

It had been the most violent bull to ever plague the region. A creature that destroyed villages and decimated herds. They called it Ygor, the evil one. It had taken almost fifty warriors to bring it down, a dozen dying in the attempt.

Jhonas would know. He had been there with his father. That was about three years before both his parents died of lung rot. Ygor was a curse on the Jotnar and, in his death, the curse had spread to everyone else.

Zora knelt by his side, looking at his wounds. His own blood was crusted across his wide bristly chest. He clutched his fractured arm; the tingling pain went all the way to his fingertips. His beard and hair dripped with melting frost. She snatched his arm, sending spikes of pain up to his fingertips. She looked at his gored chest and shook her head. She grabbed a basket and filled it with various items from her shelves. "Fool of a Jotunn," she hissed.

"At least you're honest."

She glared. Their dark white-less eyes met for a moment. "I didn't expect you this time of year," said Zora.

Jhonas shrugged. "Been tracking a golden lion."

"Yeah?" said Zora. "You and every other asshole for a thousand miles. I can hear it every time I go to clear the snow."

"I've seen it."

"I know," said Zora, kneeling next to him. "They all stumble like drunken children." She smeared green paste over his chest and blue paste over his forearm. "You're probably the only one who has a chance."

He nodded. It was the closest thing to a compliment that Zora was capable of.

"That's not why you're this far north out of season," she looked into his eyes as she slapped an adhesive bandage over the cut above his eye. "You're running from something." She looked into his eyes like she could read his mind. "The little hunter running from civilization. Running from responsibilities and a promising future *and* a fat wife with big teats."

Jhonas stared flatly, unimpressed with her skills of deduction. She could read him like a book, but Jhonas never felt the need to guard himself around her. *She knows the question, but does she have any answers?*

A kettle whistled, and Zora poured a cup of herbal tea. "Drink. It'll help."

It tasted like dirt and twigs, but he welcomed the warmth. He felt the pain subside substantially.

A pause followed and Jhonas felt himself speaking more than he had in months. "I don't know what to do," said Jhonas. "I feel trapped between two charging bulls. I know what is expected of me. I know what I should do. I just don't know if it's for me. I know what my parents would want. I want to do right by their memory."

Zora listened as she wove a brace around his arm. Sturdy cords secured his fractured bones. It was an old technique, allowing him use of his arm while his dense Jotunn musculature held his bones together.

"Can a Jotunn hunt for the rest of his days? If I keep as I am, I will grow slow and die out here. I'll end up as a ghost of the wilds."

"Would you really hate that so much?" said Zora, without

looking up from her work. Jhonas didn't answer. Zora wiped her hands on the hem of her dress. The hearth crackled and sent sparks up towards the skull of Ygor. The winds howled outside, shuddering against the hall.

Jhonas waited desperate for her response. His eyes big and pleading.

"I can't guide you on this, little hunter," said Zora. "*This* is not of the gods or wilds. This is the habits of civilized Jotnar."

He nodded, disappointed. "Thank you for listening. It did help."

"Oh, Jhonas," she put a hand on his cheek. "You mistake me. *We* are not civilized Jotnar. Who gives a damn what those in the towns and settlements think? We are of the wilds. We are closer to the gods that they can even dream. If you were to settle down to marry and run caravans, you'd turn to drink within a year and throw yourself off a mountain within a decade. You are not of that life and you know it."

She kissed him full on the lips. She smelled of herbs and hearth smoke, the true scent of a giantess.

"You have a long life ahead of you, the gods will give you as much," she said after breaking the kiss. "Do not feel the weight others give you. Torturing yourself for another's dream is a mistake. What about your own dreams? Your own will? You owe the civilized world nothing. It just takes."

He took her hand into his. Her calloused fingers interlaced with his own. He looked into her eyes and realized something: he already had a hall to return to. He didn't need anything else.

She nodded. "I'll get you some food."

"I don't need to eat right now."

She smiled. "Good," and slammed her lips against his.

He turned and wrapped his arms around her waist. She pulled the wool blanket around them. He dug his chin under her jaw, kissing her throat. Their cords of muscle slackened and trembled.

"Don't get too excited," said Zora. "I'm not fixing that arm again."

He smiled. He wrapped his injured hand around her throat and pinned her to the floor. Her smile grew wider. Her long black hair cascaded over a white fur pelt. They were lost in a soft world of earthy skins.

Jhonas unwrapped Zora from her turga, revealing her body. Her hard lithe muscles and coppery dark skin. She dragged her nails across his back as he buried his face into her breasts, biting them tenderly. Her legs wrapped around his waist as she sighed, the hair on them pricking him.

The embers of the hearth crackled and dimmed as the blizzard raged outside.

♦

In the morning, Jhonas ate a second helping of porridge. He threw a handful of bird's eggs into his mouth, popping them like candy and grinding the shells between his molars.

Zora had begun cleaning the terror bird on a cleared section of floor. Blood and entrails splattered the floorboards.

Jhonas finished his breakfast and prepared to leave, wrapping himself in his warm turga and mammoth skin cloak. His arm already felt better, usable, if a little tender. It would take a month to fully heal.

"Until next time," said Jhonas, shoulder his bag and bolt-action cannon.

"I hope you'll be less annoying," she teased without looking up. Jhonas chuckled. "See you next year, little hunter."

"Gods be with you, Zora."

"They always are."

♦

Jhonas trekked north for another few days before being diverted westward by the occasional lion scat. He found himself far more focused and pleased with his progress. He had caught several small deer for his meals. Each night brought pleasant dreamless sleep.

Within a fortnight of leaving Zora's hall, he could see peaks of the Urals in the distance, a series of blue spires like the teeth of a wolf. The mountains housed the dwarven nation of Ural-Heim, a client state of Jotunheim for two centuries. The Dwargs kept to the mountains, the Jotnar kept to the forests and plains.

Jhonas felt lighter since his stay with Zora. She was right. *I have nothing to prove. No one is forcing me into anything.* He had his places to return to each year. The oppressive future of caravans and marriage wasn't inevitable. The expectation and guilt only existed so long as he let it. He was only punishing himself for his memory of parents long dead. He cherished his memories of them, but they did not determine his future.

He knelt in the snow. A big cat print was pressed into the soft snow. It was fresh. He could smell the musk of yellow snow a few meters ahead. It was his best clue in days.

He gripped his cannon and hurried low to the ground. Before he moved ten yards he heard a feral yowl echoing through the forest.

Jhonas doubled his pace.

◆

Jhonas drew back a snow-covered branch.

His black eyes peered through the foliage, searching for the howls.

He found a pit trap made out of an old, forgotten Dwarg larder. The walls of the shaft dug deep into the frozen soil. The entrance had been covered with a lattice of saplings, leaves, dirt, and snow; it was impossible to detect. Then the golden lion had been lured by a bloody piece of meat hanging from a branch above.

Jhonas left the cover of the tree, cannon in hand, and crept towards the shaft. He looked down and found the golden-brown shoulders of the lion. It pawed and scratched at the walls, trying to find a footing. It bared its teeth and growled up at the giant.

After over a month of tracking, here it was, easy as a fish in a barrel... but Jhonas knew this was wrong. His stomach twisted at the sight of the lion's bared fangs. It roared, crying to its pack for help. He saw the criss-crossing scars across his muzzle and front quarters. The regal beast was trapped.

It was wrong to execute the lion like this.

A beast like this deserves to die hunted, not executed in a trap.

Jhonas slung his cannon over his shoulder. He glanced around before seeing a log of just the right length. He trudged through the snow before dragging it towards the pit... which was when he realized his mistake.

The smell of campfire smoke preceded the sound of boots crunching in the snow.

Jhonas dropped the log and rose to his full height. He was met with two bayonets held uncomfortably close to his chest. Akil and Heras looked like shit with their crisp clean turgas reduced to dirty rags, their faces gaunt and hungry.

"What do you think you're doing?" hissed Heras.

"I'd ask you the same question," said Jhonas. "Traps? What kind of coward traps a beast like that? It deserves to be free until the last moment."

"Shut up!" barked Heras. "We caught it. We've been out here a month with nothing to show for it!"

"No," said Jhonas. "You can still go home with your pride."

Akil held the bayonet inches from Jhonas's throat. Both Jotnar had been through hell trying to catch this lion.

"Just leave it be," said Jhonas. "Go home. There's no shame in that."

"You just want it for yourself!" Heras roared.

"You're pathetic. Both of you."

"Shut up!" Heras drove his bayonet forward. Jhonas took the blade in the shoulder. He grunted and took hold of the weapon. Akil thrust his weapon, but Jhonas used Heras's weapon to parry away the second attack and kicked Heras in the front, knocking him back.

Jhonas wrenched the bayonet from his shoulder and spun it in hand, charging Akil as he resumed the attack. Two angry bulls charged, their cannons sparking off each other, metal clanging as they parried and reposted the bayonets. Akil was larger and stronger than Jhonas, but lacked the hunter's experience. Jhonas saw his opening and slammed the bayonet into Akil's foot. Blood spurted onto snow. Jhonas brought the stock up into Akil's jaw. The huge Jotunn crashed to the ground with the weight of a falling tree.

Heras roared, diving into Jhonas with a wild haymaker. Jhonas took the strike in the jaw, stumbling back. He held onto the cannon and swung it wide.

Heras caught the firearm. "Fucking Sib."

"Oh, just shut up," grunted Jhonas, he slammed his head into Heras. He threw aside the cannon and slammed his fist into Heras's face. They traded punches back and forth, the air crashing with each heavy blow. Jotunn fists like battering rams against bone walls.

Heras stumbled back, his face bleeding in half a dozen places, one eye half-closed. Jhonas looked no better. Their breaths puffed in jets of steam. Heras growled. His blue eyes saw a boulder a few feet away.

"Don't do it," warned Jhonas.

Heras growled and went for the boulder, digging his fingers beneath the stone. With veins bulging in his forehead, he hefted it over his head, roaring wordlessly like a wild animal. He moved to crush Jhonas.

Jhonas gritted his teeth, moving faster than the half-Hyborean, and took hold of the discarded log. He swung it hard in a wide arc, and it exploded into woodchips against Heras's ribs. The Jotunn screamed as the boulder fell and pinned him under it.

The crunch of Heras's upper body reminded Jhonas too much of a smashed melon.

Jhonas's chest heaved, as he wiped the blood from his face. "Pathetic." His body vibrated with adrenaline. He checked the wound in his shoulder and concluded it was minor. He rolled his shoulder, working the feeling through his arm. The blood was already coagulating to seal the wound.

A snarl and howl echoed from the underground shaft.

Jhonas found another fallen tree a few dozen yards away. When he returned, Akil was gone. There was nothing left but a few splashes of red and the Jotunn's imprint in the snow. Jhonas wondered what stories Akil would tell. *What lies?* Perhaps it would be better to stay away from civilization for a spell.

Jhonas lowered the log into the pit, creating a rudimentary ladder. He gathered his belongings and left the scene. It would be an interesting story for the next outpost he visited. He would have a lot of explaining to do.

He glanced back at the clearing. The golden lion stood next to Heras's corpse. It sniffed the bloody mess.

It looked up with molten gold eyes. Jhonas kept very still.

An indescribable moment of mutual understanding passed between the Jotunn and the beast. It ran its tongue across its teeth before bounding off into the forest.

Next time.

Jhonas turned and began a long trek to the next outpost, content, a small smile on his face.

—The End—

CHALLENGE

The Orc Burrow was housed in the ruined remains of a temple, or church, or whatever the humans called it. The roof had collapsed in the distant pass. The broken glass of the windows still cluttered the corners, the walls were shattered, and the benches were used up for firewood.

The remains were a remarkable hollow animal. A rib cage of wooden pillars still formed the long hall, the ends still intact. The front door hung on rusted hinges. The rear wall of the church was now the front of the boss's shack. Above the door was the humans' dead god with its arms pinned to a cross. Its head had been replaced with an ugly monster glyph years prior.

The bell tower leaned precariously on its side. The bell remained, but it was now etched with strange and crude sigils. A single light flickered in the window of the tower.

A pair of orcs approached the Burrow and climbed the steps. A mob of their fellow clanbrothers followed them, the various huts and shacks that occupied the surrounding terrain emptied to see what was about to happen.

The thinner of the lead pair, Wyre, smiled with his polished white, jagged fangs. His second, his brood-brother, Brik, followed closely behind.

Wyre looked up. The sky was dank and grey, as if the gods promised rain soon. A crow sat on top of the bell tower. It cried at Wyre before flying off into the nearby trees.

Wyre knew, *Today is the day I die.*

He marched on into the ruined church, the realm of their Boss. Boss Narrok. Narrok Silvereyes. Narrok the Crusher. *Narrok the Coward*, thought Wyre.

Wyre stood in the church's doorway. His clawed hand felt the warm grip of his blade.

His blade was his only possession of note. Anything else would have been taken by the bosses. A four-foot-long blade of slightly curved and razor-sharp metal. Strong and flexible with an extended handle almost a foot and a half long. A bizarre blade for an orc. Wyre made it work.

Wyre wore a vest of blue denim, salvaged from human leavings, and a pair of billowing red trousers tied with a belt. A dog skin draped across his shoulder. A single bone spike pierced through his pointed ear.

His black, watery eyes zeroed in on the Boss's hut. A warm glow danced between the ragged curtains of the doorway.

He marched forward, Brik at his side. His brother was thicker at the chest and shoulders than Wyre, something he had been jealous of for a very long time. Brik was raw power. Wyre was forced to be smarter. A trickster. A cunning killer.

And because he was smarter, Wyre and Brik had become the unspoken leaders of the runts, the young orcs who begged and died at the behest of the Bosses and Captains.

They were a great team.

Things needed to change.

Some things needed to end.

All things gotta end.

The crowd gathered further. Orcish faces occupied the spaces between the rib cage of the Burrow. Runts and boys of all sizes watched. The captains, or caps, the minor mob leaders, stood a head or so above the rest.

Everyone watched with quiet anticipation.

Wyre stood in the centre of the former church. The stone floor polished smooth with generations of occupiers. It was cold beneath his bare feet.

An ancient pale hound chained to the dais lifted up an ear. Its lazy eye considered barking at the young orcling, but realized it was too much effort and went back to sleep.

Wyre inhaled, gathering as much air as he could muster. This was it. This was everything. He roared, "My name is Wyre! Brother of Brik. Runtboss of the SilverMutt Clan. I have come to challenge Boss Narrok Silvereyes for the SilverMutt Clan!"

There was a ripple of whispers throughout the audience. Orcs big and small looked at one another in amazement. Once the initial wave of murmurs hushed, every head turned towards the Boss's hut. A single hooded figure could be seen in the dark tower overlooking the Burrow.

A slow beat of footfalls creaked on the floorboards of the dais. A huge shadow overwhelmed the low light within the hut.

Boss Narrok stepped out on to the dais. At almost seven feet tall, he was the biggest monster in the clan, and therefore the leader. A walking mountain of green flesh. Arms like front loaders, legs like tree trunks, and a head built like a steel crate. The boss wore only a skirt of pale dog skins and the skull of a dog as his belt buckle. His wide chest was rippled like cables beneath pine-green leather.

He carried his beastly cleaver on his shoulder. Three feet of pure black steel with a silvery edge to match Narrok's, bizarre-ly-coloured, bright silver eyes. He threw back his head in a boom-ing deep laugh. "You!? You!? A runtboss? Who in the Great Green ever thought of something so stupid!

Laughter echoed through the crowd. Mostly half-hearted to appease Boss Narrok. None of the smallest runts, the majority of the clan, cracked even a smile.

Boss Narrok stepped down from the dais, still laughing, "What kind of focking whelp thinks he can challenge me! Get out of here, boy. Before I smash your skull and use it for a piss pot."

Wyre chuckled. "How can you use my skull for a piss pots when it's crushed to pieces?" *Step one: Make Him Mad.*

Narrok's silver eyes went wide. He bared his teeth in a vicious threat. The dozens of runts cackled with roaring laughter, while the caps and their immediate subordinates observed total silence. It was a stupid, pointless joke, but any gab taken at the boss's expense was an insulting defiance.

"You little git!" barked the boss. "You are nothing! Who are you to challenge me?!"

"I am nothing because this clan is nothing! We live in dirt and live off meagre hunts. If I am nothing, it is because we have all become nothing! And a nothing can challenge the Boss of Nothing!"

Narrok's patience ended. He roared, "Deff, Vav, Jaaz! Rip this shit apart."

Three of the largest members of the clan rushed forward.

A single clear tone echoed across the burrow. Crows scattered from the nearby trees. Everyone froze and looked up.

The clan's shaman, OldMutt, stood at the top of the bell tower. He held a dog's skull in his gnarled hand. His hooded cloak of dog skins shadowed his wrinkled green face. He struck it against the bell again, another tone piercing the air.

He cackled a single word: "Dishonour!"

The meaning was simple. If Boss Narrok dismissed the challenge and disrespected the corresponding traditions, he would be dishonoured.

Narrok's silver eyes narrowed at the Elder, then at Wyre. His huge shoulders sank. He set the tip of the cleaver against the ground.

Wyre's entire body shook with nervous anticipation. *Step Two: Compel the challenge to be accepted.*

Those were the two easy steps.

Wyre leaned to Brik. "Ready?"

His brother sighed. "Yeah, let's get this over with. I'd rather bury your corpse before it gets too dark out."

"Don't be so negative. It's unbecoming."

Narrok roared, "Fine, Fine! What's your issue, boy?!"

"You let this clan lie in rabble and dirt! You let us live in misery! You bully and abuse this clan like a child's toy. I won't stand it!" Wyre raised his long blade at the monstrous boss. "I will take this clan and raise us to greatness!"

Wyre had seen enough brothers killing each other. Enough pathetic hunts, enough boys lying in the dirt bleeding for daring to have a piece of food in sight of anyone else. Orcs were violent. *Fighting is all any of us has.* It did not have to be this way. *We don't have to fight ourselves. We can conquer. We can loot. We can be great.*

As the old Great Hordes were.

Step Three: Get support.

Narrok laughed. "Ha! That's it? HA! And who supports this claim? Who supports this runtboss!?"

Brik stepped forward, arms crossed. "I do. A clan that does nothing is nothing. We are dirt." He pointed at Narrok. "We are dirt because of you!"

Brik crossed to one side of the dirty arena to the other, arms raised. "Brothers! We cannot let this sad boss have us roll in the dirt and call it greatness! We must fight! We must hunt! I ask you! Do you support my brood-brother, Wyre!"

The runts shrieked and cackled in agreement. Their thin and emaciated frames were visible proof of the vile bleakness of their existence. Other boys, the worst off, the ones with poor clothes and poorer meals, joined in the chorus of support, peeling supporters away from the captains.

A clan was a pyramid. The weakest and most numerous runts and boys were at the bottom, followed by caps in the middle, and the boss on top. Only the fear of reprisal, fear of an unwinnable battle, fear of the bosses kept order in place.

Shaman OldMutt rang the bell again as his agreement that the challenge was accepted and the support genuine.

There was only one course of action for Boss Narrok.

Now comes the hard part, thought Wyre. *Step four: Fight.*

Boss Narrok stepped off the dais. "Fine. Let's get this over with." His heavy footfalls shook the wreckage of the church. He was twice Wyre's weight and a full foot and a half taller. He dragged his cleaver against the ground. Metal screeched against stone.

"This ain't gonna go well," whispered Brik. "You're not that fast."

"Real fuckin' encouraging, brother," said Wyre. He shouldered off his vest and dog skins, dropping the heavy fabric to the ground. He stretched the muscles across his chest and shoulders. He could do this. *Maybe?*

34

Wyre's blade was longer, and he was faster than Narrok. It was his only hope. He held up his blade in both hands for a low guard, as to parry and counter quickly.

Narrok held up his cleaver in an offensive guard, his stance wide and secure. He grinned.

Wind blew across the Burrow. Leaves tumbled across the dusty square in dancing spirals. Scrap metal from a nearby hut shuddered and the bell tower creaked. The grey sky watched above. The gods would be silent on the proceedings. The gods had forgotten them a long time ago.

Everything was silent.

The entire clan watched.

Narrok burst from his position, cleaver raised. He slammed it down at Wyre's head. Wyre parried it away and slid to the side. He jabbed at Narrok's shoulder and was rewarded by an ear-piercing roar.

Red-purple blood leaked down Narrok's bicep.

The boss wasn't expecting that.

Narrok turned to bring his cleaver down again. Wyre slid back on his heels, trading his sword between hands. Narrok was mad now. He had expected this fight to already be over.

Wyre smirked, just to annoy the boss.

Narrok roared and launched himself back at Wyre, a mountain of flesh barrelling right at the boy. Wyre used his speed and size against Narrok, circling and weaving around the great monster. He caught the cleaver against his blade and guided it away. Each heavy clash sent vibrations up Wyre's arms. He thrust quickly and retreated. He couldn't be greedy.

After another exchange, Wyre slid backwards again, leaving another two gashes on the Boss's arms and shoulders. Strings of saliva hung from Narrok's fangs. Tiny ribbons of red-purple blood rolled down his green skin.

Wyre's arms were shaking. He couldn't continue this for long. Boss Narrok was too strong, and Wyre was already getting tired.

Narrok attacked again.

Wyre parried again and he just slid backwards. He was cornered against one of the pillars of the church. An invitation.

Narrok charged forward. Wyre waited before the last second and dove to the side. Narrok slammed into the pillar, bricks shattering and tumbling over him. He growled before he could rise.

Wyre laughed. "Is this your boss?! Is this your leader?! The one to lead us?" Instead of attacking, as he probably should have, he raised his arms to the tribe. "Is this what we are? Just mindless monsters attacking everything in sight? Is this all we are?!"

Narrok snarled and got to his feet, dust stuck to bleeding wounds. Rubble rolled off his wide shoulders. His silver eyes were tiny within his brow. He launched himself at Wyre like a mad dog.

Wyre twisted out of the way, barely in time. He didn't have the leverage to parry away the cleaver, and it bit into his blade. Exactly what Wyre was trying to avoid. Narrok used his mass against Wyre. The sheer force locked the blades together and Wyre couldn't maneuver. He slid back on his heels.

Narrok grinned. "Weak."

He shoved with the force of a hurricane. Wyre lost his footing and tumbled across the ground.

Narrok roared and smashed his blade downwards. Wyre

rolled away. The cleaver bit into the ground, sending chips of stone flying. Wyre reached for his blade, his fingers almost grazing the handle.

Narrok slammed his foot into Wyre's side. The boy tumbled across the burrow before slamming into a pillar. His chest seized.

Narrok laughed. Wyre wiped the dust from his eyes. Narrok loomed over the runtling, a hulking shadow against the grey sky. His chest heaved with each breath. He laughed. "Pathetic runt."

Wyre gripped a handful of broken glass and dust.

Boss Narrok reached to lift Wyre by the throat.

Wyre slammed the fistful of glass into Narrok's silver eyes. Narrok dropped him, screaming, and stumbling back with earthshaking footfalls. He clawed at his bleeding eyes.

Wyre used the opening. He spun on his arms and kicked out the Boss's left leg. Narrok yelled as he lost his balance and crashed to the ground. *Top heavy beast.*

Wyre didn't waste time. He got to his feet and kicked Narrok across the jaw. Pain shot up his foot.

Wyre grabbed his blade. "Brothers! All of you! There is a human village thirty miles to the north, just sitting there. Sitting! Fat and rich! We've spent all our lives scavenging off their leavings and biting at each other. I say we should storm those fucking humies and take what is ours!"

Murmurs rose throughout the entire tribe. They weighed the options. If they exposed the tribe to the humans, they could suffer horrible repercussions. They could be exterminated like rats.

Wyre raised his blade. "We can either live like animals or we can be conquerors!"

"Stupid runt," growled a voice behind him.

A force slammed into Wyre's back and crashed with him onto the floor. The weight threatened to crush Wyre's body. Narrok lifted Wyre and slammed him against the ground. Wyre felt a crack and gasped for air.

He twisted in Narrok's grip, managing to free one arm. He jabbed his clawed fingers into Narrok's eyes. He screamed as tears and blood streamed of his already very damaged sockets. His grip squeezed harder, trying to crush Wyre with sheer mass.

Wyre jerked his hand back. Narrok shrieked and slammed Wyre against the ground. Wyre wheezed; everything hurt. Narrok stomped backwards, clutching his eyes as blood poured from between his fingers.

Wyre raised his hand. In his fingers he held one of Narrok Silvereyes' dripping eyeballs. The runts and boys exploded into cheers and war cries. One of Narrok's loyalists cried, "Bad form! Bad form! Mediocre!"

OldMutt nodded approval from the bell tower. It was a rude attack, but for a runt fighting a Boss, tradition allowed such dirty tactics for such unequal fights.

Wyre slowly got to his feet, clutching his side. He tossed the eyeball to the side. Brik rushed to him with water. He splashed it across his face and gulped it down greedily.

"You've done it," said Brik.

"Almost. I need to end it."

Boss Narrok gasped and roared with pain. Blood poured down his face, the huge mountain of green muscle on the verge of sobbing. Loyalists came to his aid with water and bandages.

Narrok roared and swatted them to the side. "I'll kill you! I'll focking kill you, runtboss!"

Wyre shoved Brik to the side. He collected his blade, barely managing to lift it with one hand. His ribs throbbed with blinding pain. Wyre wiped his face, accidentally streaking Narrok's blood across his mouth. His legs quaked.

The loyalists brought Narrok his cleaver, but he refused. "I'll rip you limb from limb, whelp!"

Narrok charged.

Wyre grit his teeth, his entire body seemed to shutter with pain. He held his position, adopting a straight back, one-handed stance. He'd seen pictures of humans in a stance like this. *Fencing, they called it.*

Narrok hurtled towards Wyre like an avalanche, his remaining silver eye barely visible in his furious and bloodied scowl.

Wyre exhaled, calming his aching pain into perfect focus.

Now.

With a single precise swipe, Wyre slashed upwards and towards the left. Red-purple blood splattered across the church ground. Narrok tumbled into a pillar. When the dust cleared, Narrok was on his back clutching his eyes. He kicked and screamed like an overgrown human child.

The entire tribe roared with either screams of dismay or cries of approval.

Narrok Silvereyes had been reduced to Narrok No-Eyes.

The great boss thrashed and kicked. "Where are you? Where are you? I'll kill you! I'll focking kill you!" He pawed like a clumsy bear searching for his prey. "Where is he?"

Wyre's whole body shuttered. *I actually did it.*

The pain in his side redoubled. Wyre fell to one knee. *What's wrong with me?* He'd broken ribs before, but never like this. His body still pulsed with adrenaline. He used his blade to prop himself back to his feet. He stared at one hand, seeing the fingers fall in and out of focus.

What in the Great Green is happening to me?

Wyre's supporters burst into cheers. Now a large majority of the tribe agreed. They would no longer be these backwoods animals living off scraps. They wouldn't need to bully and abuse each other. They would take what was theirs because it was theirs to take. Wyre raised his blade. "We will be like the Great Hordes of Old!" he screamed.

"RAAAAAAAAHH!!" roared the SilverMutt Clan.

Wyre looked to Brik, who had a neutral expression. No excitement. No pride. He had always been the quiet of the pair, but this was different. Wyre was trembling, unable to move.

Brik?

Wyre's tongue felt dull and fuzzy in his mouth.

"Fool… Fool… Cursing focking fool…" whimpered Narrok on the ground. Wyre stumbled over to him through his growing delirium, blade ready to end this. The challenge would not end until one of them was dead.

Boss Narrok still clutched his face. "You focking fool, you'll kill them all…"

"No Narrok, I'm freeing them." The words slurred in Wyre's mouth.

"You're dooming them. Attacking the humies is suicide.

Attack one, the rest of the bloody country hunts us down. We live when they ignore us. We live when we hide." He pulled back his massive hands to reveal the blinded and bloodied mess that had been his eyes. "We live when we are nothing."

"Living as nothing is not worth living."

Narrok growled. "You fool."

"You won't have that to worry about anymore."

"No?"

Wyre raised his blade to pierce Narrok's heart. Before he could bring it down, he felt his entire body seize. His back constricted like a metal cord. He gasped for air. He couldn't move. Wyre looked at Brik at the last second. Brik averted his eyes, his frown full of shame.

No.

A hand grasped his ankle.

The blind Narrok grinned as blood streamed down his cheeks.

Before Wyre could do anything Narrok thrashed him against the ground like a rag doll. Each crash sent new waves of throbbing pain through Wyre's body. He stopped feeling anything after the third crash. His face smashed against the ground. He saw Brik turn away and disappear into the crowd. Bones cracked and crunched against the ground. The crowd winced at each crash.

Narrok dropped Wyre's broken body against the ground. Wyre wheezed. He knew most of his ribs were broken, his cheek crushed, jaw dislocated, and his left arm broken in three places. His lower leg shattered where Narrok had gripped him and slapped him against the ground. Blood gurgled from his cracked lips. He was only vaguely aware of his surroundings. The shrieking runts and *boys completely shattered.*

Brik was gone. Ashamed of what he'd done to keep the clan safe from his brother's ambition.

OldMutt had vanished from the top of the bell tower and returned to his lair.

Narrok rose unsteadily to his feet. He pressed his foot onto what he judged to be Wyre's chest. Wyre gasped for air as he felt the life leaking out of him.

Narrok looked down. "Boy, you think I didn't know you'd be coming. You thought I didn't know?"

Wyre wheezed, "Didn't think I'd be that crafty, did you?"

Narrok wiped the blood leaking down his face. "Nah, I didn't. Focking little monster. We knew what you were planning. We couldn't let you lead the clan to its death."

Wyre's eyes gazed up towards the sky. His brood-brother betrayed him. The sickening disgust in Wyre's heart was beyond the pain of his body. He knew what had happened. *The water.* Wyre spat a glob of blood. *Curse you, brother. May the Great Green see you bleed.*

"Fock off, runtboss." Narrok leaned in. Wyre's sternum crumpled under his immense weight like a collection of wet sticks.

◆

With the challenge over, the Burrow was silent. The entire clan stared, trying to figure out what had just happened.

To them, Narrok had won. Wyre's shattered body stilled against the church ground. A trio of remaining loyalists rushed forwards. One helped bind Narrok's wounds, another wrapped a strip of fabric across his eyes. Sitting on the church dais, Narrok stroked his ancient hound's ears. The dull creature whimpered at its master's pain.

Narrok whispered to one of his aides, "Kill Brik."

One cap ran off.

The rest of the tribe hadn't moved. Narrok could feel their glares. He roared, "All of you! Fock off!"

His ears twitched.

Nobody had moved.

"I said fock off!"

Nothing happened.

"Do I have to smash you all! Can't you see I can murder you without even my eyes! Your blind old boss can still murder you!"

He heard the voices of several runtlings.

"Is it true?"

"What?" hissed Narrok.

"There's a human village just sitting there?"

"We could be more?"

"We could fight?"

Narrok laughed through the pain. "If we attack there, then every goddamn humie for a thousand miles will kill us all! That ain't a fight to be proud of! That ain't a fight we can win! We just die like rats! Don't you let that dead runtling poison your mind!"

"He died for us."

"He died to see us be more."

Narrok stood up. "We can't be more!" He waved his arms, unable to see where the runt voices were coming from. "We'll just die! Stupid runts! Can't you see that?!" His heart drummed in his chest.

Voices and murmurs drifted across the tribe. Voices of revenge and confusion, murmurs of Wyre's martyrdom. Narrok didn't like the sound of any of it. He roared, "All of you are nothing! Come at me! I dare you! I'll rip you all apart before I let this clan march to suicide!"

Narrok reached for one of his caps. "Kill any of the ones loyal to that runtling. Kill them all."

The cap grumbled.

Narrok pulled him close. "What?"

"We can't kill the entire clan…" The cap shoved off Narrok. "How'd you ever know if I've killed the right ones?"

Narrok's stomach dropped. The wind began to pick up and it smelled like rain.

"How'd you know if we ever listened to you again?"

Narrok reached out. "Listen you stinking pigs! I am the boss! I am the one that keeps the humies from hunting us down like rats! I keep us alive!"

"How you supposed to do that anymore, Narrok No-Eyes?"

He felt a chill down his spine as he heard, but couldn't see, activity around him. *What will happen to the clan now?*

What will happen to me?

-The End-

PILGRIMAGE TO ANOWARA

The stranger's stomach growled painfully as she walked the dank forest. *We're almost there*, she lied to herself.

The gloom was all encompassing throughout Appalachian forest trails where moisture and the aroma of moss filled the air. The stranger pulled her black cloak tightly around her body, the cold cutting to her core. The darkness of the forest offered no confidence or certainty she would reach the next town anytime soon.

Pain spiked in her stomach. *God, any more of this, I'll have to start learning to eat acorns and pine needles.* Her rations had gone out two days ago.

A twig snapped.

The stranger's hand rested immediately on her .45 Colt. The revolver was empty. *But they won't know that.* The last few bullets wasted on hunting a stringy emaciated rabbit.

The cacophony of forest sounds filled her ears. A rustling of the trees above, the dripping of condensation off a rock, the chittering of a squirrel, the bray of some distant animal.

After a long pause, the stranger continued walking down the trail, her boots crunching against the ground. The anticipation sent a shiver up her spine.

Probably just a rodent or bird. She wondered if she could catch it. *It's nothing.*

As the hours passed the path zigzagged down a slope carpeted in tall grass and the periodic conifer. The tall grass could easily hide a predator or bandit. It swayed in the breeze, the twisted oak trees at the far side of the glade formed an unwelcoming gateway in the distance.

Fuck me. She kept her hand on her empty gun and marched into the open ground.

Her eyes swung slowly from side to side, watching for threats. An owl hooted in a dead tree above that reminded her too much of the gallows. The owl rotated its head around before flying away. She grimaced, feeling the discomfort and that spine-tingling anticipation. It was too easy a place to be ambushed.

She could almost picture a sabre-toothed cougar or a featherback theropod pouncing from the underbrush.

Eventually, she reached the end of the slope and the trail curved back into dense forest. She thought she could smell smoke... The conifers and beech trees rose up around her like reed stalks and temple columns.

Rotten leaves scattered in a gust of wind. Through the debris, the stranger saw the ruins of a long-abandoned lodge. All that was left was the stone foundation, the pillar of the chimney, and the rib cage of wooden slates. The smell of sour tobacco drifted down the trail.

A man stood in the shadow of the chimney, just off the path.

The stranger's hand fell to her holster.

"Good afternoon, miss," said the man, stepping onto the path. "Nice day?"

He wore a denim jacket over a woollen sweater. Baldrics criss-crossed his chest for the truncheons hanging at his hips, red tassels on the hilts. His narrow face should have been handsome if it weren't for his yellow teeth and sagging eyes. His blonde hair was pulled back with a red bandana. Just another poor white-trash bandit, probably an exile from the lowland towns under Warwich rule.

She searched his person for a firearm but couldn't see anything. *This far from civilization, bullets can't even make their way here.*

"The weather is shit and so is my day," said the stranger.

The man whistled. "Your attitude as well."

He knocked the ash from his clay pipe against a tree as he approached, slowly, prowling like a big cat. She could smell his unwashed stench and feel his hungry eyes climbing her figure. Her cloak hid most everything, but she was sure he enjoyed using his imagination.

The stranger slipped the revolver from its holster and sneered. "It's about to get a lot worse."

"'Fraid so, darling."

The stranger raised the empty revolver. "I don't have any money or food."

His eyes undressed her slowly. He was taller and no doubt stronger than her, but he was wary of her weapons. "You got a shiny .45, a big fancy sword… all good things?" The man snickered before calling out. "Hey, Kormak, what you think? Looks like gold around her neck?"

The stranger swore, hiding her necklace.

A hulking shadow stepped out from behind a tree. A pot-bellied orc brandished an industrial hammer, the haft wrapped in masking tape. His face was covered by a long red bandana, his hide the colour of rotten leaves.

It grunted through the bandana. "Aye, a sparkly piece. Fetches a good price. What you think, Gomez?"

Foliage rustled behind the stranger. She got a whiff of something out of a petting zoo.

Over her shoulder she saw a short creature leaning on a steel-tipped spear. He had a squashed nose, dull chestnut skin, and two stubby horns sprouting from his forehead, a red bandana around his neck. A denim vest left his hairy chest exposed. His legs were covered in thick curly wool with the split hooves of a goat.

"That sword will pay a hefty price," snickered the satyr. "Let's get this over with, Leonard, I'm hungry."

"Leonard?" said the stranger.

"It's Leo."

"I don't care."

"Just hand it all over, nice lady. We won't hurt you. You can carry on with your day over to the next town."

"Last time I checked," said the stranger. "I'm the one with the gun."

"Is it even loaded?"

No. "Of course it is. What kind of idiot points an unloaded gun?" *This idiot.*

"Prove it," said Leonard.

The stranger was never good at lying. She gripped the handgrip with a white-knuckled desperation, pointing it straight at the bandit's head. She kept her face neutral. Wind whistled through the ruins of the lodge. A pair of crows watched the proceedings from atop the chimney. She imagined popping him right between the eyes. The way his head would jerk back. She didn't *want* to do it. She didn't enjoy killing. She just wished she could just to avoid the fight. She wanted to wipe that smirk off his stupid face. *Okay, maybe I'm a bad Buddhist and I enjoy killing assholes.*

The silence hung longer and Leonard's smirk stretched wider as her bluff melted away.

Oh, fuck it.

She lobbed the chrome revolver at the bandit's face. He doubled over from the wet crack of his broken nose.

The orc roared and stomped forward, but it was the long reach of the satyr's spear that was the real threat.

She spun around and drew her black sword just in time to parry away the spear. Her cloak flared around her like wings. The satyr grinned. The orc swung his huge hammer.

The stranger ducked just in time for the hammer to whistle past where her head had been and smashed into a tree, blasting out wood chips. She knocked away the spear tip, slashed backwards, slicing the orc's shoulder, and drove forward, rushing the satyr. She bounced between engaging the two inhuman creatures, countering their clumsy attacks but forced to remain on the defensive between two fronts of attack.

The chestnut creature giggled and pranced backwards with delicate hoof clops. He struck back with a flurry of spear thrusts. The stranger parried each strike with gritted teeth and mechanical precision. She had been trained with worse than this, but her hunger sapped at her strength.

I'm already tired of this. She left an obvious opening at her right side. The grinning satyr took the feint and thrust out his spear.

The stranger jerked sideways, allowing the spear to pierce her black cloak, but with a sharp jerk of the fabric, she had control of the weapon. She yanked the spear hard, pulling the satyr with it. He was caught off guard and sent off balance.

His terrified face met her apathetic glare. She chopped downwards with the edge of her sword, bisecting the satyr from shoulder to hip. Blood gurgled from the pieces as he slumped to the forest floor, red pooling over the dirt.

The orc roared in protest, seeing his comrade fall. He went for an overhead strike, she wove away like liquid and spun the spear like a staff, striking the orc across the face. It broke with a snap and the creature tumbled off the path.

She cast the spear haft aside, taking her sword in both hands.

Leo charged, leaping over his remaining comrade. Blood streamed down his face, hideous now. The stranger caught both his batons on her black blade. "You bitch!" he screamed.

"Is that seriously the best line you have?" she hissed.

He dropped one arm and swung at her stomach, the tassels on his sword like the tails of a fox dashing. She caught the truncheon her on the crossguard of her sword. The blade bit into the truncheons, their faces inches from each other. His breath reeked.

"Why'd you have to do it the hard way!?"

"Oh," she growled. "Just something to do. Fucking pig."

He was stronger and would soon overpower her. Instinctively, she dug her heel into his foot. He grunted and jerked backwards. She moved to strike him down, but his counter was too blinding fast. He knocked her on the side of her head, rattling her brain. The skin split and blood trailed down her temple.

He hooted but was met with the hard heel of her hand in his jaw. He stumbled back and she flicked her sword, cutting him at his ribs.

He roared with pain.

The stranger kicked him in the chest, knocking him to the ground.

She didn't have the chance to recover.

The orc sent her to the ground, striking her chest with the haft of his hammer. The wind knocked from her lungs, she let out a ragged gasp. When she opened her eyes, she saw the orc standing over her.

He chuckled, his face still hidden by the bandana, and raised the hammer.

She saw the satyr's broken spear shaft a few feet away. The stranger rolled away just in time. The hammer threw up clods of dirt. The orc roared, and the stranger was forced to roll away again from a barrage of hammer attacks.

She rolled over the broken spear, snatched it, and unfurled into an upwards thrust just as the orc raised his hammer.

The ripping sensation of piercing a leather bag of Jell-O went up the broken haft. The spear impaled the orc through his pot belly and out his back. Red-purple blood flowed down the splintered ash.

The orc roared with pain, but, before he could attack again, the stranger jumped to her feet, levering the creature down to its knees. She wrenched the weapon out, blood spurting from the wound, and drove it through its mouth and out the back of its head.

Though his face was covered, the orc's eyes leaked pain and hatred before he fell to the ground with a heavy *thunk*.

"Kormak!" bleated Leo.

The stranger picked up her sword with a fluid dash and held it out with both hands, ready.

Leo stood, clutching his side, stared horror at his dead comrades. His bloodied face twisted with anger. "Fuck you! I'll get you for this!"

He fled and vanished into the forest.

When she was sure he was gone, the stranger sheathed her blade. Her chest rising and falling, sweat glistened across her face. She swore, touching the ballooning bruise on the side of her head. She wiped the blood with her sleeve.

"Fuck everything…" she growled.

She collected her revolver and her bag, then proceeded to search the bodies.

Nothing but a couple copper coins, a squished chocolate bar, and an empty lighter. The chocolate bar at least helped against her hunger. She also took the orc's sheepskin vest. It reeked and needed the blood washed out, but it would be warm.

She left the corpses where they died.

"Is this how it's going to be?" she said to herself. *Every day a new fight?* A world full of lawless bandits, corrupt officials, ravaging monsters, and otherworldly forces. Things beyond her tiny little life. What hope did she have? A sliver of certainty that she would try? That didn't mean much against a world like this. What hope did one person have?

"I'm just one woman."

Was it impossible? Was it hopeless? She had a group of men to find, and she was alone. The men with black cloaks and black-bladed swords. In a vast world of a thousand dangers, all she had to go on was rumours from scared peasants. Those who spoke said: south. South. South meant everything and nothing. She had to find these men… she had to find them.

She kicked a rock, hissing a colourful curse. "This will never end."

The winds whistled through the trees, reminding her of the encroaching cold of the night. The terrifying noises of the forest, the constant solitude, and danger were her only companions.

She whipped around when she heard footsteps approaching, hand on her sword.

From down the winding trails of the forest came three cloaked figures, their faces obscured with hoods, hunched, and leaning on staffs. They marched in perfect order. Silent, aloof, and indifferent. They didn't even notice the corpses off the trail.

The three old men with scraggly white beards turned to the stranger.

"May the gods bless thee," said the leader. They all bowed.

On reflex, the stranger bowed with her palms together, the sign of respect that she had learned when living amongst a sect of lost monks. "Buddha bless this meeting."

The monk nodded before turning and returning on their path.

The stranger straightened, realizing this was the first meeting with people in days… well the first one that didn't result in violence. She hurried to follow the cloaked men.

"Excuse me. Excuse me, sirs—holy ones," she asked. "Would you know how far it is to the next town?"

The three men stopped, frozen like statues. The stranger leaned down to see the leader's face, but he kept his cowl lowered. "We do not aim for town. We ascend Anowara."

"Anowara?"

"Anowara. The great turtle," said the old man. He pointed with his staff. Ahead of the path, through the forested hills, fog, and mists, the stranger saw the vague outline of a distant peak. "Our pilgrimage has been long."

"Pilgrimage?" *They must be ascetics of some denomination.* "What is at Anowara?"

"Wisdom. Knowledge. Truth"

The stranger chewed her lip, still trying to meet the eyes of the old monks. They were immovable statues, and, before she could say anything, they continue their slow meandering march. Their faces remained hidden beneath hooded cowls. She walked along with the monks. "I could accompany you to your destination." *For food.*

They did not answer.

They simply walked onward through the trails of the Appalachians.

The stranger followed along, only certain that these old men would need food and she hoped to get some... and maybe be a little less alone.

Hours passed and the monks still walked silently onward. The regular shuffle of their feet and staffs became just another note in the perpetual hum of the forest. Birds chirped, rodents scurried, insects buzzed, and the monks walked on.

They crossed an old wooden bridge and through miles of gloomy dense forest before beginning the ascent up the hills towards Mount Anowara.

The stranger followed silently at the back of the line. The sheepskin vest under her cloak reeked to high heaven but was a godsend for keeping back the damp cold.

She hoped to avoid violence, but this was not a world that allowed the luxury of pacifism. *This is not the monastery, my only refuge. This is not my home. This is not my world... not like I can return home.* Exposure meant she was trapped on the Wrong Side. The Veil, some force or gods or power, kept the planes of existence separated.

It had been four—maybe five—months since she left the monastery at Chateau le Jean. She had lived with the lost convent of Buddhist monks for the five years following her Exposure. The first thing she did when she left was order the biggest, meatiest steak at the first inn she found. Five years of vegetarianism had been more than enough.

She smiled to herself, remembering the cruel tutelage of her Master. Some memories were okay to return to.

That crotchety old bastard. She could picture him with his wrinkled light brown face, like a piece of wood, never displaying a hint of compassion. Too much of a maverick in his own right to ascend to the position of abbot. Too useful and knowledgeable to kick out. He had been a tough-love kind of mentor, never displaying a hint of praise. *You don't speak our language; you don't call me Sifu. You call me Master, idiot Exposed girl.* The second lesson he ever gave her... after kicking her ass.

She hoped to see the old bastard again one day.

The trees rustled. The stranger's eyes narrowed and surveyed the forest. *If it's that fucking yellow-toothed bastard Leonard again...* her hand rested on her sword. *I can non-lethally beat his ass.*

A huge footfall crashed in the undergrowth. The stranger's eyes went wide. It was not Leonard. Something enormous was approaching. She drew her sword. A wrinkled hand grasped her wrist. The monk at the rear of the line shook his head slowly. His eyes were as pale as milk.

Footfalls crashed closer. Trees swayed and shuttered under the immensity of the encroaching creature. Heavy booming footfalls.

The monk continued, oblivious to the encroaching danger.

The creature crashed through the forest. The stranger readied herself for an attack. From between the treetops came a furry animal head, not unlike a deer. Its blubbery lips, long eye-lashes, and long face floated twenty-feet in the air.

It took another heavy step forward, revealing its body.

"A giraffe?"

Like a giraffe, but not, it was dark brown and beige, a tree trunk-like neck covered in a mane of shaggy brown hair. It reached up to graze on the tree tops. Its long legs, half its height, ended in wide padded feet. On its sloping back was a sagging hump covered in more brown fur.

It nibbled the leaves peacefully.

The stranger let out an immense sigh before eyeing the monks. They continued down the path, ignoring the dangers that surrounded them. The horrors that could pluck them off the road at any moment. Their indifference to disaster was only an invitation to predators. *They will get themselves killed.* She couldn't let them get devoured by some creature or killed by bandits. She hurried to catch up to their tireless march.

The stranger glanced back and saw another creature approach. A calf. This one was only six feet tall and still struggling on its shaky awkward legs.

The ascending trail grew rougher. It twisted with zigzags around clefts of rock jutting out from the mossy ground. The air was noticeably colder. The sun had already vanished behind the distant eastern hills. The cloudy sky darkened to charcoal.

"It will be dark soon," said the stranger, feeling the fatigue drag on her. "Shouldn't we camp?"

None of them answered. They kept marching at their own beat.

The stranger sighed and continued, even as her legs screamed to stop. *They are going to be worse than Master, aren't they?*

It rained that night, but the monks didn't stop until it was impossible to see more than a few feet ahead. The stranger felt like she was about to fall over from the weight of her drenched cloak. She followed the outline of the old monks through the downpour that leaked through the forest canopy.

They took shelter beneath a huge oak tree whose dense branches provided some cover. It was too wet to start a fire. The stranger huddled within her sheepskin and her cloak. The hood dripped water in front of her face.

The monks sat in a circle and passed around a canteen, one of them offering her a sip. She thanked him and took a sniff. It reeked like sour garbage, but her stomach pained for some sort of nourishment. The taste was worse than she imagined. Whatever fermented swill they were drinking burned on the way down.

She shuttered. "It tastes like onions and bananas." A burped slipped from her mouth. "And pickles."

"May the gods bless thee," said the lead monk.

The three monks began to hum and chant in a low droning chorus.

It wasn't any prayer she knew or a dialect she recognized. The stranger shuffled back into a knot in the tree and curled up tighter in her cloak, using her bag as a pillow. The sheepskin only helped so much in the damp misery, and she shivered.

She found the prayers comforting. She had spent a long time waking up, going about her day, and falling asleep to similar sounds. Life at the repurposed Chateau had been peaceful, but the stranger was restless. Her skills grew over the five years and, after she did a tour with a Franco militia, she knew she had to leave. She needed to find the men who took her from her world, who took her life.

She had to find the men with the black-bladed swords.

Maybe there would some truths at the summit of Anowara.

She closed her eyes and prepared herself for a miserable sleep.

♦

The clap of hands and deep throaty prayers woke the stranger from her sleep. She'd been dreaming about warm beds, hot food, red wine, and eager younger partners. She sat straight up, rubbing her eyes. Everything hurt. Everything was stiff and strained. It was still dark out. The horizon lacked even the hint of the nearing dawn. *Jesus, Master was never this bad.* She brushed her long black hair out of her face, her braid coming undone and hair fraying at the ends.

The three monks were praying around their canteen, each taking a ritualized sip in turn before rising.

The lead monk offered the stranger a sip. She took it reluctantly and shuddered at the sour taste. Her stomach began cramping from hunger. Her period was late from sheer malnutrition, which was a very bad sign.

They continued their journey up Anowara as dawn light made the landscape visible, the trail becoming progressively steeper and rockier. The forest grew thinner until there was only the periodic pine between mossy rocks. The monks continued, undeterred. Over the next ridge, the mountain rose before them, a huge cleft of rock reaching up into the clouds. The summit was shrouded with wisps of mist.

After a few hours of walking, the stranger's thighs already burning from the incline, they reached the edge of a fissure in the mountainside, a sheer drop into unfathomable depths where sloshing water echoed below. Across the chasm, the ascending slopes lead further up Anowara. *Only thirty feet away. Insufferably close… impossibly far…*

The lead monk stamped his staff and continued. They walked along the edge of the canyon until they came to a path leading downwards.

"Are you sure this is the way?" asked the stranger, leaning against the rock, taking the pain off her knees.

The monks didn't answer. They wandered down the trail along the cliffs.

Alright. She followed and wondered why she was doing this. Was it the challenge? The promise of knowledge? Was it her own self-loathing and suicidal tendencies that made her glutton for more punishment? She wasn't sure. She looked up at the mountain, a ringing echoing in her ears as she felt herself following the path.

They followed the narrow path well into the afternoon, never stopping. The barren walls dripped with condensation. It was abysmally cold. The stranger hugged herself, trying to keep warm, and told herself, *One leg in front of the other. One leg in front of the other.*

She would periodically check to make sure the monks were still in front of her, but wasn't sure if she'd just passed out and imagined them being there.

The opposite wall of the canyon was a mere ten feet away

now. *Could I jump it?* It zigzagged through the mountain, descending deeper and became darker and colder. The stranger chanced a glance over the edge.

Her heart raced at the hundred-foot drop into a rushing river.

Maybe? Certainly not in my current condition.

If they kept following this, it would just lead them further from their destination. She looked passed the monks and peered into the distance. After a curve in the canyon there was a bridge of stone. A natural crossing that led to a series of switch-backs climbing up the sheer face of the mountain. The titanic precipice of Anowara loomed above, disappearing into clouds and mists.

At that moment, everything became very dark as a shadow enveloped the canyon.

The stranger turned and immediately froze. Her entire body rigid with complete terror, eyes wide. *You gotta be kidding me.*

A huge spider stretched across the walls of the canyon, straddling both walls on stilt-like legs. Its bulbous body was the size of a bathtub, and its dripping fangs were like kitchen knives. Bristly white hair covered its body and its legs. Its clusters of beady black eyes watched the stranger motionlessly, reflecting her terror back at her.

Oh, fucking god, why did it have to be a spider?

The stranger slowly drew her sword. The wolf-crossguard offered no encouragement as her legs trembled.

"Run!"

Over her shoulder, she saw the monks marching towards the crossing, remaining with their tireless meandering pace. They didn't seem concerned or even aware of the threat.

Are you kidding me?

The stranger turned back just as the spider struck.

It slammed her hard against the wall. She caught the fangs with her sword, gripping the blade like a crossbar. She screamed, feeling the furry mandibles paw towards her like thrashing arms, wrapping around her sword. Disgusted chills crawled up her skin. Revulsion churned in her stomach. Her entire world were the glassy black orbs set into its bulbous head.

The spider lifted her off the path and slammed her against the wall again. Pain webbed across her back.

In the distance, she saw the monks crossing the canyon.

Do no harm, my ass. Monsters and bandits didn't care. She let go of the blade, still holding the hilt, and drew her revolver by the barrel. She hammered the polished grip like a club, smashing the spider's eyes over and over again.

It shrieked and let her go, reaching back and thrashing its forelimbs and mandibles at the pain.

She slid down the wall, landing hard on the path. Her knees buckled under the landing, unable to take the fall. She holstered the revolver and gripped the sword with both hands.

The spider struck again in a blur of motion. The stranger held the blade straight out, like a thorn, arm screaming from the weight.

It crashed into her with meteoric force, slamming her against the wall again. A piece of its thorax burst open like an overripe pumpkin.

The creature shrieked, retracting and fleeing a few feet higher up the wall. A long stream of oozy ichor spilled out of a gash from its back down to its bleeding mouth. A mandible fell into the river. She had missed; her attempt to impale the spider on her sword had gone off-course.

The monks had already crossed and were climbing the switchbacks.

Why'd it have to be spiders!?

The spider resumed the attack, its eyes splattered with its own blood. Its legs blocked the stranger's avenues of escape on both sides.

She swung her blade uselessly trying to repel its attacks, jabbing at it but unable to reach the creature's vulnerable parts. It swayed its body back and forth, trying to throw her off before it struck. It was unsettling to watch.

Fucking spiders. Those emotionless eyes, all those legs, and the morbid horror-show way they ate.

The stranger put it from her mind. She wasn't able to reach its body and could only defend direct attacks so many times. The spider would win an engagement and that's all it needed.

Master had taught her how to attack when already engaged. *Be aggressive when forced to, it's not our way to start violence...* said the old man. *End fights. Defend the powerless.* That's what he taught her, despite the monastery's pacifistic principles.

She dashed below an attack and struck at the legs, carving through them like branches. She sheared off the ugly little clawed foot. It shrieked and, before it could attack, she cleaved off another leg. Ichor spilled over the pathway. When the severed leg tried to grip the wall, it slipped on the bleeding stump.

She spun around and attacked the other legs, chopping off another section. The twitching pieces fell down into the river.

It brought its other legs from the opposite wall to reinforce the front, its body in reach. It was about to lose its grip and teeter into the abyss.

The spider knew that and attacked, but it was clumsy and the stranger easily dodged. She spun and slashed off the last front leg. The spider shrieked and pawed uselessly at the path along the cliff. It failed and lost its footing.

It fell towards the river, shrieking and snapping its mandibles.

But one of the remaining clawed legs caught the front of the stranger's sheepskin vest.

Oh shit.

The weight of the spider yanked the stranger right off her feet.

◆

The narrow river came quickly.

The spider crashed into the water, sending up a plume of white spray. It shrieked and thrashed its legs as it was carried down the river.

The stranger screamed as she fell. Hitting the water was like hitting a wall at that height, but she kept a solid grip on her sword as sound and oxygen were cut out. The water was ice cold. Shivers sliced through her body.

The world spun as she tumbled in the rushing river. Her free hand searched blindly for a rock, a vine, anything. She found a grip on a spike of rock. She pulled against the rushing water and wrapped both arms around a stalagmite. She gasped for air and blinked the water from her eyes.

She hugged the spike of rock for a long time, catching

her breath in long ragged gasps. She shivered at the icy embrace of water. As water splashed her face, she searched for a route back up the canyon wall.

She could see the crossing a few hundred yards up the canyon. Further above she saw the monks ascending the switchbacks.

The stranger grit her teeth. *They are beginning to get on my nerves.*

Another few shoots of rock led towards the canyon wall. The river cut through the mountain throughout the centuries. Seasonal irregularities created levels and jagged handholds. She tracked a way back up towards the path. It would be a long and painful ordeal.

She began her ascent, mumbling more creative streams of curses at each moment of progress.

By nightfall, the monks had found shelter under a huge shard of rock. At the summit of the switchbacks was a steep slope that led towards the peaks. Through the inhospitable landscape, great shards and pillars of mossy stone rose like a garden around the trail.

The monks had made a small fire where they set a small teapot, the sweet aromatic smell of tea drifting from the hiding place. The stranger was still damp and too tired from her hours of climbing as she stumbled into the firelight like a shambling ghost.

She collapsed into the shade of the shelter. She rolled onto her back, her chest heaving and limbs tingling.

A monk placed a cup of tea next to her.

She drank the hot liquid slowly. *Nectar of the gods.* Its warm earthy flavour rejuvenated her body. Warmth flowing through her limbs and to her numb fingers.

"Buddha bless," she mumbled.

The monks didn't respond.

Their contempt for her actions was clear. They didn't say anything, but they obviously did not approve of her actions. She had harmed a living creature. *A creature that would have killed me anyways.* She was too tired to protest. She did what she did to survive. *Why am I following them? Why? Why torment myself with this?* She looked up into the darkness of the mountainside. That unnatural draw calling her forward to the summit like the great groaning of a god.

I need what it has… I need to know. She needed to see the peak. She needed to… She slipped immediately into sleep, sprawled out on the rocky ground. Dreamless as death.

♦

A synchronized clap and throaty prayers jolted the stranger from her dreamless sleep. Her body groaned as every fibre of her being protested. It was dawn, a line of colour along the distant horizon. Below the lowlands were rippling forests and moors. They were in the deep wilds that the kingdom of NeoAnglia could not conquer.

The monks gave her another sip of their onion-banana juice. She didn't even protest and was pleased to have something in her stomach. Everything hurt. Callouses had long ago formed on her hands, her skin like leather from fighting, but blisters were forming and tearing in new places. She pulled the cloak tighter, trembling from the cold. Shivering down to her bones, deep in her chest, the type of cold that meant you'd get sick very soon.

The group began their ascent towards the summit, which had vanished into the mists. The stranger followed her silent companions. The garden of ancient stones rose along the steep slope.

Hours passed. The grey clouded sky gave little warmth or light, and the stranger kept her focus on putting one foot in front of the other. The agonizing pain she awoke with devolved into perpetual numbness across her body.

She began to struggle to keep up with the monks. Their even-measured footsteps took them farther than her slow hobbling pace. She realized how her urgency exhausted her and how their measured pace saved energy. *I've been so desperate and eager...* Looking up, she saw the cloaks of the monks growing faint in the mists. She swore and hurried to keep up.

She entered a world of swirling mists and fog, only able to see a few feet of rocky terrain around her ankles. Everything was an impenetrable wall of grey.

She could still hear the ring of their walking sticks, but they grew fainter in the mists.

The stranger hurried to catch up, running, teetering on her exhausted, unsteady legs. Closed in within a labyrinth of boulders and crags, she pushed herself, but her legs just wouldn't cooperate. She rushed through a curtain of fog, but found no one. She didn't even seem to be on the path.

She spun in a frantic search for a sound before realizing she was completely and utterly alone. Silence wrapped around her. Her wobbly legs fell out from under her. She swore as she slipped and rolled down the slope until she halted against the side of a boulder. She rubbed the pain lancing across the back of her head. "Jesus Christ."

Why am I doing this? She asked herself. She didn't need to join this pilgrimage. It meant nothing to her.

What possible truth could be worth this? It sounded like a fairy tale. It was probably a lie anyways. *Those old fools.*

Rocks crunched nearby. Footsteps approached through the mists.

"Did you forget about me?" said the stranger.

"Never," said a man's voice.

Leonard stepped out of the wall of mist. His narrow face still crusted with blood. His torso wrapped tightly with soiled bandages and tape.

The stranger's shoulders sank. "Fuck me…"

"Exactly," said Leo. "Fuck you! You killed my boys!"

The stranger got to her feet, using the boulder as a brace. "And I'll kill you the same way."

She knew she was in no condition to fight. *But neither is he.* His body favoured one side and the deep cut across his side left every movement a visible pain. The stranger was freezing and exhausted, and her heart raced in her chest. But she had no choice. She drew her sword, leaning back into a crouch with the point aimed at Leo.

"Well, I'm waiting," she said. She didn't have the energy to come up with a better comment.

Leo obliged, face red with fury. He drew both his red-tailed batons. He dove into an attack, knocking away her leading thrust.

He went for a low slash, like last time. She dropped her crossguard to defend.

But it was a feint, and she was too damn tired to see it.

He slammed his fist into her face, knocking her backwards into the boulder. Pain burst across her swelling cheek. She growled and launched herself into a clumsy attack. He dashed away, slid around her guard, and knocked her across the chest, then

67

again across her face. Hot pain exploded and the skin split. Her head rang, brain vibrating in her skull. She slipped back, clumsy as she swung her sword in an arc, trying to cleave him in two. He was fast, like a cobra, and he dove and struck, leaving her wrist and arms tingling and numb. Her fingers were barely able to hold onto the sword.

Leo grinned with his yellowed teeth. "This is for Kormak and Gomez!"

He attacked, anger blocking out his pain.

"Will you shut up!?" She played defensive, retreating up the slope, forcing him lower.

The pair dashed through the garden of stone. The stranger used the boulders as cover, trying to control the avenue of attack. Leo was fuelled by blind rage and continued attacking in a swimming motion, with arcing strikes followed by the red tassels. He hit her twice more on the back and in the knee, leaving tingling pain. He was so fast.

He dove around her guard, forcing her back further and further through the rocky terrain. His focus was intense. Each attack, parry, and counter in perfect rage-fuelled form. All the stranger could do was defend with slow trembling movement, adrenaline pumping through her veins. She flicked her blade at the last moment, knocking the truncheons with the flat of her blade and sliding away.

She stumbled backwards and moved around a boulder.

She yelped, her arms windmilling to regain balance. She stood at the edge of a sheer drop. Below was nothing but an abyss of swirling grey mist.

Leo roared, charging into his next attack.

She swung hard, cleaving through his two truncheons as he tried to block her. "I've had enough!"

He ducked under her follow up attack, her crude attempt to end this, and he drew a long knife across her stomach in a single fluid movement.

Blood splashed the boulder.

She screamed as crimson streamed down her front, pain exploding across her stomach. She couldn't even spare a glance to see if anything of her spilled out. She couldn't judge the depth from the pain. Only that nothing *felt* like it was falling out of her.

Leo reached forward to grasp at her hair, ready to plunge the bloodied knife into her.

"ENOUGH!" she snarled and launched herself forward, everything red-blind adrenaline and ringing in her ears.

She dropped her sword and grabbed the man by his denim vest. His eyes widened with surprise. She used his own weight against him, spun on her toes and tossed him off the precipice.

He screamed, waving his arms as he fell towards the sea of mist.

The stranger dropped to her knees; her entire body as cold as if she jumped into ice water. *Stay awake. Stay awake.* Her eyes just felt so heavy...

◆

The stranger was surprised when her eyes fluttered open. Her head swam, vision blurred, and everything ached. Above was only swirling mists. Her fingers the rocky shale around her. Her fingers were sticky with blood. She felt hot and wet everywhere.

She looked down and peeled back the flap of fabric. The

wound looked worse than it was, a mess of glistening red. The blood had coagulated, sealing the split across the flesh of her stomach. It would have been debilitating if the fight had continued and she would have lost.

She ended it. *Fuck. I sure did.* The surprise of an unarmed takedown had done the trick.

The stranger felt her arm and shoulder; if they weren't fractured, she would be lucky. Swollen welts grew in all the places she'd been hit. They would be purple and green. The worst one throbbed on the back of her head. She touched her face, feeling the swollen flesh that oozed scabby blood.

She surveyed the sea of mist she found herself in. Trails of wisps fell down the cliff like a waterfall. Leo's knife sat beside her at the edge of the outcropping. It was a broken-backed seax with a red-threaded grip.

Where is he? She looked over the edge and immediately wish she hadn't.

Leo had landed on a series of jagged spikes of rock.

She shuttered at the sight and looked up. It would be an excruciating climb.

Why? She wondered. She thought about just laying down and closing her eyes. *Why keep going? Why keep going ever again?* Let the peaceful doom take her. It would be like falling asleep.

Something cracked.

Her eyes went wide as flakes of shale broke around the outcropping. Pieces fell and shattered on the jagged spikes below. The knife teetered on the edge of the outcropping. The entire formation shuttered, a crack forming along the cliff wall.

"Shit!"

The knife almost tipped off the edge. She grabbed the tip of the blade, spun it in hand and drove it into a crack in the cliff.

The entire outcropping fell beneath her. She screamed as her arm took all of her weight, pain spiking all the way to her shoulder and chest. She hung over the jagged rocks as shale cracked and tumbled down the mountain.

She exploded in a new stream of expletives as she held on for dear life, pain ripping through her whole body like she'd been stretched on a rack while touched with torches. Her hands and feet pawed for a handhold. She gasped for air as she clung to the mountain side.

Her boots caught a lip of a rock, gaining a footing.

She roared against the mountain and began her ascent, cursing the gods as her wounds reopened, bleeding across the stone face.

The stranger grunted as she hauled herself on to the rocky ground. She tossed Leo's knife aside, the edge ruined from being used as a climbing spike. Her arm burned from the climb. She lay on her back, panting.

She looked down at the reopened gash on her stomach. Blood pooling and staining her pale flesh.

"Fuck you, God."

She laughed, but that hurt. The laughter descended into heaving sobs. Tears leaked from her brown eyes and streamed down the side of her face. She gasped, pitifully, her broken voice sobbing.

Between raging gasps, she coughed. "It's impossible."

And she didn't just mean the climb.

Her vision swam as the blood loss took its toll. Everything became hazy as her eyes fluttered shut.

♦

Metal screeched and sparked. Flashes of gunfire echoed in the night along the highway. The bus swerved, teetered, and finally tumbled off the road and down the slope along the ditch. Trees snapped and cracked like reeds.

A woman screamed, and everything went black.

When the woman woke up, everything was noise, fire, and screaming. She was pinned beneath a piece of the wrecked Greyhound bus. She strained to free herself, but couldn't. Her face was covered in scratches, and she bled from a gash across her chest.

She looked up and saw horrors. Huge men strode through the wreckage, slaughtering the survivors. They were more like spectres, or reapers, in their billowing black cloaks. Maybe a dozen of them, faces hidden by the shadow of their cowls. They killed everyone: men, woman, girls. The only ones they left were the younger boys. Those vanished within their cloaks and were hurried away.

It had just been a bus ride between Toronto and Montreal. That's all. Then something hit the highway. Something huge and inhuman. Something the woman would one day know to be a monster from the deepest corners of myth and magic, though she had no idea what it had been specifically. Something that attracted the cloaked murderers.

People whimpered and sobbed as their loved ones were ripped from their arms and killed. Bones crunched as swords cleaved into them.

The woman grunted trying to free herself. "Where... where are they?!"

Her eyes searched for... she couldn't remember who they were. They were formless. Featureless. Ghostly blanks in her memory. Cherished memories whose importance was lost to her.

She caught a glimpse of one of them, one of her... she just couldn't remember who. Two of the big men threw them to the ground. The fires danced light across their blank faces. They bled from a gash above their eye. The woman reached out for them. She just couldn't remember who they were.

Have you forgotten?! echoed the monk's voice, disassociated from the nightmare.

Tears streamed down her face.

One of the men, a titanic bear with huge shoulders and a broad back, drew his long onyx blade. The silver crossguard in the image of wolves leaping from a blood drop, firelight dancing across it.

"Where are they!? Where are they?!" she screamed. *God, who were they?*

From within the cloak of one of the killers, she caught a glimpse of a small child. Nine years old. The hooded man pressed the child's head to his chest, blinding him to the carnage. She had no idea who the child was. She couldn't even recognize his face, she just knew he was important.

A sword flashed.

A headless body fell to the ground. The woman remembered the pain, her scream, her horror. She just couldn't remember *who* that person was. Why they mattered to her so completely.

Her wailing scream, long, ragged, and terrible, alerted the spectral killers to her presence. They pulled her out of the wreckage. Five of them loomed over her. Ghostly reapers with black cloaks and blades with silver hilts. They looked down on her... not with contempt... but indifference.

"This one is yours," said one, as casual an order as ever there could be. A child whimpered within his cloak, held to his chest.

One with a cross-shaped scar on his jaw drew a huge black-bladed longsword. "I'll deal with it away from the boy. Take him."

They vanished, leaving one to stand over the poor injured woman.

Have you forgotten what they did!? echoed the monk.

The man dragged her towards the front of the wreckage, his iron grip around her throat. He cast her roughly to the ground. On his belt hung a knife.

The voice echoed. *You have gone beyond death and madness. You have been beyond what most souls have ever seen and survived. You have passed the Veil of this world. Have you forgotten what they took from you!?*

The man raised his longsword.

You are stronger than you could have ever imagined! commanded the voice.

The woman exploded into action, firing off her injured leg. She snatched the knife off his belt and plunged it into his neck. It felt like cutting meat, soft under the keen edge. Blood spilled out and down her arm. The man fell to his knees, the sword hanging limp in his hand.

Have you forgotten!?

"Where is he?!" she screamed into his face. The man didn't answer. She ripped the sword from his hand and plunged the blade deep through his chest and out his back, puncturing his make-shift armour. "Where is he!? Where did you take him?!"

Blood gushed over her hands as the man died.

"Hey!" barked one of the other cloaked killers. Three appeared out of the shadows, flames flickering around their boots. "Get her!"

She kicked over the corpse. Blood dripped down her arms. She swung the blade in reckless wild arcs, fending off the warriors.

Have you forgotten!? shouted the voice.

The woman screamed. "Where did you take him?! Where is he?!"

Moving like a pack of feral wolves, the men moved at once to impale her as a team.

Little did any of them know that that the fires finally hit the fuel line and whistled to the leaking gas tank. An explosion ripped the massacre apart, setting trees alight and burning the remains of the dead.

The force of it knocked the woman knocked off her feet and threw her through the air. She slammed into a tree, hitting her head. The body of the man she just killed landed on top of her.

Darkness.

When she awoke in the light of the next morning, she was drenched in blood and soot. Two small men in saffron robes stood over her. Her mouth cracked. "Where is he?"

She fell back into darkness.

Have you forgotten?! Have you forgotten?! echoed the voice.

The stranger's eyes shot open. She gritted her teeth and

forced herself upright. Scraggly lengths of her dark hair hung in front of her face. Her brow furrowed with anger, her big brown eyes intense.

"Never."

It was night. The mists had cleared. The intense darkness was cast away by the cascade of stars above. The milky way dazzled across the night in a shower of diamonds and gold flecks. Whatever gods watched, they expected more from this woman.

Her black longsword sat nearby.

Rocks clattered. The garden of boulders and rocky crags danced with shadows and starlight. From behind several boulders crept three feline shadows. Their eyes shone gold through the low light.

The stranger's body burned with pain.

The mountain cats spread out to surround the easy prey. Their lithe panther bodies moved as smooth and silent as shadow. From the dim light, the stranger could see their yellow coats spotted with black. Knife-like fangs jutted down from their upper lips. Long swayed tails back and forth.

I will not stop now. "This fucking mountain won't stop me. Nothing will."

Fighting through the pain and exhaustion, she crawled towards the sword. One of the creatures bared its teeth, lines of saliva dripping between its fangs. Her fingers gripped the wire-wound handle.

The stranger pried herself off the ground, using the blade as a crutch. Her wobbly legs took her weight. A half-insane smirk grew across her face. Blood dripped from her stomach and onto the rough shale ground.

The cats paused.

The stranger raised her blade into her fighting stance, her arms held back with the point aimed at the nearest threat. "Well, I don't have all night."

The eternal starlit sky twinkled above. The wind howled, flapping her cloak like the ragged wings of an injured raven. When the mountain cats leaped into action, she met them head on.

♦

The sun basked the mountain summit in light. The endless perfect blue sky stretched from horizon to horizon. The wind whistled against the stone-faced summit of Anowara.

Blood-stained fingers reached over the edge of the plateau. The stranger hauled herself and climbed on top of the rocky shelf before the final leg of the ascent. Her dirty, stringy hair blew in the wind. Her face was dirty, and she had a spotted cat skin draped over her shoulder. The yellow fur seemed to shimmer in the morning light.

She looked like a wild barbarian from some forgotten land at the end of a journey.

A swirling sea of cloud and mist circled the summit, likely the tallest in the Appalachians, invisible to her world. The final sharp crag of the mountain sat on a flat plateau. It seemed like a lonely island in a vast ocean of cloud.

The stranger had tended her wounds and satiated her hunger on stringy cat meat. Her body hurt, but her eyes narrowed as she focused away from the pain.

She looked up at the final stretch of the pilgrimage. Another fifty feet climb up the dome of stone.

Over her shoulder, she looked out towards the distant

horizon and the eternal sea of clouds across the horizon, vanishing into the distance. She was on top of the world.

She inhaled, taking in as much air as her lungs could. With the world laid out before her, she screamed. "I will find him! I will never stop! One day I will find you! I will find them all! I will put them down like the dogs you are!"

Her words echoed across the infinity of skies and clouds.

It felt so good she smiled.

Suddenly, the whole world shook. The mountain quaked with violet tremors. The stranger swung her arms to keep balance as she tried to make sense of it. There were no fault lines here. No way could an earthquake occur.

Then again, what did she know about this world anymore?

A huge echoing exhale sounded behind her.

The stranger gripped her sword, feet wide as she prepared for the next threat.

The mountain quaked again. The summit itself shuttered and began to move. From within the rock moved a huge leg, ending in spade-like claws. The animal was nearly indistinguishable from the mountain rock, with flesh like scaled shale and wind-blasted stone.

The foot pushed against the stone plateau, raising itself off the flat surface. Below the immense bulk of the creature were strings of moss, fungus, and an entire ecosystem of flora and fauna. The mountain-top, a huge shell, rotated towards the stranger.

From a gap in the stone shell, a titanic head loomed over the stranger, a beaked turtle's head the size of a school bus. It opened its eyes of dull starlight. It might have been blind, but she couldn't tell.

The stranger stumbled back and fell into a sitting position.

A colossal turtle capped the summit of Mount Anowara. It looked down at the tiny human, blinking slowly. Its face was deeply lined and wrinkled, resembling coral. Strings of moss filled the wrinkles and hung off its flabby neck. Its nostrils flared, gusting hot earthy air. Its beak clacked open, revealing a tongue like a slab of wet granite.

"They… said… you… were… coming…" Its voice shook the ground, deep and rasping, like hurricane winds, but slow and intentional.

Its ancient eyes blinked again. The stranger could see herself in the reflection. She was minuscule compared to this god. Its eyes, as big as car tires, were swirling pools of silver. Old beyond human understanding. Wells of eternal cryptic knowledge.

The stranger licked her lips with anticipation. She struggled to her feet and stood proudly before this god.

"You… ask… for… truth?"

"I do."

"For… knowledge?

"I do."

"On… whose… behalf?"

She had no doubt that was a test. Its eyes studied her carefully. She could lie and say enlightenment or purpose. Divine revelation was full of ego. Revenge was unworthy.

She decided to tell the truth. "On behalf of what I've lost. The child whose name I cannot remember. For the person I was with. The family I lost. I don't know them anymore… I don't know what they were to me."

Its bottomless eyes twinkled. "What... do... you... wish... to... know?"

"Do you know where the black swordsmen are?"

The turtle raised its head. It extended out of its shell with a snake-like neck. It swung its neck, surveying the endless sea of cloud. Its silvery blind eyes narrowed and peered into the distance. The corner of its beak curled down into a frown before returning down to look at the tiny human.

"I... do... not... I... am... sorry."

Its voice did sound sad.

The stranger frowned. Her shoulders sank as disappointment spread through her chest and climbed into her throat. She kept it together, feeling the absolute despair.

She saluted and bowed before turning back towards civilization. *Where do I go now? All that for nothing?*

No, not nothing. She had gained plenty for this pilgrimage.

"Wait..." rasped the turtle. Its eyes drifted to the hilt of the sword.

She looked up at the god.

"I... see... one..." its head arced towards the south. "Far... to... the... south... go."

The stranger nodded. "Thank you, wise one." She turned once again.

"Beware...."

She paused. "Beware?"

Its swirling eyes fell on her sword. The leaping wolves

still stained with blood. The silver crossguard twinkled in the light. "Beware… Beware…the… Brotherhood… Beware… the… blood… Beware… their… violence…"

"What are you talking about?" demanded the Stranger.

"No… More… Rest…" The great turtle shuffled around, shaking the mountain with each step. The stranger kept her feet this time.

"What are you talking about?!" she shouted. "What brotherhood!? What blood?! What does it all mean?! Who were they!? Where did they take him?! The child. Who was he?" *Was he a nephew? A son? A brother? Who?!*

Her questions fell on deaf ears. The head vanished into the mountain side. The legs became nothing but boulders once again.

She sighed, knowing her questions wouldn't be answered here. That's when she noticed a piece of paper stuck between two rocks. She plucked it and saw old writing on the front that she couldn't comprehend.

Between the two rocks she found a wooden container. She opened it and smiled as the sweet earthy smell of tea leaves filled her senses.

The stranger looked out from the plateau, the stunning sky overhead, resolute in her determination. And now she had a clue of where to search for answers. She adjusted her weapons, her cloak, and the animal skin before beginning her descent down Mount Anowara and towards civilization.

-The End-

TRAIL TO
IRON RIDGE

"Mom. Mom. Mom," said Tyler, shaking Mallory's arm.

"Not now, hush." She returned her attention to the peddler with the frayed purple coat. "You were saying?"

"We can take ya, sure," drawled the peddler, a thin white man with dirty brown whiskers across his chin and a gunbelt around his waist. His cattleman's hat pressed against his chest. "Always need another hand on the trail."

"What will that entail? Mr...?"

"Isaac is all the name my mama needed. But to answer your question, ma'am—you're Exposed, ain't ya? You're a woman, ain't ya? You cook, clean, you can drive, eh? You can read?"

"I... Yes," said Mallory. "I can cook, clean, and read. If by Exposed you mean I wasn't aware of this world until four months ago, then yes."

"Good! Then havin' ya around will pay off plenty." He gestured her to follow him.

She nodded and followed the peddler, holding Tyler's hand tightly. There were eleven mismatched vehicles, all customized with huge tires, engines, water tanks, and spiked bars around the rims of the car. They were like armoured turtles and beetles, something out of *Mad Max*.

Black and Latino men sat on turrets with rifles in several vehicles. Fifty or so people— settlers, ranchers, wanderers, and others—had joined the convoy heading westward.

"And you're heading to a..." *God, how do I explain it*

without sounding ignorant? "A modern place?" *That's even worse,* she thought, her anxious mind long since returning since coming to this world. A world without pharmacies or her medication.

Instead of being offended the peddler, Isaac, laughed. "Of course, ma'am! I'm heading to the Underground, they got a big ol' department that handles Exposure cases like yous. You'll be right at home."

"Mr. Isaac, please. We'd just like to find somewhere safe." *God, what am I do trusting a stranger like this?* What else could she really do in this situation? Stay in this dead end town out of an old spaghetti western, or try the Oregon Trail for something better. *Maybe that's all my ancestors really had to go on too.*

He put his hat over his heart. "I understand all to well, ma'am." He gestured down the convoy of vehicles. "There's plenty of families and civilians, single women, bachelors, and old folks all coming along. You'll be plenty safe."

She nodded, trying to convince herself they wouldn't be left for dead in a desert with... she gulped, glancing at a corral nearby full of strange animals braying and snorting, pawing at the dusty ground. "I'd—"

"Mom! Mom!" said Tyler. "Those are hadrosaurs."

"Mhmmm," she agreed. Terrified. *Dinosaurs, alive, today. Great.* It was something like that which sent them stumbling into this strange world. The hadrosaurs were above head-height with pine green hide covered in reddish stripes. Their horse-like heads ended with wide duck bills, their eyes tiny black jewels. The four muscular legs ended in hoof-like feet. Mallory glanced down the walkway of the town, seeing people bidding friends and associates farewell, workers moving crates and bags. *Being left in the desert for prehistoric monsters to find us.*

A huge rhino-like monster was being led into town by

some rancheros with sombreros. Its frilled head was like a medieval shield, ringed with short studs flushed orange and red. Foam and dust gathered at the corners of its beak and its tiny black eyes. Across its back and tail were quills like a porcupine, or the rib of a bird feather. It carried huge wooden barrels across its back.

"And we have to head west to get to the modern place?" she asked Isaac.

"Yes, ma'am!" he said cheerfully. "Through carnivore territory!"

Mallory grimaced, seeing two cowboys in the saloon eyeing her. She was a Black woman in her thirties, she wore a coat over her vest and blouse, a heavy Pullman suitcase with all their worldly possessions in hand. She wore a wide hat to keep the sun out of her eyes and her tightly-wound braids in a curled bun. Tyler had small jeans, a button up and a coat three-sizes too big, his hair's tight curls beginning to grow out. He rubbed his eyes again—exhausted from rising at dawn—then blinked himself awake at the sight of the prehistoric creatures.

She held onto his tiny hand, terrified of losing her grip on him.

"Over here, ma'am!" shouted the peddler, holding open the door to a modified minivan.

Around the hubcaps and bumpers were the scars of claw marks and dents... two of the rear windows were covered in tape and plastic to hide impacts of cracked glass. Inside the back were boxes, crates, barrels, and baskets of supplies with blue water tanks were bolted to the roof.

Inside the cabin sat another thin white man in the driver's seat. He wore denim overalls, a straw hat, oversized shirt, and sandals. His watery eyes studied the family, not offering a word of welcome or encouragement.

84

"Clyde! This is Mrs. McQueen and her son," said Isaac. "They ride with you. Treat 'em right."

The driver, Clyde, grunted.

"Don't mind him," said Isaac. "He's been a bit touched since a donkey booted him in the head."

The man was far from dumb. Just silently miserable. Mallory and Tyler climbed up into the long bench seat of the vehicle. It smelled of cigarettes, old leather, and dust. Mallory secured their behind the seats and pulled Tyler into her lap. He was heavy, but she refused to let him out of her arms.

Isaac smiled cheerfully. "We have a five-day journey until Iron Ridge Station. Then it's a smooth ride to the border. We'll get you to a safe place, ma'am. Don't you worry."

Mallory nodded. "I'm putting a lot of trust in you, sir."

He nodded and donned his hat. "I understand that, Mrs. McQueen." He closed the door, locking them behind bars like it was a cage. *To keep us in or keep other things out?*

Vehicles roared to life after a few minutes, engines clattering and people shouting their final goodbyes. It wasn't long before they pulled away. The faces of the old frontier town passed by at a leisurely pace. Riders passed into town, only adding to the time-displaced feeling that Mallory struggled beneath.

"Mom. Mom. Mom." Tyler pointed out the window. "Is that a centaur?"

Her wide eyes looked out the rear window and she gaped. It hadn't been riders.

She stared forward, ignoring the spiked bars on the hood of the van. She pretended it was just a normal drive. Just a normal everyday road trip. She tried to convince herself she wasn't on a different plane of existence, away from everyone and everything she ever knew.

Just the very thought of that made her want to cry, and she held onto Tyler with both arms.

◆

The first day was mostly long and boring. The sun blazed overhead, wisps of cloud distant and unconfident. The mountains were a craggily mass of blue along the horizon and only grew larger as they travelled, rising into titanic walls of stone flecked with white and gold light.

Clyde didn't say a word. There was a cassette playing, and he didn't say anything when Mallory put in some Marty Robbins. As the mountains passed them, she saw huge swaths of untouched land, like something out of an old painting.

Tyler sat next to her, unwilling to sit on her lap anymore. He was a small ten-year-old. She had finally let him watch *Jurassic Park* when they visited Denver last summer. He'd been asking for months, but it was just too intense for a nine-year-old. Now he could quote the film verbatim. He eventually leaned against her and slept, rocked to sleep by the rhythm of the vehicle and the slow guitar strum of the cassette playing.

By nightfall, they'd crossed many miles through the mountains, the convoy winding through the valleys and trails like a silvery snake. Birds cried over the landscape. The convoy came to a stop and pitched camp, the vehicles brought up in a ring.

Mallory was told to help out at the chuck wagon, a Frankenstein-ed Volkswagen and old van with an entire kitchen that opened out of the side. The camp cook, Mrs. Alexandra, a willowy Black woman who wore her hair in a wrap, got Mal chopping onions and carrots. She kept glancing around as mechanics worked at the vehicles, men and women stretched their legs or got campfires going. The men with guns patrolled the perimeter of the cars.

"If it's so dangerous, why did we stop?" said Mallory, only to herself.

Mrs. Alexander heard her. "Because it's more dangerous to drive this route at night."

"I'm sorry, I didn't mean…"

"It's fine, girl." The older woman looked at Mallory's work. "Fine job. More fine than necessary." She gave Mallory a look like she was reading her mind. "You're all Exposed, ain't ya?" asked Mrs. Alexander, as she stirred a cauldron over the crackling campfire.

"Yes," said Mal. "Four months now."

"Hard to believe it all, ain't it. Read some books from your world. Felt more like a fairy tale. Automobiles in every house, everyone with electric lamps and phones. Incredible." She glanced at Tyler who sat in the grass, bored. Several of the children played tag within the ring. He watched. They didn't ask him to play. They saw him and kept running. He was content with one of his few remaining kid's dinosaur books. It was peeling and worn, well loved, still brightly coloured. "It's like anything, Mrs. Mallory, he's different. Give it time."

Mal nodded, biting back her sorrow. "He struggled with friends back home too."

"Many intelligent boys do. Leave him be." Mrs. Alexander stirred the cauldron—rice, salted beef, and a few wild herbs. Mal added the vegetables.

"I've accepted this is our world," said Mal. "I know we can't go back, I'm just trying to learn to live in it." She glanced at

Tyler. Her heart sank seeing him so alone in the rough grass. "I just wish I could keep him from that."

Mrs. Alexander met Mal's eyes. "You can't, Mrs. Mallory. You really can't. Not here. Not on This Side. I met my husband along the Mizizippi and gave him two sons. Well, my husband died of cholera. My young son died when our townlord called a draft for every boy over the age of fourteen. My elder son has been gone for nearly twenty years. You can't protect your son from this world. You can only prepare him the best you can."

Mallory's stomach twisted. Her eyes glistened and she forced herself to finish her tasks before taking a step out of view behind car.

He can't see me cry. Not now. She needed to be strong for Tyler.

Mal pressed her face in her hands, sobbing silently. The withheld terror almost too much to bear. At home, she was worried about Tyler making friends, eating right, getting outside, paying their rent, and other pedestrian worries. *Why did I stay with Jason as long as I did?* Now she had the constant fear of diseases that had been exterminated in her world, monsters, and powers beyond her understanding. There were no police, no doctors, no family, no one to reach for. *No one to hold her and help her.*

Why did I have to leave?

A noise echoed in the distance. A long waling shriek that echoed across the mountains and valleys like the crash of waves. It sent icy chills up Mallory's spine and she instinctively pressed herself against the side of the car, the spiked bars poking into her back.

Mr. Isaac ran up, his hand on his belt. He saw the fear in her eyes and offered a small smile. He patted her shoulder. "Please stay in the ring, Mrs. McQueen. Get some rest. Let us worry about the rest."

Mal nodded and obeyed, her eyes constantly glancing behind her.

As they ate, Mrs. Alexander told Mal that there were cities within the mountains further north. Cities ruled by goblin warlords, modern cities. Underground cities with every modern convenience. It felt like such a distant goal. *We will reach it,* Mal told herself.

Mrs. Alexander continued talking about how every year the Goblin King continued to spread his influence to the towns and counties north of the Colorado River. The Navajo and Apache Sovereignties were nervous about that. Those Indian tribes had managed to build their own countries in this world.

Mallory didn't understand it. Any of it. It was just more to learn, more to adapt to.

The worst part of that was... that big stuff was the most comforting. She had grown so numb to the news, the politics, the hysteria—knowing this world had its own problems was comforting.

◆

Mal sat next to Mr. Clyde with Tyler under her arm. The long hours on the trail wore on. The sun hid behind some clouds as they drove deeper into the Colorado Basin. The shadows danced over the endless landscape. The mountains ringed with trees, the wide rivers and rolling hills of deep green trees. The convoy, even with its off-road modifications, only made a slow crawl through the landscape. The silvery snake of vehicles slunk along, avoiding obstacles and rivers.

"Mr. Clyde?" asked Mallory, absentmindedly.

The man grunted.

"How long have you been doing this?"

He spat. "Fort-ey y'ars, miss."

"Everyone says this is a dangerous trail. You keep working like this?"

"Nowhere else ta' go. The lizards been on my back a dozen times. I don't mind 'em," he rasped. "Just keep an eye on ya'r boy."

She was about to ask another question when Tyler jumped in his sleep. He hadn't sleep the entire night, uncomfortable and complaining in a tent, but, the instant they started rolling along the trail, he clocked out. He moved a lot in his sleep, but didn't wake up.

"What's out here?" she asked. "If you don't mind me asking?"

He leaned around, looking far behind the convoy. "Take a look for ya'self."

Mal twisted, looking far into the distance behind the convoy.

It might have been a dog or coyote. Mallory wished it was.

The shadow of a bird-like figure stood on the crest of a hill, well outside the perimeter of the outriders. It followed the convoy, hoping to scavenge food. It reached up with its switch-blade claws and scratched behind its head. It shook dust from its short feathery coat.

"Lizard is looking for scraps," said Clyde, grimly. "It's a small one, thin too. Probably be dead in a weak."

"What is it?"

His eyes narrowed. "Muckback raptor. That ain't a worry."

The dusty valley they crossed fell behind the bends in the mountains and Mallory prayed that the creature was gone.

But she knew that there could only be more of them ahead.

♦

The next night, Mallory sat around the campfire with several other travellers. Tyler still hadn't played with any of the other children, but she was beginning to think that might not be a bad thing. This journey would end and everyone would go their different ways.

Mallory sat on a small folding chair, chewing a biscuit with a small bowl of beans and pork. Mrs. Alexander sat down next to her, finally her own turn to eat.

Around the circle were two younger men, a family of three, and a lone middle-aged woman. Everyone ate quietly, unwilling to talk, the awkwardness of travel seemed to silence all around.

Isaac, a few spots away, was eating from a mess tin.

"Mr. Isaac," said Mallory, poking at her bowl. "Tell me more about where we're headed? This modern place?"

"After Iron Ridge, we have another week on the trail until we get Highhold, old dwerg settlement. It's a gateway into the realm of the Goblin King. Then it'll be a train ride to where you'll need to go."

"But what is it like there?" she asked, her arm around Tyler, who stopped eating. "What will it be like for us?"

"For you, ma'am? You'll be just alright. Exposed folk do well there. You'll probably find a job just like ya had on the Right Side, maybe even better. You'll slip into it like a glove."

Tyler sat cross-legged, nibbling his biscuit, eyes studying their compatriots.

One of the passengers pulled out a harmonica, ready to fill

the silence with a tune. "Not out here," snapped another traveller. "Not now." The man nodded, guiltily returning the instrument.

Silence filled the camp until Tyler looked up at a lone middle-aged woman. "Why are you crossing?"

"Tyler, hush," said Mallory.

The woman's frown deepened. She was a nasally woman with a long miserable face. She poked at her food. "It's alright," she chirped, her voice higher and less accented than Mallory expected. "I'm going to meet my son. He's found work to the west."

"What's he doing?" asked Tyler.

"He's a good lad, working as a clerk under an earl," said the woman. "My name is Marga Petrov."

"Where are you coming from?" asked Tyler.

"You're curious."

"That's enough, Tyler," said Mallory, reaching for his hand.

"No, it's quite alright," said Marga. "NeoAnglia, but my family came to America many years ago... but were Exposed during the Great Chicago fire."

"That was nearly two hundred years ago," said Mallory, slightly stunned.

"I believe so, my family has moved around, from fief to fief. We settled in NeoAnglia until my son managed to cross over to the mountains. Now it's time to meet him there."

"NeoAnglia?" asked Mallory.

"Kingdom of the Warwichs and bastion of Angleland," chirped one of the younger men, raising a flask in a mock toast. "Fucking blessed kings."

"Language," snapped Mrs. Alexander.

"You left there too?" asked Mallory. He was young and strong, like he'd been doing hard work his whole life. His face framed by scraggly brown-sideburns and a premature receding hairline.

"Aye," he said, drawling with an accent. "Names James Corwich. Worked southside of Dunwich docks meh whole life, ma'am. Bowed and gave lip to the lords and ladies that passed by. No more. I'm going to the west, finding my own way."

"So said a million before you," said the other man, younger, darker. He reached out and shook Mallory's hand with soft hands. His spectacles hung around his neck. "Godwin Corredor, graduate from Miskatonic University, Dunwich."

"What made you leave, then eh?" asked James.

"Well, while I can sympathize with rejecting the monarchical norms of our country, I'm not searching for far reaching isolation. Something nearly impossible in our time." He brushed off his smart vest. "I am joining a corpfirm in New Barci."

"Where is that?" asked Mallory. "I'm sorry, I'm... I'm Exposed. We both are."

"We know, m'lady," said Godwin. "It's plain as day. It's not a worry. I am heading to a city state along the Pacific Coast. A Latin heartland, centuries old, trades well with the Indigenous Sovereignties. Free from goblin or kingly rule."

Three others burst out laughing.

Godwin scoffed. "Have I missed something, good people?"

The mother of the family of three laughed. "If you think for one second that goblins ain't coming for New Barcid, you got another thing coming." She was a pretty white girl, a few years younger than Mallory. "Goblin King is spreading everywhere he can."

Godwin, somewhat deflated, sighed. "I suppose you're right, m'lady. One can only hope and do ones best."

"Hope is for northside folk," said James.

Godwin rolled his eyes. "My mother was a Latin-born immigrant, sir. She came to Dunwich with nothing. I'll hear nothing of old classist rivalries here."

James didn't say anything; he just ate another biscuit.

Mallory was nearly dizzy trying to keep track of everything. She looked at the young Godwin. "Are those modern places?"

"As modern as this world can offer, ma'am," he said, smiling. "I assure you, you'll find a home."

"What's it like?" she glanced to both Godwin and Isaac. "There's schools for Tyler?"

"Of course!" Isaac chuckled. "Schools and universities, aplenty. Whole district for magic schools too! You're a yankee, ain't ya? Well, they got doctors and health coverage! Took my dad, rest him, when he had kidney trouble and they fixed him right up. Didn't cost me nothing."

"Goblin bribes," sneered the mother of three.

Health care? Seriously? She could have burst out laughing if it wasn't so ridiculous. They'd have coverage in an underground city ruled by storybook creatures when they couldn't get it back home without her husband's insurance. At least until he lost it...

"Go on." She continued to stroke Tyler's curly black hair. She felt him nodding off in her arms.

"There will be a secure modern life for you, Mrs. Mallory," said Godwin. "Not to worry. Exposed rarely go hungry. Even a high school education is sought after in this world. I've seen high school kids from troubled homes on the Right Side be employed by corpfirms on the Wrong Side."

"Exactly!" said Isaac. "I'll get you to an official in High-hold and you'll be set. You'll see—"

A patter of feet against the grass preceded a shadow that slammed straight into Isaac, knocking him off his spot.

A woman screamed. Blood flecked Mallory's face. She blinked and finally realized that a huge bird-shaped body had crashed into Isaac. The creature, feathery and squealing, ripped into the peddler with its switch-blade claws and its long narrow snout clamped over Isaac's throat.

Everyone screamed, leaping to their feet and scattering to the vehicles.

A gunshot echoed, knocking the creature of Isaac. Its dusty grey feathers splashed with dark brown. It thrashed on the ground with a spade-shaped tail and talons at the end of each limb. Mallory came to her senses, held Tyler to her chest, and bolted for the nearest vehicle. She threw open the door and leaped into the cabin where Mrs. Marga was hiding. Mallory instinctively passed her Tyler and twisted around to close the door.

She screamed.

A second raptor was barrelling right towards her. It moved so fast it was nearly a blur, its talons outstretched and jaws wide open like a bear-trap.

Mallory pulled the door shut onto its head. It thrashed and snapped its jaws, squealing. Its claws raked at the window and metal, ringing and scratching. She pulled with both hands, getting her feet under her. The raptor wiggled its narrow jaws, prying open the gap with its scaly snout. Its skin pulled back to reveal the whites of its eyes.

Mallory grit her teeth, twisting in the driver's seat to get her legs between her and the door. She pulled with all her might, squeezing the raptor's head until it began to squeal with pain. It jerked back. Mallory kicked it, knocking it out and slamming the door shut. The scream ended.

Mallory laid back, gasping for air, her heart drummed in her ears. "God." She looked up, seeing Mrs. Marga holding Tyler against her heaving chest. A look of complete terror fell away to relief.

Mallory grabbed Tyler, holding him to her chest. Stroking his curly hair. He'd shut his eyes. "Thank you," said Mallory, her breath ragged.

"Of course," said the older woman, shaken.

"Is it over?" squeaked Tyler, finally opening his big brown eyes.

"Yes—"

The raptor slammed into window. Mallory and Mrs. Marga screamed. The creature pawed and snarled, leaving surface scratches in the glass. It fell back and leaped again, slamming its switchblade talons against the glass. The window held up, and it didn't try again.

A gunshot echoed from one of the truck turrets. A ranger worked his repeater, firing at the raptor, finally killing it when its chest was blown out.

Mallory covered Tyler's eyes.

She looked out the window and saw two more raptors had appeared and had been eating at Mr. Isaac. His stomach opened up in a mess of glistening red. Mallory's stomach churned and she averted her eyes.

Another gunshot and the creatures scattered.

The attacks stopped just after midnight. One of the rangers was killed when the raptors got a hold of him.

Exhaustion dragged at everyone as the convoy moved out at first light. The rangers rallied them, barking orders and driving the passengers forward, but it was slow going. The rangers were at their weapons at all times as the vehicles rolled along the trail.

As Mallory and Tyler rode with Clyde, she held Tyler so tightly he had to ask her to stop.

"I'm sorry, baby," she said, voice croaking.

He looked up at, eyes huge. "It's alright, mom. It's just the circle of life. Dinosaurs got to eat too."

Clyde chuckled for the first time. "Boy, you understand right. Just don't give 'em the satisfaction of an easy dinner."

♦

The hours passed and they didn't stop for a lunch. They ate biscuits, homemade granola bars, dried meat, and bags of dried fruits as the vehicles continue their crawl through the untamed landscape. There were no car games or conversations or songs... just long surveying glances and constant shoulder checks. Everyone was scared. Everyone felt eyes on their backs. Everyone knew they would be hunted by whatever was out there.

Clyde was silent, without his grumbles or curt commands.

Mallory felt the stone in her throat, the desperate need to cry. To release her fear, terror, and anxiety that had been building for months now. She'd never had many chances to release herself of the pain that sat in her chest. She needed to be strong for Tyler.

He can't see me cry. Not now.

The convoy was looping around the slope of a mountain, flanked by forests. Clyde adjusted the gear and they took the curve in a slow studied motion.

As the convoy passed a forest, everyone watched the trees with terrified anticipation. Eyes scanning every bush, fern, conifer, rock and tree. Shadows danced across their fearful eyes as sweat beaded down their brows and necks.

She looked up, seeing a shadow loom.

She yelped.

"Mom! Mom! It's okay!" Tyler, yanked at her arm. She was ready to snap at him, but then she saw. "Mom! It's a sauropod!"

A huge greenish head rose out of the treeline.

The huge head was wide and flat, almost like a whale, with nostrils on its forehead, its jaws crunching vegetation that it plucked from fern-like trees. It raised its head higher, showing its huge trunk-like neck covered in wrinkly skin.

The entire convoy stopped. The engines cut out. Clyde put the vehicle in park. None of the gunners fired their weapons. Mallory looked around, confused and terrified.

"Can't spook 'em," said Clyde, leaning on the wheel. "They stampede worse than an avalanche."

Another head rose above the canopy. From their huge barrel throats came whistling songs, like a pod of whales. The haze of the hot day, the insects, the distant calls of animals were all flooded away by the siren song of the sauropods.

They watched in awe and wonder. More great long-necked titans appeared. A juvenile appeared in the tree line, its oversized head nearly to the tops of the trees.

The herd left the shelter of the forest. Feet like curled fists dug into the earth. The huge greenish titans passed through the convoy, peacefully avoiding the vehicles as if they were nothing more than rocks. The two herds passed one another by. Both on their own journey. Both simply trying to survive in the unforgiving worlds they found themselves in.

"Clyde?" she spoke softly, as if something would hear her otherwise. "Why do people take this route, if it's so dangerous that is?"

"One of the few routes west that isn't run by goblins, lords, or rich folk."

Mallory nodded. "Shouldn't someone have built a train or something through?"

Clyde grumbled. "Somethin' you gotta understand about *This* Side, Mrs. Mallory. There never was no westward expansion and killin' of all the native nations. There was NeoAnglia, Franco, and the southern principalities along the east. Then there was the Dwergs in the mountains in the west, 'til the Gobs took over. Then there's lots of pockets of this world across the continent." He looked at Mallory with eyes that seemed less annoyed and simply tired. "No one strong enough to kill off the beasts here to give time to build a rail. The Centaur King could, but he won't. The Sovereignties won't."

"If it's so dangerous," whispered Mallory. "Why do we stop at night? Why don't we just drive through?"

He looked at Mallory with a grim expression. "Much worse things stalk the night than big ol' dinos'ars."

The last of the sauropods left the forest and passed the convoy. The herd marched deeper into the rugged countryside, immovable and unconquerable. Tyler watched with sparkles in his eyes.

Their eyes followed the herd into the distance and into a valley to the southwest, the bottom of a lost sea, with lakes and rivers catching the run off of the mountains above. From there grew lush scrublands with huge Savannah trees, thick prairie fields, and flowering glades. The empty basin was immense...

In a distant lake, rose more whale-like forms of sauropods. Along the shores, where pines and conifers painted the land green, were herds of animals, little more than dots at this distance, but Mallory could hear their trumpeting calls. In the shadows of a nearby group of trees was a trio of huge lumbering rhino-like bodies. They shook their horned frills and snorted before going back to chewing at hard thorny bushes.

Tyler nearly yelped, but Mallory clapped a hand over her son's mouth. When she was sure he could control his excitement, she lifted her hand and he whispered. "Mom, its... it's a triceratops." He blinked, unable to comprehend the wondrous place they had stumbled into.

As long as Tyler whispered, Mallory let him whisper the names of every animal they passed. He was ecstatic, terrified, and in sublime awe all at once. The way only a child can be.

◆

That night, the convoy was pulled into the recess of a huge monolithic slab of stone. It leaned over them like the awkward thumb of a great giant. The trumpeting calls echoed through the starry night. The convoy formed a tight box and torches surrounded the perimeter. The rangers patrolled in teams and kept throwing weary glances over their shoulders.

Everyone was uneasy. No one slept, and they weren't allowed to cook food. Only biscuits and hard barley bread with preserved fruit or nut spreads.

Everyone gathered around lanterns and hoped that the absence of smells wouldn't attract predators. Mallory sat on a small folding chair, chewing her biscuits. She held the food with both hands to keep from shaking.

Mrs. Alexander sat down next to her and passed Mallory a flask. "Drink up, dear. It'll calm you down."

"I don't drink."

"Drink."

Mallory sniffed the flask, winced, then took a sip. She coughed. "What is that, grain alcohol?"

Mrs. Alexander shrugged then took a sip and passed it around the circle. Mr. Godwin took a sip and passed it to James. The poor Anglo dock hand nodded, begrudgingly gracious.

"Forgive my impertinence," Godwin said to James. "Who awaits you, sir?"

"No one," said James, throwing back his head with the flask. "I got tickets for carriages from Iron Ridge to Los Diablos. Took everything I saved. I'll find work. Always work."

"Do you speak Espanol?"

James Corwich paled. "Church Latin. It's the same, ain't it? They're all Latins."

"You do know that most menial jobs in these regions are performed by Latins, mixed-bloods, and Black folk, right?"

"They have'ta have some Anglo."

"They are all gonna be using working man's Espanol in the industries you are skilled in, sir."

James sat, eyes widened, the realization hitting him that he had made an immense mistake. Picking up his whole life, fleeing across the continent rife with danger… then going to find jobs he may not even have the language for. Mallory felt that immense sense of fear, the knowledge of a total mistake long since committed to. She understood that feeling. She'd made mistakes like that. That welling feeling came up in her throat and she squeezed Tyler's hand to secure herself.

Godwin, Mrs. Alexander, and others all howled with laughter. He passed the flask onward, then buried his face in his hands.

"Not to worry, old boy," said Godwin. "I'll get you conversational before we arrive. Church Latin is an excellent base, but nothing compares to a mother forbidding Anglo around the dinner table."

James nodded, silently stunned at the herculean miscalculation he made and the study he would have to endure to fix it.

"And your destination?" asked Mrs. Alexander to the mother of three, her husband bouncing the toddler on his knee. Mallory believed they were the Austins, a white family with a three-year-old boy and twin seven-year-old girls. They all had a slight southern accent.

"We're heading for an oil town, new vein discovered north of Mexico, long way ahead, but we'll get there," said Mrs. Austin. "We'll find a new life."

"Where were you from?" asked Mallory.

"Oh, just a barony from what you'd call Georgia, if my memory serves."

"What happened?"

"Another baron tried to take over," said Mr. Austin, not looking away from his blubbery sunburned son. "We got out before the fighting started. Got out with much of what we had. Better than most."

"The town we lived in is gone now," said Mrs. Austin, very matter-of-factly.

Mallory wrapped herself around her son, hoping and praying and thinking about their future. *They are all lost, looking for a new life,* she thought, looking across all those faces. The father from the family half-hugged his wife, kissing her head. *They are all just searching for that better life in a world they can't control.*

Mallory felt a lot less alone than she'd been since her Exposure. In a world she didn't understand. A terrifying dark world where she had no control. There was something to be said knowing that she wasn't the only one—

A piercing roar echoed in the distant night.

The entire camp went silent. All watching. There was a shuffle of the outriders crossed the camp with the case that housed the bazooka.

Everyone was frozen and watched.

No one slept that night.

Everyone just froze and watched and listened to the sounds of predators on the hunt.

◆

Nothing came that night. They survived and continued their journey, exhausted, sleepless, and paranoid. As dawn cast light through the mountains and forests, everyone loaded up. Children whined and cried, some older folks needed help moving around.

Clyde was shockingly more amiable. He elbowed Tyler,

handed him a set of binoculars, and pointed out the window. Mallory perked up from her stupor, watching the interaction.

"That there, boy," said Clyde, he was pointing to a huge sloped forest at the foot of a mountain. "Wolf Mountain. Not that there's any wolves."

Tyler nodded. He rubbed his eyes and used the binoculars. "I see hadrosaurs in the forest."

"Aye, duckheads always in the forests or in the fields, they get bigger up north."

The convoy was passing through a prairie of tall grasses. The waist high foliage crunched beneath the tires.

The small colourful heads of huge birds sprung up from the grass. First a few, then a dozen, then nearly a hundred. A huge flock of gazing ostrich-like creatures. They chirped and warbled, flapping their feathered arms. Many of them had turkey-like red flaps under their beaks or on their heads.

Tyler pointed. "Those are ornithomimosaurs, Mom. I don't know which one. Hard to tell."

Clyde chuckled. "We call them turkey storks. Get one, can feed a family for a month."

"You eat dinosaurs?" said Tyler, stunned.

"Ain't no deer around, some folk gotta eat something." Clyde chuckled with a high-pitched cackle. "Tastes just like chicken."

Tyler wasn't disgusted or hurt like Mallory expected. He just looked back at the creatures in awe. Mallory watched the creatures chirping back and forth. She put her arm around her son and hugged him tight.

"Moomm… I'm fine."

"I know," said Mallory. "I was just thinking about how much you've grown and adapted to this world."

"Mom," he groaned. "I'm just doing what animals do. They adapt to new surroundings—"

The truck bucked and jerked to a halt. Mallory held onto Tyler and the door handle. When Clyde put them in four-wheel drive, it only dug them deeper into the soil. Mallory was frozen. Clyde leaned back, cursing under his breath.

"Lord is testing me," hissed Clyde. "Hit a flood bed… Shoo."

He honked the horn in a pre-set pattern, announcing to the other trucks what had happened.

The convoy came to a stop. Men sat in their turrets with their guns while three drivers dropped into the muddy ground and hurried to Clyde's truck. They all kept wary eyes on the grass. Mallory felt her heart hammering in her ears as they used a board and their own strength to push the vehicle out of the trap.

Mud and grass fibres sprayed. The truck rumbled around them. Mallory watched the tall grasses swaying in the wind, terror leaching into her heart. She looked through the rear-view window and saw Mrs. Marga wave from the other vehicle, an encouraging smile on her face.

Tyler waved back with a wide grin.

Clyde pushed the gas, the tires squealed and sprayed more mud. The drivers cursed and with a heave the truck came free.

Mallory let out an exhale.

Clyde seemed to share her relief. He leaned out the window to talk to a driver, a tall Black man with suspenders. "We better get going—"

"Agreed," said the other drive. "Our fuel is—"

Before he could finish his sentence a huge shadow leapt out of the grasses. It slammed into the driver, jaws around the back of his neck. A wet crack snapped his spinal column with a quick jerk.

Six more huge shadows leaped from the grass. Seven raptors. Not the small, turkey-sized Muckback raptors—these were long, lithe beasts with black and white feathering and quills along their necks, several with pure white heads instead of patterns. They screamed and slammed into the other driver.

Gunfire echoed, but it was too late.

Four went for the vehicle behind Clyde's. Screams echoed from the other vehicles.

The seventh saw Clyde's window was open. Its huge head full of sawblade teeth clamped onto his wrist. He screamed. Mallory pulled Tyler back, the moment freezing in time. Its white feathery head was set with spikes just above the dilated yellow eyes.

Mallory slammed her foot on the gas. The car was jerked into motion.

Clyde screamed right in her ear as his arm was torn from its jaws. Blood sprayed the cabin as Clyde's entire forearm was ripped from his elbow with shreds of skin and flesh. Tyler wailed, his hands over his ears.

More gunshots echoed. Mallory drove as Clyde yelped with pain, clutching his bleeding wound. They cut through fresh grass, away from the convoy.

In the rear-view, cars to the rear of the column scattered,

but the one Mrs. Marga was in remained stationary and surrounded. Upright tails thrashed back and forth as the raptors worked their way into the vehicle. One of the big dune-buggies rolled by, and a man fired pistols, which knocked a raptor off the vehicle.

Another raptor, hidden in the grass, leaped onto the buggy. It drove off-course and disappeared from the view

Clyde swore, his voice growing faint. "I can drive."

"Your arm is off! Shut up and let me drive!" She knew that's what she should had said to someone else a long time ago.

The convoy pulled out of the fields in a scattered pattern and rallied back into a long train, like ants that got lost, and re-knitted their marching line. They'd lost two vehicles: the patrol buggy and the van that carried Mrs. Marga.

They didn't get much farther before they had to stop to give medical attention to Clyde and make repairs. They took position on a rise in the river basin, the vehicles drawn up in a ring with everyone packed tighter as they waited out the danger of the night. They all took turns watching and waiting, unable to sleep, unable to move. A few of the children slept, and that's what mattered.

Mallory found herself standing by the chuck wagon, looking out at the sunset, the strands of burning orange clouds against the picturesque landscape. The mountains and forests teemed with prehistoric life. Mallory could see the bobbing heads of sauropods and the hear the orchestral cacophony of calls made by the hadrosaurs. She continued to look over her shoulder, seeing those open jaws and excited dilated eyes flash in her mind.

They watched and waited, hoping to see the sunrise they knew wouldn't be around for many long hours. Mallory brought a basket of dried fruit packets to a ring of folding chairs. Tyler was curled up on one, dozing. Mallory sat down next to Mr. Godwin who was tending to Clyde's arm.

"On my word," said Godwin. "I regret coming by this way."

"What other way was there?" asked Mallory.

"Oh there's routes across the continent, few and far between, but they exist. Far to the north is the Yarldoms of the Eastlandes, Canada in your world. To the south are the ships of the Latin Viceroys and Carib-born nations. Here is simply the most direct."

Clyde hissed as the bandage was pulled tight over his stump. "Bloody lizards."

Mr. Godwin nodded. "Indeed. You will live, sir." His eyes seemed to say, *as well as you can, however.*

Clyde didn't have it in him to curse or have a complaint. He just leaned back, his arm in a sling. He seemed to fall asleep quickly with his hat over his eyes.

Mallory looked westward, nearly forgetting their destination through the horrors they faced. The mountains nearly leaned over them. The titans of rock and stone were close enough to touch.

"We must be almost there," said Mallory.

Mrs. Alexander sat down next to them, handing out biscuits and cookies. "We'll reach Iron Ridge by tomorrow afternoon."

"Then why don't we just drive through the night?" said Mallory.

Mrs. Alexander took a long sip from her flask. They all knew how close they were. It was simply the impossible matter of surviving the final leg of the journey. The older woman glanced in the westward direction, then at everyone around the lantern. "It's risky to try this terrain at night."

"It's just as dangerous if we sit here and wait," said Mallory.

Mr. Godwin, James, and several others shared looks. A

long silence followed. Everyone weighing their options. The drivers with their repeaters and rifles mulled it over too, whispering in hushed concerned tones. They knew this land and its dangers, but this convoy run had taken more out of them than the others. The sun dipped behind the mountains, casting the primordial land into night.

"Oh fine," chirped Clyde beneath his hat. He peaked from beneath his cap and threw something into Mallory's hands. She barely caught it and realized it was the keys. Clyde grumbled and rolled back over to his misery and pain. Mallory smiled.

"I can't but agree," said Mr. Godwin. "This place is defensible, but at the state of things, I do believe the risk might be worth it."

"But this just ain't no road," said Mrs. Alexander. "This is the rough wilds. We hit a single ditch or get stuck, we are more vulnerable than we've ever been."

One of the drivers stood up, seemingly ready to get going—

A call echoed in the night.

Everyone knew what it meant.

Mallory and Mrs. Alexander shared a look. The older woman swore. "Alright! Let's pack up and get going! GO!"

The camp burst in a flurry of activity. Mallory reached for Tyler, but when she found nothing, her heart stopped.

Anyone with firearms ran to the cars, taking position for an outward defence. Anyone without a weapon ran to secure the vehicles and the children. Three of the trucks roared back to life with their lights illuminating the insects in the air. Tyler was no where to be seen.

"Tyler?" Mallory spun, already dizzy. "Tyler!"

A driver pumped his gas and called for any passengers ready to run when he was ready.

"Where's my son!" yelled Mallory, heart racing, trying to grab the shoulder of a driver "Tyler!"

Mrs. Alexander grabbed her arm and they shared that terrified horror that only a mother can share. The older woman nodded and they both went to check different wagons. Mallory ran, throwing back canvas, checking under the wagons. "Tyler! Tyler!" *If I find him...!* "Tyler!"

Mallory's vision was red, she ran, checking behind trucks. She stopped.

She froze.

Between two trucks, just at the edge of the light, she saw him.

Tyler stood, hugging his backpack, looking up at a huge shadow in the darkness.

Mallory gulped. She felt the wind against her back...

Tyler was so small, wearing his little button-up and slacks. He was as still as a statue, like he knew not to move or was captivated by what he saw, staring up into the darkness. The shadow blinked its reflecting yellow eyes, its huge head low to the ground.

Mallory looked back, everyone was looking the wrong way. She whimpered, seeing her child alone in the firelight. She was alone, frozen, with nothing to reach for.

The shadow took a curious step forward into the light, nostrils flaring, its bulldog-like face was creased and wrinkly. Horns on its brow hid its eyes in deep black sockets.

Tyler remained motionless.

Mallory wanted to scream, but knew she couldn't do a damn thing.

If she screamed, the creature could attack. If she did nothing then Tyler would be killed. Terror froze her in place, cementing her to the ground. Her hand reached out, wishing only to grab Tyler by the back of his shirt and wrench him back from certain death.

The theropod raised its head, vanishing back into the night, rising like a demon. Its jaws opened, revealing the glimmer of stringy saliva that stretched between its serrated teeth. Its eyes reflected the light like haunted blue orbs.

"Tyler!" she screamed.

Before the creature could strike, a shotgun barked, the flashing light illuminating the monster. Nearly twenty-feet long with comically vestigial arms, skin like wrinkled leather covered in crocodilian armoured studs. Its ghoulish face striped grey and white.

At its side were two more, one with a broken horn the other with stripes down to the end of its tale.

The first creature took the buckshot in its meaty shoulder, stumbling back and bellowing with pain.

Over Mallory's shoulder, she saw Mrs. Alexander had fired the weapon. Eyes focused and narrowed. The barrel of the shotgun smoking.

Mallory didn't think. She acted. She bolted for Tyler, grabbing him by the torso and wrenching him back just as the broken-horn pounced. Massive jaws chomped where her son had stood, a wet clap slapped the air. Mallory nearly tumbled, wrenching herself back through the ring of cars. She clutched her son to her chest, running hard as the campsite collapsed in on itself.

The theropods charged, knocking over a souped-up charger. People scrambled, people screamed, firearms cracked, and the beasts cried out. Two cars peeled away, tires screeching. A driver screamed, struggling to get the modified minivan to turn over. The theropod slammed into the vehicle's flank, knocking it onto its side with a huge crash.

Mallory ignored everything. Everyone. She didn't see what happened to Mrs. Alexander or Mr. Godwin, or James Corwich, or Clyde, or anyone else. She ran, desperate to save her son. He was pressed to her chest, despite trying to see over her shoulder.

She saw Clyde's truck. She didn't think, she acted. She swerved to avoid a theropod chasing fleeing people.

She threw open the driver side door and tossed Tyler into the passenger seat. She still had the keys and the vehicle started without issue. The engine hummed and she was about ready to step on the gas when she looked in the mirror.

A lantern had been thrown against the ground, scattering oil over dried grass. The fire bloomed into a carpet of bright orange light, illuminating the beasts from beneath.

The dinosaurs busted their horns through the windshields of the trucks and ripped out the people inside, shredding flesh and clothing against the broken glass. Arms and body parts were torn from the vehicles, chomped down and gulped the way a birds swallow prey. Wet smacking perforated the screams.

The animals knew that the metal containers held food, like turtles in their shells. *All* the predators knew that there was food within. Each time someone took this trip, it only reinforced that behaviour. It drew the animals to them. The theropods lost themselves like a fox in a chicken coop. They snapped their jaws, biting down on anything they could, shaking people until their bones snapped or another target presented themselves.

A theropod raised its head, under lit by flames, with eyes

like pinpricks beneath its horns, demonic and terrifying. Primal fear ran through Mallory's spine. It raised its thick neck, bird-like, before stalking towards the truck.

Mallory yelped and slammed the gas.

They peeled away, leaving the monster in a cloud of dust. It charged back into the massacre like an excited dog.

Mallory looked back for the briefest moment.

The fires grew and the entire camp was a vision of hell. Horned demons surrounded by fire, bringing its fury down on those it deemed worthy of its hollow mercy. A beast bit down on a wounded traveller, who was unable to escape, whipping its kill back and forth to break its spine before gobbling it down like a fish.

The car hurtled through the prairie, dirt flying from the tires. The blue of the moonlight glimmered off the mountains, like waves of diamond dust. The forests of the valleys teeming with prehistoric life. Terrifying monsters of a bygone age. She kept the speed up until the gunshots and roars died down behind her.

She looked up at the bright waxing moon, then down at the landscape.

Where do we go? Where can we go? She turned to avoid bushes and kept on a clear part of the ground where animals had stomped the grass down. Wilderness went seemingly forever. Mallory didn't know which way to go and she didn't know what was out there. She had nothing. She had no one. She was alone and everything that stood between her son and certain death.

She ran her hands over Tyler's head, feeling his hair. His small arms clung to her. He blinked again in the darkness.

Mallory started to cry. She needed to be strong for Tyler.

He can't see me cry. Not now.

It was never the right time. Never the right moment. She tried to swallow back the tears but failed, and they rushed down her cheeks. She tasted salt and fear.

Why now?

She had cried in front of him before. When Jason, her husband, came home again without a job. He'd been so sweet for so long, but, as Tyler got older, she realized that the sweetness was armour and his sadness was a trap. Jason was weak, and Mallory needed help. She put Tyler in a car and said she was going to Denver to see her parents.

"I can come with you," he said.

"I'll call you." Said Mallory, shutting the door. She looked at his pathetic face, his sagging shoulders. "Please, Jay, please find work. I'll start applying in Denver. See what we can find."

He nodded. He was a broad-shouldered white man, with a clean shaven jaw and curly brown hair. Tyler took after Mallory far more in colour, but his frame and face were entirely Jason's. "I'll join you when I have something."

He'd been a worker in a Chicago factory before the recession and another wave of closures.

"Yes." *Maybe.*

Tyler sat asleep in the back of the car.

"Please, Mal. I love you, I love you both." He said the words, but she saw that calculated look that she'd finally learned to recognize. That hidden deep frustration. That insecurity that forced her to always stay.

"I'll call you."

He stepped forward, arms out to hug her.

"I'll call you." Her entire body felt a wave of shivers and disgust. She slipped into the driver's seat. He looked through the window with huge eyes, but still with that calculated, pathetic look. She drove out of the lot of their apartment building before he had any chance to appeal to Tyler.

She watched Jason's sagged shoulders and hopeless expression pass from view.

Before they could leave the city limits, she looked into the mirror, tears in her eyes, and saw with horror that Tyler was awake. He shut his eyes and pretended to go back to sleep, his head resting against the car door.

She needed to be strong for Tyler.

He can't see me cry. Not now.

She needed to be strong for Tyler because Jason wouldn't.

When she blinked away the tears, guilt and shame rose in her chest. It was their flight to Denver that got them Exposed. It was a crash in her anxious delirium and fear that drove them to this unimaginable world.

That's what everyone told her. *Fear, isolation, anxiety… the preconditions for Exposure to the Wrong Side.*

"It's my fault we're here," she whispered to herself.

When the lights of the camp had been gone for a long time, she stopped. Silence filled the car. They were on a rise in the prairie, the mountains opened up in the distance. The sky shone with more stars than she'd ever seen, but it wasn't the time to appreciate it.

Mallory looked at the console and saw that the gas was in the red. She turned off the engine and the lights.

She looked out across the flat grasses and bushes, the trees were all far away. *Shit. Shit. Shit.* "I'll be right back." She reached behind the seat for one of the half-full Jerry cans.

Tyler nodded, holding onto his seat belt with both hands.

Mallory checked around the vehicle, seeing nothing but hard soil and grass when she cracked the door open. She slowly slunk out car. Her boots crunched on the soil. Her ears vibrated with adrenaline, heart racing in her chest as she crept around the side of truck to the gas port. The wind blew against her face, pushing at her braids, the smell of soil, grass, and cold filling her lungs.

She exhaled and hurried around the back. Her breath caught in her chest and she skirted round the bars and spiked bumper, then to the fuel port.

SNAP.

She turned with her hands held up, expecting open jaws to clamp shut on her throat.

It was only a piece of tumbleweed that got caught on a stick.

It blew away, making more snapping sounds each time it bounced across the landscape.

She exhaled and hurried again to fill the tank. Each desperate glug, glug, glug, of the can pouring petrol into the tank. She adjusted her pour, too urgent and awkward. It flowed easily and faster.

She looked east, back to where the campsite had been. *I left them.* She shook her head. *No, they'd understand.*

When the can was empty, she hurried back to the driver's seat. She tossed can in the back, slammed the door, reached for the ignition—

Tyler's hand clapped down on her wrist.

"What."

"Shhh."

Mallory froze. Tyler had never hushed her, ever. She turned very slowly from the boy and looked up.

No.

Beyond the rise, less than a kilometre away, was a ripple in the landscape. Something Mallory had taken as a shoulder of dirt or collection of upturned stones. Tyler was silent and still and Mallory followed his example.

An exhale shot dirt from the end of the ripple of earth.

It put its massive feet under it and pushed itself up to its full height. The huge beast rose like a piece of the landscape. Another theropod, but massive, bigger than a school bus. It lacked horns or another kind of ornamentation. It simply had a massive rounded snout that could swallow a horse.

It shook the dust from its back and stalked towards the silent vehicle. Each footstep sent a slight shudder across the ground. Its bulk seemed to float elegantly through the air. Its vestigial arms hugged its chest.

Mallory gripped the wheel with both hands until knuckles white as she kept from trembling.

The beast lowered its huge head to sniff the vehicle, the moonlight revealing scars across its scaly snout, the tufts of proto-feathers across its head and neck and its huge eyes. It was the eyes that made Mallory bite back as gasp of pure terror. A chill went across her arms and legs. Tyler was frozen, eyes glistening as he watched the predator study them.

The eyes were more like an owl than a reptile. It was intelligent and knew exactly what it was looking at. It saw them.

It didn't attack. It didn't rip them from the vehicle and devour them. Mallory's mind played the image over and over again, but it didn't happen.

It sniffed, circled the car. It was immense. She saw scars on its side and back, claw marks across its snout. It was dirty red with a darker colouration across its back.

Then it simply walked off. Each silent footfall quaking Mallory in her seat. Its tail bobbed behind it and it marched off into the distance.

Silence filled the vehicle for a long time until the dinosaur was long gone into the darkness of the night.

"Why..." she touched Tyler's shoulder, making sure he was okay.

"We weren't enough for it, mom," squeaked Tyler. "We weren't a threat."

She reached over and hugged Tyler, squeezing him tight to her chest. "I'm so sorry, baby. I'm so sorry. I brought us here."

Tyler shook his head against her. He didn't say anything. Mallory could never tell if he knew what she meant or not, or maybe he just couldn't figure out what to say or how to express it. He was just so smart and so much stronger than her.

When they broke their embrace he looked at her with his big brown eyes. "Mom, I want to go home."

"Me too."

With the rock in her throat becoming unbearable, Mallory finally let the charade drop.

"I'm so sorry, baby," she gasped, patting his face. "I'm so sorry I took us away. I'm so sorry I brought us here. I made a huge mistake. I made this happen." Tears fell down her cheeks. She gasped, holding onto the wheel.

"...But not to dad," he said, finishing his original thought. "Dad didn't make us happy." That's when the tears came, and Mallory sobbed in front of her son. He wrapped his tiny arms around her and stroked her hair. "I just want to go home."

It's hard when a child realizes their parents are only human. That they aren't flawless or indomitable paragons. *The fact is that we are just as scared and uncertain as we were when we were kids ourselves.* It's harder still when a child confirms they already knew how flawed and scared they are.

Mallory sobbed into her tiny son's arms and finally gave up the burden that she couldn't bring him back.

When her heart was finally bearable, she let go and kissed his head and cheek. "Thank you, baby."

He nodded and sat back down.

She turned the key and the engine hummed back to life. She followed the compass in the console westward.

◆

Daylight came, a rippling wave of warmth over the distant eastern horizon.

Hadrosaurs and sauropods sang as they stirred in their herds and families. Ceratopsians bashed their shield-faces over a territorial dispute. A pack of raptors gathered in their den, falling into an interlocked sleeping pile as they finished a long night's hunt. The mass herds of animals stamped down old grass, scattered seeds, and fertilized new growth in the constant cycle of rebirth.

They would follow a cyclical route through the mountain valleys and canyons,

A ribbon of smoke loomed back towards the camp.

The last of the petrol carried them to rising cliffs at the edge of valley. The mountains loomed above Mallory, like more prehistoric titans. This time they promised safety and survival from their pilgrimage through the wilderness.

The wall of Iron Ridge was a bastion. Two stone monoliths climbed well over two hundred feet into the air. Worn and weathered from millennia of erosion, they remained the stalwart markers for every traveller and tribe for a thousand leagues. Between the two monoliths, up a gravel road, was a crude fortification, the palisade built from scraps of sheeting and timber and repaired with regular dabs of cement.

Mallory looked up at the wall as she slowed the vehicle. Her eyes watering as the sunlight glinted off the metal. She turned off the vehicle and got out, Tyler in her arms despite his size.

"I can walk, mom."

"I know," she hugged him tight before setting him down. She held his hand as they hiked up the road towards the gates of Iron Ridge. There were shouts and activity on the walls. There were a set of huge metal doors, covered in thousands of claw marks and scratches.

With a huge shudder and a whining squeal, the doors opened and let the pair in.

They survived the badlands and their host of prehistoric terrors. *Now we just need to keep on surviving,* Mallory said to herself, and passed into Iron Ridge.

The call of a beast echoed in the distance.

—The End—

THE
SHATTERED CLAN

The knuckle bones clattered on the ground, ringing with the words of the gods. Zakar didn't understand them the way his brother did. Prophecy was a fickle business. *Things happen, just never the way one expects,* thought Zakar Moon.

The bones clattered again.

Nar Moon sat cross-legged on the ground, his narrow shoulders wrapped in a wyrm-skin cloak. Zakar's brood-brother was the clan shaman. The tent was musty with smoke and animal sweat. Furs and sleeping skins covered floor, bowls, crates, and braziers in the corner. Armour and weapon racks against one side and a gaggle of clan elders on the other.

The bones continued to clatter.

The flickering flames sent shadows across the canvas walls. Against the back wall, the ragged banner of the BlackDragon Clan was draped above the lord's crude wooden throne.

Lord Dracar Wyrmbak watched Nar Moon's ritual with silent trepidation. He glanced at the elders, all wrapped in lizard and saurian skins, faces hidden beneath cowls. Dracar's own hollow face set with blazing brown eyes. He was the brooding titan of the BlackDragon Orcs. His massive chin rested on his titanic fists, his skin like the face of an ancient worn shipwreck.

Zakar paced at the entrance like a caged beast as he waited for his brood-brother to complete his consultation with the gods. At nearly six-feet tall, Zakar was the smallest of the captains. His broad shoulders were bare and swirled with the black wyrm tattoos of the clan; his long apish arms and square chest were scarred from years of fighting. His face was feline and cunning, with narrow reddish eyes. He wore a simple sleeveless tunic and trousers, patched and repaired regularly. A long-crooked sabre hung on the belt at his waist.

Zakar was Captain of the First Warband. The other two captains, Bruce Kal and Mog Bane, were tending to the clan, watching the perimeter and organizing foragers.

It had been a bad winter for the BlackDragon Clan.

Spring had arrived and, with it, new dangerous opportunities. A representative of the Goblin King had brought a message from the mountains. An offer of employment. An offer of resurrection.

Scum.

The bones clattered one final time with the weight of crashing tides.

Silence followed.

Shaman Nar looked up, his long face set with bright red eyes, a pinched nose, and long sharp fangs. Nar was just over five feet tall, always the runt of the brood, but more dangerous than any of them. Nar was a fox where Zakar was a panther. Nar was clever beyond his age and had been marked early to become a shaman by the elders. He communed with the gods and dragon ancestors, but even his powers hadn't been enough to save the clan.

Zakar stopped his pacing, waiting for his brother to speak.

"I don't like what the gods are giving me," said Nar, half-joking. "Slimy bastards…"

A cloaked elder hissed at the blasphemy.

Lord Dracar's sour calm was at breaking point. He glared at the shaman, growling deep in his chest.

Zakar squatted next to his brother, trying to make sense of the bones. His body ached for action. He hated waiting. *But like the great predators, like the dragon ancestors… I will wait.* He had to. He bristled against patience but knew it essential.

"Speak plainly, Nar," growled the Lord.

"The gods will not aide us in this," said Nar, flatly, his fangs glinting. "We are on our own, as we have been for near a year."

Lord Dracar rose from his throne like a rhino stirring from sleep.

Zakar rose too, meeting his chieftain's gaze.

"Call the clan, Zakar. Gods or not, we march. We strike under the cover of night. We attack this Lord Goldstein."

The order fell with the force of an executioner's axe.

"Aye, Lord," said Zakar. He left the tent, shoulders clenched and fist gripping his sabre.

The gods had truly abandoned them.

The mountain air was cold and unforgiving, winter claws still dragged at the campsite. The clan had retreated to the mountains, finding a canyon to hide in and wait out the winter. Dozens of peaked shelters filled the crevasse, patch-work tombs of canvas, skins, and scavenged materials.

The BlackDragon Clan had endured a very bad winter, but this opportunity could help them escape their fate. If they could succeed, that is.

Zakar found one of his vanguard boys, Brig, poking at a campfire. The coals glowed low. There was no soup pots or roasts tonight. Brig was as thin as a reed, but still quick as a snake, a runt of his brood. His eyes studied the coals with an intelligence that reminded Zakar of Nar.

"How ya, Briggy," asked Zakar, kneeling to the boy.

"Been better, Lord. And I ain't no runt anymore."

"But you're *my* runt," joked Zakar.

That got a smile out of the boy. "Go sod yourself, Zakar. I'm too hungry for that."

Zakar put his hand on the boy's shoulder. "I know. Me as well. I'll see what Mog has brought."

"Nothing! There's no deer or pigs. Only rabbit and weasels, we're vermin starved. Not even a dog…"

Zakar sighed. "Soon, lad." He patted the boy's shoulder.

Brig looked up, eyes wild with intellect beyond his few years. "Why'd they do it? The humies? We did our job, why'd they do us in like that?"

"I don't know, lad. Might be in their nature, like cats and wolves." He stood up, the runt rising with him. "Get your brothers ready. We march tonight."

Brig nodded and hurried away.

As Zakar moved through the camp, he was reminded of how they got to their current sorry state. Orcs of all shapes and sizes languishing and loitering with no spirit or hope. Bored eyes, sad faces, and slouched stances. There wasn't even any fighting. The orcs clung to themselves and each other, piled like starving jackals waiting to die.

The BlackDragon Clan had lived in the foothills of the Rokki Mountains for two hundred years. Their progenitors were exiles from dark forest tribes of Germania who came to the Americas as stowaways. They were blessed by ancient dragons in millennia past, a story they still held to their hearts.

They lived amongst the great redwoods, taller than spires and thicker than boulders in this new continent. The forest was a bastion that protected them. They traded, trapped, and even worked with Chinook clans and some Cascadian settlements. When called to war, they ran as mercenaries, or they were forced to raid when needed to. As any needy did in hard times.

Last spring, Lord Dracar made an unimaginable mistake. They took the offer from a Baron Jupiter Suez. A lordling to the south, on the edge of Cascadia. He had a border war with another lordling, though the BlackDragons never knew the reason—land rights, an insult, or an alliance gone wrong, perhaps. Dracar and the elders agreed to the offer of money and loot as mercenaries. It would feed the clan for another two winters.

It seemed a good deal, like some skirmishes and battles they had joined in decades before. Nar was the only one who spoke against it. A distant strange baron they knew nothing about? It seemed suspicious to him. Zakar cursed himself for not siding with his brother.

It had been six months of battling. The BlackDragons were an auxiliary force. They skirmished and attacked when Lord Dracar saw fit, working with the captains in the Baron's army. They aided Baron Jupiter when called. In the battle, just before the first snowfall, the Baron Jupiter defeated his foe. The terms called.

The BlackDragons retreated to a conquered farmstead and waited for their payment.

That had been their second mistake.

When the wagons and trucks came, they didn't bring food or money. They brought weapons… and men the used them.

The BlackDragons didn't stand a chance. Jupiter's men burnt their camp, killing and murdering orcs with reckless abandon. Zakar fought, trying to cover his clan, rally with his lord and the other captains. They were beaten before it had even started. The orcs were unprepared. Jupiter's men blasted them with shells of rock salt, iron nails, and silver filings, like the superstitions of old. They burnt the orcs' bodies and beheaded them. Made an example of them. The snow fell hard that night and the fires burnt black. Zakar remembered the fire and blood like a nightmare. The squeal of the baron's snow-machines and crackle of automatic weapons.

Zakar and Nar had lost the remains of their brood.

Arar and Nurar...The Moon brood. Born under an auspicious full moon seventeen winters prior. Now only two remained.

The battles for Baron Jupiter had been brutal, but his slaughter of the BlackDragons had been unprecedented. He didn't just want to *not* pay the orc mercenaries, he wanted to exterminate them. Remove them from memory and song.

The BlackDragons' escape into the mountains had been devastating as the cold and hunger of winter further decimated them. Their BlackDragon banner flew for no victories. Their hunters came back with nothing. Their messengers were slaughtered when they reached out for aide.

On the brink of extinction, they were faced with another hopeless battle with the promise of aide for their victory.

Zakar entered the camp plaza. where a bonfire crackled with what slim timber they could harvest from the mountainside. Sullen orcs, the larger warriors of the clan, surrounded the pit like bored lions without a sun or hungry wolves in lean times. They sharpened weapons, oiled their few remaining rifles, fletched arrows, and honed knife blades. They tried to keep their minds occupied from their plight.

A pair of brothers from the First Warband rose to greet Zakar, Con and Ran, their shoulders capped with scavenged rugby pads and leather armlets. Anger had soured their faces since losing a brood-brother to Baron Jupiter's attack. Captain Bruce Kal stepped into view from a shelter, a hulking beast with a bare chest and arms covered in scars and tattoos. Another First Warband runt, Nickle, had his rifle on his shoulder. Two more, Broom and Booker, turned with feeble terrified eyes.

Zakar drew his sabre, the scrape of the scabbard ringing across the yard. The brass hilt was scrawled with Nar's runes. "War!" he shouted.

Orcs jumped to their feet, weapons in hand. "WAR!" they screamed, their feral calls like a chorus of tigers and jackals.

The camp burst into organized anarchy. The collapsed tents, packed away or buried remaining possessions, and gobbled down their rations as they prepared for combat.

Zakar went to his tent and prepared himself for war. Over his tunic, he strapped on his pauldrons of hammered steel, a vest of scavenged nylon, spiked greaves and bracers, a sash of green wool he used for cover, and a belt with tassets of leather and bone. He checked his remaining firearm, a heavy calibre pistol, and a pouch of ammunition. When he was ready, the runts took down his tent and packed it away.

Zakar kept little left for himself. He gave everything to his clan.

The entire encampment collapsed in on itself as if it had never existed, leaving only the bare grey canyon.

Lord Dracar stood at the entrance of the canyon, completing his final rituals, with much of the clan in attendance. The lord knelt before the surviving elders with his honour guard—five large orcs all wearing heavy steel armour, scavenged ballistic nylon and stiffened padding. They all had heavy calibre automatics and riot shields the size of door frames.

Lord Dracar carried a crude chainblade in the shape of a great axe, and his left arm was wrapped in a flamethrower device, as if his arms both held snarling steel dragons. On his shoulders stretched sheets of heavy steel armour covered in spikes and theropod skulls.

Zakar fell into line with the other Caps behind the lord, and the honour guard. Just over two hundred BlackDragons—all that remained of their once-mighty tribe—filled the canyon. Pine-green orcs dulled from the winter, ready for war with blades, fire-arms, armour, and rough cloaks.

Nar stood in the shadows of a rocky outcrop above the clan, waiting, watching, always separate from the rest of the clan.

The elders raised their dragon-toothed daggers and spears. "War!"

Lord Dracar rose, turning to face the entirety of his clan, his face hidden behind a snarling dragon battle mask. He raised his chainblade, revving its steel teeth and screaming, "WAAARRR!"

The rest of the clan replied by, firing off a few shots and clanging weapons against armour. They roared. "WAAARRRRRR!"

Zakar raised his sword, but he didn't answer the call. His fear for his brothers was stronger than his bloodthirst.

◆

The BlackDragons marched into the night. They moved fast under the cover of darkness through the forests, through the old redwood trails they had once dominated. The skyscraper trees were like titans that watched the roving band of orcs. The First Warband led from the front, spread out to ensure no threats could catch the central column off guard. Lord Dracar would never let that happen again.

Zakar and Nar were marching ahead of the column. Zakar had his pistol in hand, ready to engage at a moment's notice. He glanced through the underbrush, eyeing his boys.

The First Warband—the vanguard—took the smartest and most cunning of the clan, many of the boys were runts that Zakar trained through many hunts and skirmishes. The vanguard led the combat, preparing the way for the rest of the clan, which was divided amongst the two other warbands under Bruce Kal and Mog Bane. Once there had been seven warbands amongst as many captains.

Nar walked along with his dragon-skin cloak trailing behind him like a tail. He carried a long theropod femur-bone as a staff, scrawled with long lines of squarish runes. It was equally dangerous to bash skulls in as it was to help focus his will and power.

The moon bled through the trees, beams of white light cascading from the canopy and onto the rugged undergrowth. In the spaces between trees, Zakar saw flashes of memory. Vignettes of nightmares and the darkest events he had witnessed. The battles, the betrayal, the burning of orc bodies with kerosene and torches.

Burning us… the notion sent fingers of anger through Zakar's limbs. There was no greater insult to an orc. Burning an orc denied their spores from spreading. It ended their bloodline. It ended their clan. It destroyed them. Burning an orc was worse than castrating a mammal.

"The gods really have abandoned us," he muttered.

Nar chuckled.

"What?"

"The gods don't care."

"You've never believed in them."

"Not true," said Nar, playful as ever, despite everything. "They are real. I've met them."

Zakar didn't know how to respond to his brother in the best of times. Ever since his final tests of becoming the clan shaman six summers ago... he was different. He had come back from a pilgrimage with scars and a dragon skin.

"Speak plainly," said Zakar.

"The gods are simply far beyond our little lives," said Nar.

"Why must they be silent? If you—"

"There is nothing *I* could do," hissed Nar. "They don't care. What are we to them? So great and powerful? How much thought do you give to the mites in your bedrolls or the ants under that tree?"

"And you wonder why the elders hate you..."

"They hate me for my truth. We are one very small cog in a farcical machine."

"Then what's the point?" said Zakar.

"The point, *dear brother*, is that there is none. We are beasts, ants to the gods, seeking survival when life can be so randomly taken." Before Zakar could argue, Nar cut him off. "That having been said, I once met a wise man who told me that only in the absence of meaning can true purpose be found."

Zakar glared at him. "Talk plainly."

Nar sighed. "And you wonder why I keep to myself. It means that when the world wants us dead... when honour is a whisper... the only things that matter are those we choose to value. You, our clan, our brothers..." Nar stopped, looking into Zakar's eyes with the intimate familiarity only brothers can share. "By all the useless gods and my feeble powers, Zakar Moon, we will survive this fight."

Despite everything. Zakar smiled, a crack in his grim armour. Only Nar could do that. He patted his brother's shoulder. They both missed their brood-kin deeply and would avenge them when they had the chance.

For now, they had a fight to win.

♦

"Oh, curse all the grimy gods," said Nar.

The next night, the pair scouted out the enemy's bastion. It rose up in the crook of the mountainside, hills embracing it like a protective mother.

The clan would have to attack from the front.

The fortress must have originally only been a trading post or milling settlement. Now, it boasted a curtain wall of concrete slabs and scavenged metal. A quilted bulwark nearly fifteen feet high with a wire-fence gate—complete with metal slabs that could be drawn out for additional protection. Twin timber watchtowers fitted with gun-nests flanked the gates. Behind the walls sat a huge estate manor and mill, the smokestacks silent and only a few lights visible in the windows. Electric lampposts and spotlights flooded the yard with incandescent light.

Outside the walls were several lodges and cabins, like scattered bricks across the landscape. The bones of a growing town, connected by powerlines, yards of empty garden beds, and lumber shelters. Zakar narrowed his eyes, studying the buildings: a smokehouse, an empty stable, a few depots. Lord Goldstein was tending his flocks tenderly. Mercenary soldiers—humans in slap-dash armour and carrying firearms—patrolled the grounds inside and outside the walls. *Perhaps that's why the Goblin King wants him removed?* Was Goldstein a growing tumour in their flank? Or had he betrayed them in some unseen underhanded way? It wasn't Zakar's concern.

Nar took the scope from Zakar.

"You only see the attack, not the rest of it," said Nar. Zakar hissed. "They have electricity," commented Nar.

"So?"

"You see any powerlines coming in? Only coming out. No smoke from the timber."

"It could be underground. Petrol generator."

"Ah, but no vehicles, only an empty stable yard. They have power from somewhere within the mountain… it's why the mill looks so unused. Perhaps thermal? I've heard tell of that. Perhaps that's why the Goblin King wants Goldstein removed. Oh, there's a captain."

Zakar stole the scope back.

The wire fence gate rolled sideways and a human woman—armoured in red—stepped outside. Her narrow pale face set with piercing eyes and a blonde crew-cut, flanked by spiked spaulders. Soldiers saluted before speaking to her. Her neutral expression displayed calm command of herself and her men.

Zakar adjusted the scope to study the men. Most of the mercenaries carried simple rifles, revolvers, and the odd automatic weapon. Hatchets, cavalry sabres and bayonets were their only close-quarters arms. Cheap, but could be very effective, especially in a group. He focused closer to study the captain, but the image grew hazy. On her hip she carried a straight-backed cutlass, the hilt connected by a wire to a powerpack on her back, and her handgun in her holster had a similar cable. Zakar didn't recognize

132

the weapons. What he didn't recognize he didn't like. Uncertainty crept into his chest.

This was going to be a hard fight.

"I don't like this," said Zakar. "It's going to be a slaughter."

"Aye," said Nar. "Go tell the lord to begin the attack." Nar crawled back from the lookout, prowling into the shadows of the forest, his cloak vanishing into the underbrush.

"What are you doing?"

"Oh, just something very dumb." The disembodied voice echoed back before trailing off into the darkness.

Zakar cursed, never able to predict his brother's plans. He snarled before retreating to the clan.

◆

They began the attack at midnight. The light of the moon was enough for the BlackDragon orcs, but the humans were blinded by their reliance on lamps and lanterns. Zakar crouched low in a line of hedges near a lodge. The vanguard led the way, preparing the enemy for the main attack.

The entire clan, two hundred orcs, surrounded Lord Goldstein's fortress. First up were the thirty or so orcs of the First Warband, who slunk like cats to dispatch the outer patrols with merciless efficiency.

Zakar's tattooed arm shot out of a hedge, wrenched a soldier back, and silenced him with the wet crack of his neck. The human didn't feel a thing.

Brig and Broom crouched nearby. They checked a warehouse, disappeared inside as if eaten by the structure. After a few tense moments they gave an all clear. Broom exited with a new rifle and a bloodied bandolier of bullets. Every bullet mattered.

Con and Ran and dragged a mercenary beneath a wood-shed, his yelp muffled by a crunch. Nickle pulled another soldier into the smokehouse. Sharpshooters Farns and Hotsnap barbed two others through the head with their crossbows, their strings echoing a muted *thunk* before bodies fell twitching to the ground.

There was no margin for error. No risk left to chance. No hesitation or weakness. Zakar was finished playing games with humans. The BlackDragons were here for a total and decisive victory.

An archer, Split, loosed an arrow, the missile lancing through a soldier. His gurgling cry followed by a quiet *thunk*. Split grinned at the kill. Hotsnap pulled his brother back into a collection of ferns as another patrol came.

The orcs were wolves amongst blind and deaf sheep.

Zakar gave the signal.

His warriors burst from cover, pouncing and bringing the men down with brutal efficiency. They broke necks and slashed throats, knives rising bloody in the low light. The final yelp of surprise was silenced.

Zakar broke cover, keeping low and out of sight. They were three hundred yards from the watchtowers, their spotlights swerved predictably away. He gave a nod of approval to his party's swift efficiency. They moved to take the weapons and hide the bodies—

A voice crackled.

The lurking orcs froze.

A handheld radio on the ground crackled. "Squad Seven. Squad Seven. Report! What's going on out there—"

Zakar's boot crushed the device. "To the walls. Fast." The warriors nodded and broke into low sprints. They were on the edge of losing the element of surprise. They needed to push the full attack.

They cleared the final approach along a fence-line, past a lodge, and into the ditch that encircled the walls. Slabs of timber and gravel formed the bridge to the chain-link fence gate.

Thirty orcs clung to side of the wet ditch, soaked to their knees and hidden from sight with their green hides and rough cloaks. Their wyrm tattoos and war paint made them nearly invisible. The spotlight swerved over their heads and not a single human noticed.

Zakar was satisfied they were ready.

He reached into his belt and aimed an electric light back towards the forests, flashing it thrice. After a pause, a line of horned shadows appeared in the undergrowth of the forest with two hundred pairs glowing eyes. Packs of dozens of orcs rushed forward like a wave of shadow.

The soldiers in the towers peered out, taken by the growing quiet of the night. The silence of their patrols made them nervous. Their shouts and confused voices rippled behind the wall just as they realized what was happening.

Zakar exhaled, readying himself for the battle. *Please. Just no more dead brothers.*

A mighty chorus of roars, like a hundred feral lions, echoed across the mountainside from the attacking wall of monsters. The noise echoed for miles, scattering birds and freezing the blood of men. Lord Dracar sent a burst of flames from his gauntlet, sweeping it around like a dragon intimidating a rival. They used the terror of their war cries to replace the loss of surprise. They had evolved the psychology of war.

An alarm sounded. Someone screamed. "Orcs! Orc raid!" The wail of a siren went off.

Zakar watched the gunners in the towers ready themselves to fire. Mercenaries looked out from the watchtowers with scopes and binoculars. They searched, unsure of where the attack would come. They didn't look right under their noses.

That was the BlackDragons' skill. They were hunters. They knew how to misdirect attention, lure prey, encircle it, and go in for the kill.

The clan, the shadows of over two hundred orcs, swept through the settlement, amongst the clear-cut forest and empty yards. A mass of wolves, bears, lions, and all the beasts of nightmare... all moving in scattered packs. Orcs had been the undead, the wild spirits, the uncivilized barbarians of the forests. Tonight, they reminded mortals why they feared the dark.

If people lived in those lodges, they made no sound, they clutched their children, and hid. No weapons fired. The orcs weren't here for them. The attack was only for the lord's keep.

The clan finished off whatever patrols or resistance they met in quick firefights and brawls. Light flashed in pockets across the settlement. Orcs with bows, rifles, and other ranged weapons fired at the walls, chipping the concrete and biting into the slabs of corrugated steel. The cries of the patrols confused the defenders. Hooting and roaring echoed from the warriors of the clan, echoing, booming like they were coming from everywhere.

Just before the clan could get into range, Zakar gave the signal to his warband. Booker and Hotsnap loosed bundles of rope and hooks from their belts.

Lord Dracar and Bruce Kal marched up the main road towards the gates, a column of grunting beasts in blackened armour, boots thumping like drums and weapons glinting behind them.

The honour guard and their shields led the attack. The titanic lord marched patiently behind the shieldwall.

"Orcs!" the alarm wailed from within. "Get ready, boys!" Their rifles and automatic weapons clicked into action. A huge wall of steel rolled out behind the wire fence gate. *Bruce Kal will enjoy that.*

Zakar smiled, he could see the distress on the soldiers in the watchtower. "Now!"

Booker and Hotsnap jumped up, twirling their grappling hooks. The warband snapped bows and crackled firearms at the watchtowers. Pure music. Zakar smirked, seeing the horrified surprise on the mercenaries' faces as they fell from view.

The grappling hooks flew. Months of practice for such an occasion finally paid off. They bit into the beams of the tower. Instantly, Brig and six others ran forward to help.

They all took hold and were ready to pull when a surviving mercenary rose, bloodied but brandishing an automatic weapon. Before Zakar could raise his pistol, the mercenary shot the weapon, bullets flying and cutting into three boys, including Booker. Zakar's pistol drummed, sending shudders up his arm as he emptied the chamber, knocking the human from his perch.

Two more boys from the ditch ran up to replace their fallen brothers.

"War! War! War!" they roared. With three sharp jerks the tower shuddered, swayed, and finally broke over the wall like a pile of children's blocks, wood and corrugated tin squealing and crashing.

A shout of surprise came from the other tower. Broom and Farns, along with others in the warband, fired their weapons. The towers were destroyed or cleared.

The clan approached the bastion with minimal opposition. The way was clear. Two small orcs dragged the wounded into the ditch for cover.

Zakar looked up and saw, on the roof of the estate manor, more soldiers were setting up a gun emplacement: a big tripod gun with a belt feeder. It would shred the clan if they didn't get it removed somehow.

"Warband—UP! Up!" yelled Zakar as he reloaded his pistol.

The machine gun above roared and tracer rounds flew, whistling and scattering Mog Bane's fighters. Bullets sparked off the honour guard, but Zakar saw BlackDragons orcs fall in the light of the gunfire.

Hotsnap knew immediately, Brig hesitated as he retrieved Booker's grappling hook. They threw the hooks over the walls. Hotsnap's landed, but Brig had to try again. Zakar ran forward. *First over the top. First into the fight. Always.* The warband rushed from the ditch, throwing more grappling hooks and clattering against the lip of the walls. Some dug picks or hatchets into gaps, dragging themselves up like panthers up a tree. Lighter boys simply climbed the remains of the collapsed tower.

Zakar saw at least six more orcs fall from the illuminating gunfire.

Zakar hauled himself up the rope. They had to fight. He pulled himself up and over the concrete slabs. Shouts echoed below, and Zakar threw himself over the edge and dropped down into the courtyard. The corded muscles of his short legs groaned.

He stood in a courtyard. Behind the gate were layers of barricades and firing lines. He landed amongst a group of soldiers with bayonets, prepared to counter anything that made it through the gates. They didn't expect a long-limbed orc to appear in their midst.

Zakar threw himself into the men, sabre in hand. He roared, spit flying from his fangs. He cut them down with wild hacks and slashes before they could even respond, limbs flying as he cleaved through bone like dried kindling.

"WAR! BLACKDRAGONS!" he roared.

Heavy feet landed beside him. Con and Ran snarled and launched themselves at the nearest humans with choppers and revolvers. More orcs cleared the walls, dropping into the courtyard.

Stables, sheds, and other small buildings were scattered around the gravel yard with the mill and manor against both sides of the jagged cliffs. More men rushed to take cover at sandbag lines or behind the corners of structures. *Lord Goldstein expected an attack and fortified his position accordingly.* Orcs caught climbing the wall were shot and fell. A few stubborn boys got up, bleeding from their wounds but fighting on. Zakar cleared his cover line and pulled Hotsnap aside from a volley of the soldiers. More orcs fell into the nearby squads, chopping, roaring, and clawing. Humans died screaming as they tried to run away.

Between the fortifications, a sergeant on a stallion charged, waving a cavalry sabre. He thought he could save the day, slay the warband leader. He decapitated an orc mid-gallop. Zakar countered the sergeant with his sabre and claws. He chopped through the horses' neck and the rider's chest in a single slash and threw them to the side.

The rider landed in a plume of dust. blood pouring from his vest. Zakar didn't give him a chance; he rushed forward and brought his boot down on the rider's head, bursting it like a melon.

Zakar roared, drawing his pistol form his belt. "Get the gunners!"

The dozen or so remaining of the First Warband fired their weapons; rifles crackled, and bowstrings snapped. Split and Farns loosed their missiles up at the gun nest, and the fire hiccupped. They must have hit someone.

The courtyard devolved into close-range fire fights. The orcs flooded the area around the gates. Bullets, bolts, and arrows flew in every direction, cutting into sandbags, sparking off corrugated metal, and killing fighters on both sides. Zakar crouched behind a crate, thumbing bullets into his pistol's chamber. He glanced over the cover, seeing a line of riflemen gather for a bayonet charge to retake the gate.

Over his shoulder, he saw two boys shot as they tried to open the gate. The remnants of the First Warband needed to give the rest of the clan time to breach the gate.

The main doors of the manor flew open. The woman-captain stood, face grim, with a dozen more mercenaries at her side. Heavily armoured men and women in suits of red plasteel and blank-faced helmets with swords, sabres, and heavy handguns wired to powerpacks.

Zakar grit his fangs. *The real fight begins.*

With a thunderous crash, the gates shuddered. A chain-blade revved before metal squealed against metal, sparks sputtering on the flank of the gate. Orcs roared, bashing against the gates. Dozens more with ladders and grappling hooks began pouring over the walls. The soldiers fired their rifles. Some BlackDragons fell, and some landed, rolling, squatting, or simply launching themselves forward. They were a wave of green beasts washing over the walls and into the courtyard. They needed to get in quickly. They didn't have the numbers to overtake the bastion through attrition.

The red woman barked orders, gathering mercenaries and riflemen into a defensible position further up the yard. The gunners overhead continued to pour fire, now strafing the walls and shredding orcs to pieces. Green and purple flesh flew and splattered the concrete slabs. Piles of corpses began to fill the courtyard.

Zakar and his warband had done their job. They had reached the gates, taking the enemy by surprise, and cleared the way for the main force. Now they had to survive.

Zakar noticed a feral runt chopping at an already dead and grabbed him. *Klap. His name is Klap.* One of the runts. He threw them both behind a maintenance shed as rifles cracked against its corrugated steel sides. Zakar saw Con and Ran circling around the stables.

"Fire!" screamed the red-woman.

Five orcs were shot, their bodies lit by the spotlights, Hotsnap amongst them, his head cracked open like an egg bleeding pink liquid.

"Cap! What do we do!" squealed Klap.

"We fight!"

Zakar threw his sword into his belt. He dug his claws into the side of the shed, his muscles bulging as he pulled. The soldiers fired another volley, slaying more four warriors as they cleared the wall. The piles of dead grew. The gates shuddered again with another crash. The machine gun above halted again, the gunner slayed by orc gunfire. If they didn't silence the machine gun permanently when Lord Dracar and the clan poured through, the BlackDragons would have no chance.

The red mercenaries charged through the yard. They would hold where the riflemen had failed. Their heavy handguns pattered with yellow flashes. Nickle and Farns both fell, and Zakar's warband dwindled to only a few survivors amongst the chaos.

Zakar roared and ripped the side of the shed free. Two more orcs, Brig and an axe-fighter named Scale, had taken cover by the shed, and Zakar had to protect them, these little brothers. He had lost too many BlackDragons.

"Stay here!" Zakar hefted the debris.

"Never!" Brig held his rifle bayonet like a spear.

Zakar didn't answer, using the debris as a shield and joining five more orcs they charged. The gates shuddered again, sparking as the chainblade broke through its side. The surface of the gate bent inwards. A pack of reinforcing orcs used the grappling hooks to ascend the side of the estate manor. Soon they'd halt the roar of the machine gun nest.

Just a little longer.

Zakar roared wordlessly, leading with his shield. They rushed for the line of red armoured mercenaries, who fired their heavy pistols shuddered; one blasted a hole in the debris near Zakar's head. Shrapnel cut into his cheek, and red-purple blood streaked down his face. On Zakar's right, Klap was blown in half. More orcs joined the charge, screaming and hooting, weapons raised.

"NO!" roared the orc cap. He threw his shield like a discus. It whistled through the air and bisected a red mercenary at the waist. Zakar drew his sabre, roaring with the mad wail of a wounded dragon. "No more! No more! No more dead! WAR!"

A chorus of war cries echoed that could shake cities.

A line of twenty orcs slammed into the mercenaries, crashing in a tidal wave of violence. Some orcs threw themselves into the blades of their enemies to pin them, giving their brothers a chance to go in for the kill. The unbelievable savagery erupted across the yard with wild chopping, biting, stabbing, and screaming.

The stink of burning meat hit Zakar's senses. His eyes widened. The strange swords wired to the mercenaries' backs hummed and glowed a faint orange, like that of iron in the forge.

142

Zakar cracked the helm of a mercenary with his fist. Blunt pain shot up his arm. He parried a sword and realized his mistake too late.

The enemy sword cleaved straight through his sabre, leaving nothing but melted orange metal. Zakar spun around, wrapping his arm around the mercenary's throat. "Watch the blades!" he screamed as he tore the helmeted head off with a wet pop. He slammed the head into another helm, shattering the blank face of the mercenary's visor.

Another booming shudder hit the gates. The edge of the metal door was curling inward, the inner wire-link fence was buckling like a broken net. Arms reaching through to rip at the edge.

Zakar scooped of one of the enemy's swords. The cord had been cut, leaking sparks. The hilt of the sword was more complex than a normal hilt; it had circuits welded into the blade, turning it into hot burning iron.

A mercenary slammed into Zakar in his moment of distraction. He managed to bring up the stolen weapon just in time and the burning blades bit into each other.

The mercenary had the advantage, sliding his blade around Zakar's guard and slashing at his bicep. Burning pain exploded through Zakar's shoulder, and a bubbling gash decapitated his wyrm tattoo.

Zakar roared out. He reached out, taking the mercenary by the throat. The mercenary struggled, sawing his sword deeper into Zakar's arm. Hot metal hissed in Zakar's flesh, blood bubbling down his arm. He snarled, digging his claws through the mercenary's collar, he lifted the human off the ground. Zakar saw his ferocious snarl in the blank-faced helmet as he tore the human's throat from his neck and tossed the body aside.

Zakar groaned, reaching up and tearing the burning blade

from his shoulder. He stared at the weapon, seeing it stained with his blood, steam rising from the edge.

"CAP!" screamed Brig.

The little orc shoved Zakar aside as a handgun thundered and Brig fell to his knees. His rifle dropped, and a light poured through the gaping hole in his chest.

When Zakar realized what happened, he screamed. "NO!" He rushed forward, killing the mercenary with a crunch.

The gates thundered again, squealing as they finally flew opened.

Time seemed to stop; the battle swirled around Zakar as his clan died around him. They bit and clawed, struggling against humans armed weapons more advanced than they could have even dreamed. Orc bodies fell heavy like clumps of wet leaves, their eyes vacant, caught in fury and lost in confusion. They died. They would all die. Zakar looked to the estate house, where a few of his clan threw the soldiers at the gun emplacement to their deaths.

Lord Dracar Wyrmbak and the rest of the tribe flooded through the gates. Gunfire sparked off the shields of the honour guard, and some orcs fell, but the gates were open. The rest of the orcs swarmed through, a wave of a hundred beasts, killing humans with the ferocious abandon of a fox in a hen house. Lord Dracar charged through a squad of riflemen, bayonets scraping off his armour. The howl of his chainblade split three men in half. He blasted his flamethrower at a squad of red mercenaries charging towards him. Their armour was untouched, and they thrust their weapons towards the chieftain. He discovered the same thing Zakar had in an instant when his armour was pierced by two blades and another bit through the chain of his weapon.

A woman's grunts and orc howls cut through the noise. Zakar looked up at horror at the entrance to the manor.

Con and Ran had flanked and engaged the woman-captain, a cyclone of blades in the foyer of the building.

Zakar bayed, knowing he had to save the brothers. Lord Dracar could handle the rest. Zakar couldn't lose anymore brothers. He'd lost so many already. He'd lost his brood-kin, his warband, the runts he trained since they were yearlings.

Con and Ran had realized the danger of the burning-blades before Zakar had. They snapped in and out of the woman's guard like a pair of vipers, their weapons sparking off each other. They tried to break her guard, but she was too fast. They couldn't parry or pin her down. She was a blur of motion, air rippling around her cutlass.

Con and Ran were no match for her. It was only a matter of time.

Zakar killed another soldier, cutting through his outstretched rifle and down his chest. The blade, cooling, was already bent backwards like a crude sabre. He swam through the battle, knocking enemies aside, uncaring to finish them off.

Ran ducked low to get under the woman's guard. He went in for the kill.

"No!" roared Zakar, seeing the mistake. He struck a mercenary aside, cleaving into a breastplate.

Ran hooked his axe at the woman's ankle—her eyes snapped wide—Ran jerked backwards, committed to his mistake. She twisted with his movement and struck downwards. A wet hissing slap froze Ran as the burning blade impaled straight through his neck and into the floorboards of the foyer.

Con screamed in protest and brought his blade down onto the woman. She was too fast. She wrenched the blade from Ran's body and thrust it through Con's chest. He chopped with his weapon at the woman's shoulder, but it was deflected off her spaulders. She gasped, tore her weapon free, and decapitated Con.

Zakar roared, flying like a berserker up the steps. He slammed into the woman, knocking them both through the doors into the lobby of the manor.

The manor's lobby extended towards a huge staircase with polished oak baluster and banners on the walls of the upper balcony. The balconies wrapped around the lobby, overlooking the entrance where the two fighters rose. They stood on a huge dragon-faced rug cast across the floor, as if the Great Dragons had indeed come to observe the BlackDragon orcs latest trial.

Under the flickering light of an electric chandelier, Zakar glared into the woman's eyes. They both gathered themselves from the floor, holding low stances. Her blade glowed with the orange of fresh coals, her blue eyes unmoving. His own weapon, now cooled, was as bent and useless as a forgotten stick. He drew a broken-backed knife from his belt, falling into his long-practised duelling stance.

A crash echoed from outside, followed by the shudder of firearms and the howl of a broken chainblade. The BlackDragons were massacring the garrison.

Zakar and the woman stared at each other. "Give us the lord. Leave."

"HA!" the woman, "Mercy from orcs? I think not."

"We just want the lord!"

Now that *did* surprise the woman. She stood up straighter, eyes studying the beast across the lobby. She no longer saw wild animals. She saw something else. She glanced up at the balconies.

Screams and roars from outside signalled the orc victory. Armoured orcs cleaved into the garrison, putting them down like wounded dogs. The First Warband was decimated, but their sacrifice had ensured the survival of the clan.

"RedClan," said the woman. She put the clues together quickly, as if she'd been expecting such a play. "Wasn't it? The Goblin King's dogs."

Zakar didn't answer.

The woman drew herself into a stance. "I think not."

Boots clattered around Zakar. On the balconies above, more red mercenaries took position, each armed with a rifle or automatic.

Zakar grit his teeth. The clan would be shredded the instant they entered the lobby. Their raid would fail and they would be exterminated. The BlackDragons wouldn't survive a month once other settlements heard they raided this barony. The extinction of the BlackDragons. Death of all Zakar's bothers and clan.

There wasn't even a chance to warn Lord Dracar.

Zakar's fingers tightened around the knife. His instincts howling over what to do. Warn the rest of the clan before dying? Face this woman? Charge the warriors? He was desperate to find a solution. Desperate. His red eyes scanned the balcony. The faceless mercenaries all aimed for him. He would die before having a chance.

Sometimes there was no way out... He felt trapped the same way Lord Dracar felt when they received the offer to kill Lord Goldstein. Nothing but a series of equally bad decisions that all led to death.

Then he saw a space in the ranks above. An open door, darkness beyond. A pair of red eyes reflected the chandelier light, identical to Zakar's own.

Zakar narrowed his eyes.

The red eyes winked at him.

That sly little imp.

Zakar raised his weapon to the woman. "What is your name?"

The woman almost smiled. "Trick Smithson."

"Trick Smithson," said Zakar. "I am Zakar Moon, Captain of the BlackDragons." His eyes trailed along the mercenaries. "We are the BlackDragons! We are of the Great Dragons! Worshippers of Sun and Moon! For those who survive tonight, you will carry us in your nightmares forever! But you, Trick Smithson, you die tonight."

Trick smirked, sword brought up near her face, sweat glistening across her brow.

Zakar met the eyes above and winked back.

Lord Dracar Wyrmbak filled the doorway, at his back Bruce Kal and a dozen other armoured orcs. Their weapons were bloodied, warped, and half-melted in places. The Lord's battle-plate was slashed and pierced, still glowing in spots from the heat with blood dripping onto the floor. The Lord realized the situation, but, before he could scream the order to halt, smaller orcs rushed forward, caught up in their war lust.

The mercenaries readied their weapons. "On my mark!" said a commander.

"WAR!" roared Zakar.

"WAR!" responded the clan.

The lights cut out, casting the entire hall into darkness. The only light was the orange glow of the burning blades. Men

148

yelled in their confusion. The orcs could see just as well in darkness. The humans were light blind, reliant on their electric lamps.

That is when Nar Moon burst from the darkened doorway, eyes blazing yellow and casting arcane light into the blackness. His cloak flared like the wings of the Great Dragons and energy rattling from hands. He screamed the words of power, casting his spell.

A shock wave slammed the opposite balcony, exploding in a cloud of heat and dust, taking five mercenaries with it.

Before the others could react, Nar was already on them with spellfire and his bloodied bone staff.

Trick's sweat-streaked face was illuminated by her weapon. She cursed before charging at Zakar.

The surviving mercenaries fired their weapons, but confusion and surprise robbed them of their discipline. Lines of fire criss-crossed the lobby and the chandelier exploded in a shower of shards and sparks. The BlackDragons charged through the lobby like an avalanche of shadows. The men on the stairs were swarmed by the orcs, unable to see their enemy, but with the glowing blades signaling their positions like flares. The howls of human voices and bestial orc roars deafened the chamber.

Zakar and Trick attacked each other with meteoric force, sparks flying off their burning blades. The battle around them fell away to distant noise and flashing light.

Trick was far faster than Zakar, making her lethal blade all the more dangerous. Zakar's shoulder wound left him open, forcing him on the defensive. He caught her sword, burning edge biting into his cooling one, but he countered by punching her square in the chest instead of thrusting with his knife.

She stumbled back, her armour taking the brunt of the attack.

Zakar didn't give her a chance to recover and fired his boot upwards, kicking her in the chest. Cracks appeared in her armour as she flew backwards again, crashing against a wall.

She picked herself up, spitting up blood on the floor before launching back into the attack.

NO MORE DEAD BROTHERS.

They resumed their combat as the battle swirled around them with the silhouettes of axes and weapons chopping into red armour. Trick was wary of Zakar's strength, keeping just out of reach. She was attacking his sword, preparing to disarm him when his blade cooled.

He studied her as their battle became clumsier and more exhausted. Her armour, her training, her technology, and her command. Whoever she was, she was closer to the lord and his feud with the Goblin King than she let on. What did the BlackDragons really know about this? Nothing. They took the deal and ran with it. They couldn't ask questions. They couldn't find out why they were sent back into the meat grinder. They were desperate.

That's all these lordlings do. Find the desperate and make them slaves.

The locked together, Zakar trying to shove her off her feet, but she spun away with a decapitating slice. He jumped back, but that was his mistake. She slashed his sword off at the hilt. Zakar retreated, but Trick was on him in an instant. He caught the hilt of her blade on his knife, holding her back. The heated blade began to bite into the knife.

He raised a fist.

Pain exploded in his leg, knocking him backwards. A bodkin knife lodged into his knee. Trick spun away, smiling at her success, like a viper she moved to finish him.

150

Zakar could only roar in defiance.

Another shock wave exploded above as Nar erupted between the dust and debris. His scream and glowing yellow eyes transformed him into a demon. Cloak wingspread, he landed and launched a beam of white light from his staff.

Trick dodged sideways, avoiding the spellfire.

Nar snarled, fangs bared. He stood between the mercenary and his brood-brother, his pointed-ears like horns, dragon-skin cloak like folded wings on his back. He snarled like an animal protecting its young.

Trick glared and burst into an attack. Nar spun his staff in a blur, diverting her sword with perfect elegance. It was a battle between dancers, each strike as precise and elegant as it was brutal. They forced themselves towards the centre of the lobby, the eruption of flames from Lord Dracar's weapon illuminated their battle.

Zakar pushed himself up, his destroyed knee unable to take his weight. *I have to help him.* He crawled towards their duel, rolling away from battles between orcs and men. *No more dead brothers. No more!*

Trick growled and a feint and slash cleaved Nar's staff in half. He jumped back, dropping the broken pieces. His wild words of power in his fanged mouth gathered power into his claws. Trick rushed forward to slay him, but Nar caught the blade in his enchanted hands, sparks flying from the connection, squealing under the pressure.

Zakar crawled, arm over arm. He found a discarded blade, a serrated backed knife. He looked over his shoulder when he took it in his hands.

Nar forced Trick back, her blade in his control. He raised a clawed hand wreathed in crackling flames. They fought, drifting through the chaos towards Zakar. He pushed on his good leg, reaching for Trick.

He gripped her leg.

If he died saving Nar, it was a good death.

Her eyes snapped wide.

Zakar plunged the knife between the plates of her armour. Trick screamed. She spun her sword in hand, stabbing backwards. He grit his teeth, accepting the death.

"No!" Nar slammed into her.

The trio tumbled across the floor; the burning sword shattered in shards of hot metal.

In the mad scramble, everything became limbs, screams, and the struggle to survive. This was the worst kind of battle, not a glorious charge or exchange of blades. This was a scrambling, violent wrestle.

In the roll, Zakar ended up beneath Trick. His claws around her throat. She scrambled searching for a weapon. Zakar squeezed, unable to do anything else. Her felt the tendons in her neck crunch in his grip. Her face flushed red, then purple, veins popping in her forehead.

Trick found a hatchet on the floor.

Zakar rolled, forcing her beneath him. She chopped at his shoulder and side. He nearly fainted as pain exploded across his body. His rugged orc system threatened to shut down after more trauma than a human could even comprehend.

Vision red, he roared like a lion bearing down on its rival.

Her neck snapped with a wet crunch. Her body stilled, eyes frozen wide and her sword-hand limp on the floor.

Zakar tried to sit up, but the pain was too much. He held himself up with trembling arms, his side a mess of bloody wounds. His shoulders vibrated with pain as his system tried to shut it out. He felt on the edge of consciousness.

Nar laid next to them. Completely still.

No.

Zakar pulled himself to his brother, moving mechanically, his mind disassociated from himself.

No.

Trick's broken blade, stilling glowing at the hilt, was thrust through Nar's neck. His eyes lost their glow, leaving nothing but a dull lifeless red.

Zakar's throat chocked. "NO! NO!" His wail cut through the chaos of the battle. The noise shuddered to a stop as the final mercenary was cut down.

Lord Dracar roared, kicking one mercenary to the ground, heavy boots cracking the breastplate. Flames erupted from his weapon, the burst of light made the orcs shudder and cry. "ENOUGH!"

Lord Dracar stopped fighting when he saw his Moon brood die. He watched Zakar kneel over Nar, weeping over his last brother. The warlord, Dracar Wyrmbak, bloodied and wounded, held out his chainblade to the door, motionless as a statue, one eye visible through the battle-damaged helmet.

Then, the orcs sacked the manor, mill, and anything within the walls. They burnt it to the ground when they were finished.

◆

Zakar sat on the steps of the manor, his shoulders, arm, sides, and knee wrapped in bandages. His face was covered crusted in blood. He nursed a bottle of spirits they took from the Goldstein's kitchens, slowly numbing the pain and loss. The shrapnel buried in his cheek would need more advanced surgery to remove. If he avoided infection, the bits of metal would remain in his cheek.

The surviving clan members had celebrated Zakar for clearing the way, defeating the enemy champion, and ensuring their swift victory but... *By the Dragons... we still lost so many.*

They had gathered the bodies of the BlackDragons in the courtyard and stripped their weapons and armour, unless brood-brothers demanded a particular charm, tool, or weapon remained with the fallen. Zakar ordered Brig to keep his rifle, Con and Ran with their axes, and Broom and Farns with their crossbows. Hotsnap's brother kept his remaining boots and tools.

The bodies would be left to release their spores to the air. Their deaths would bring more BlackDragons into the world. If the clan survived the next few years, they would return to this place and find their new brothers, reborn from the fallen.

There were just so many dead brothers and friends. The First Warband was destroyed. Zakar had lost everyone.

Zakar sat alone, bloodied fists in his lap. The sorrow set in his chest and tightened around his throat like a noose. He took another swig of the bottle, exhaling a low growl with a jet of breath in the cold air.

Lord Dracar's heavy boots sounded behind Zakar.

A bundle landed next to Zakar. Nar's dragon-skin cloak.

"I don't deserve it," said Zakar. "I never earned it."

Lord Dracar knelt, with his helmet removed, his boulder-like head scoured with new scars. His chest and side were wrapped in bandages the size of bed sheets. His heavy brow hid his eyes, less they betray the deep loss they all felt. "I think you have. More than any have this night."

The chieftain placed the bundle in Zakar's lap.

The cold pebbly skin was smooth, the black scales of an ancient predator. Nar battled dragons and supped with gods to gain his powers and title as shaman. It symbolized the old ways, the wild ways. For all its grand history, what brought tears to Zakar's eyes was its smell. He pressed it to his face, taking in his brother's scent before it was gone. He cried, wheezing deep breaths for his brother.

"Did..." cracked Zakar's voice. "Did we find Lord Goldstein?"

"Yes," said Dracar, but with no pleasure in the victory. "In his chambers with his wife and daughter. They'd all taken poison. Their guards defended to the last man."

"Then it's done."

"I don't know," said the lord. "He reached into a pouch and produced a bundle of crumpled documents. "I can't read these without Nar. With him, we could have understood why the Goblin King sent us here. Why was a single rural barony such a threat? Why did he have such formidable guards?"

Why was Nar so fixated on the electricity? Zakar felt his stomach churn. "What have we done? What game have we entered?"

"A dangerous game with dangerous masters."

"That's exactly what got us into this..."

"Aye, lad," said Dracar. "What choice did we have, little brother? You, the cleverest of my clan, tell me? What choice did we have?" He sighed, leaning on one leg. "I'm sorry about Nar.

I'm sorry about all the runts, all the dead. I sent you to your death. Sometimes there's no right way out."

Zakar didn't have an answer. Only his pain. He looked out over his surviving clan. So few remained. They tended to the wounded and their grief.

Dawn crept over the distant Rokki Mountains, a halo of gold against the grey and blue peaks. The mountains felt oppressive, looming in the distant like a line of peaked hoods of the goblins.

The BlackDragons had completed their task. They could only hope it would save them from extinction. They needed to re-build. They were one more clan collected into the Goblin King's hordes, one more group of monsters enslaved to the dark lord of the mountains.

—The End—

PART 1
SHADOW OF TERROR

The stranger crouched by a stream where cold clear water rushed over smooth pebbles and into her metal canteen. *Please. Please. Don't give me the shits.* She was dehydrated and exhausted, but she'd have to wait to let the water boil over her pathetic crackling campfire.

It had been three weeks since leaving Penn Valley, ten days since leaving Grandton, and almost five months since leaving the Monastery. There was still an ache in her side, but it was healing well.

She had nowhere to rest.

The morning was grey, like much of NeoAnglia. *No wonder everyone is so fucked up here.* Summer should have been bright and warm, but here it was just more rain and grey; the days were just more humid. The countryside of rolling hills and valleys remained covered in swirling mist each morning. The villages grew sparser the further she got from Grandton.

It'll be better in the south, she told herself. At least there wouldn't be wanted posters with her face on them.

Rustling in the trees sent a chill down her spine. She sighed, exhaustion pulling at her shoulders. She stood up and took a long thirst-quenching swig from the canteen. *Shits it is.* She tossed it against her bag. She wore blue flannel shirt, the sleeves slashed off, jeans, heavy leather boots, and a bandana around her neck. She had seen better days, with bandages over her knuckles and arms, one over her cheek. Her black cloak hung off her shoulders, the hem frayed and caked with mud.

Her hand rested on her holster.

"I'm waiting," she called. *So sick of this shit.*

A glade filled the crook of the stream. Wild grass and flowers swayed in the breeze. The dense forests of birches and evergreens caged her in. The forests of NeoAnglia had been her only constant.

The bushes rustled and pair of cloaked figures stepped into view. Two young women threw back their hoods. Twins. *Clones?* Round, plain faces with short black bobs. Lips curled into smiles like they'd won a bet.

"You the one who killed Julian Clark in Grand-ton?" asked one.

"Depends," said the stranger.

"You visited Skerhol, Steigford, Norwich, and escaped from Matslock—"

"Jesus Christ, yes. I'm *that* bitch. You want to get to the point?"

"She's feisty," said the sister on the right.

"Yeah, no wonder everyone's gotten their panties in a knot about her," said the one on the left.

The stranger drew her gun beneath her cloak. "You want the bounty? Come and get it."

Both girls burst out into nasally cackling laughter that went on far too long. *Should probably just shoot them,* thought the stranger.

"We don't care about the bounty!" said one.

"Why would we—"

158

"Can you get to the point!" snapped the stranger.

"Oh," said the one on the left.

"How rude of us," said the one on the right.

In a horribly well-practised routine, they threw off their cloaks in a flourish. Both girls wore close-fitting front-buttoned tunics and leggings, their arms and legs wound with fighting wraps.

"I'm Lea!" announced the one on the right as she drew a pair of sai, spinning them with a flourish.

"And I'm Kae!" announced the other, drawing a short katana.

Their parents were evidently not very creative.

"And we're!" they landed in a dramatic pose. "The Ellis twins! We're the best pair of fighters north of the Mississippi! And we'll be damned if some old bag is going to take that from us!" They were like two cats thinking they found a hapless mouse.

The stranger stared flatly. "You two are fucking freaks, you know that, right?"

"Scared, hag?!"

"Nah, I'm just wondering how many times your parents must have mixed you up. You sure you're Lea and you're Kae? Like it doesn't matter much now, but I guarantee it was the other way around at some point."

"Shut up!" said Lea.

"Yeah! You're just afraid," said Kae.

"No, just really fucking bored of this shit." She thought about shooting them both between the eyes. *I'm no fucking mouse.* She tossed her gun aside and drew her sword. The chalky unreflective black metal with the crossguard set with wolves leaping from a tear drop.

She gripped the sword in both hands. A knife was strapped to her belt. "You two freaks sure you want to do this?"

"We're sure," said one.

"Old bag," said the other.

The stranger inhaled deeply, letting the air fill her lungs before expelling it through her lips, the tension in her body and mind melting away. The pain in her side from her fight in Grandton grew dull.

Both sisters dashed in opposite directions. In perfect synchronicity, they attacked the stranger. She defended, and their rolling attacks hammered against her disciplined guard. Their weapons clanged against her sword with a rhythm that echoed through the forest.

Lea locked the sword with a twist of her sai. Kae moved to bisect the stranger across the stomach, but the stranger spun on her toes and threw Lea into her sister. Both girls bounced back and charged in perfect mirrored movements. *It really is like fighting clones.*

The stranger zipped backwards, deflecting their lightning-fast movements with her longer, heavier blade. In most fights, she was the smaller, weaker, and faster opponent. That was her advantage against bandits, monsters, and mercenaries. This was different. These lighter cat-like opponents put her on the defensive. When Lea tried to control the stranger's sword, she kicked the girl in the stomach, knocking her off her feet before Kae charged.

The girls pressed the stranger towards the stream. Their attempt to corner her in. They pounced and retreated in perfect concert. Their dumbass routine proved how perfectly in sync they were. Snapping vipers goading the stranger backwards until she stood in the stream, ice cold water soaking into her boots.

Both sisters attacked at once, never uttering a word or making a signal. The stranger caught Kae's sword, but Lea ducked under and punched the stranger with the butt of her sai hilts. The stranger grunted—pain burst across her side—and retreated to the other bank.

The stranger grit her teeth. *I'm done with this.*

The stranger held her guard. The twins circled around and charged. She drew them in for the trap. They were overconfident. Kae moved to a high attack. The stranger feigned high, and Lea went low. *Got you.* Lea was overeager and off balance, her face sporting a demented doll-like grin, on the edge of orgasm thinking she was about to win.

The stranger caught the sai with her sword and snatched Lea's wrist. By diverting the attack, the stranger guided the sai straight into Kae's chest. Both sisters' eyes went wide. Lea screamed. The stranger threw them, and they tumbled into a pile, carried by the momentum.

Lea whimpered over her sister, trying to pet Kae's face. The sai had plunged deep into her rib cage. Kae's torso was a mess of red. "NONONONO! I'M SORRY!" screamed Lea. "Kae! NO!"

Kae went limp before she could say anything.

The stranger returned to her defensive stance. A gash across her forearm where the other sai had scratched her.

Lea snarled, spinning and throwing her knife. The stranger, distracted by her injury, didn't move fast enough. The narrow blade slashed her across her thigh. "Jesus!" she stumbled back, forcing her leg from buckling under her. Lea charged with the katana and her remaining sai.

She hammered at the stranger, howling, her bob becoming a wild mane, frenzied with rage. The clang of swords drummed through the forest. Lea locked the stranger's sword with her sai, the katana raised to chop at the stranger's face.

The stranger exhaled. *Like water.* Before the blow could land, the stranger swerved to the side and diverted Lea's attack into the ground. The girl slammed into the muddy grass. When she whipped around, the stranger was already bringing down her blade in an overhand chop.

Lea's eyes went wide, and she screamed.

Blood flecked the stranger's face.

Silence.

An owl hooted and flew off.

With a trembling hand, the stranger touched the gash across her thigh. Blood poured over her jeans. She gritted her teeth, looked again, and concluded it was only the first layer of muscle. The gash on her arm was minor, and she felt bruising on her stomach.

She spat on the dead girl, her frustration growing uncontrollable. She needed to leave NeoAnglia. She'd been stuck in its counties for nearly two months, unable to escape its moors and gangtowns. Trouble kept finding her. *I should have stayed with Pac and Trevor…*

She tended her wounds. She kept one of the Ellis girls' sai. As she wrapped her thigh, closing the wound as best she could, she hissed, "I need to leave this fucking country." If more bounty hunters were on her trail, she couldn't hold them off indefinitely. She had tried to avoid populated centres when she could, but small towns remembered strangers. She had tried to disappear in Grandton, but that failed spectacularly.

162

"I just need to escape," she said, just to hear a voice. She tugged the tourniquet tight. She glanced at the stream. "All water leads to the ocean." One final gamble to escape southwards. She just needed to find one ship heading south.

She got up, gathered her things, and followed the stream. When she offered a glance back, the snout of a scavenging theropod was visible from the bushes. Sniffing for the dead flesh of the Ellis sisters. Its long gracile form stepped into the glade, hungry for the kill.

The stranger exhaled. *Throwing away everything for something so stupid.*

♦

The stranger managed to get a ride with a farmer to the next sea-town, hoping to find a boat out of the country. He crossed his little wagon, the packed with baskets of eggs, onions, garlic, apples, and canned preservatives, through the winding countryside of farming hamlets, lodges, and way stations. Pastures where cows and pigs were raised. The year's crops were growing like carpets of green.

A gull flew overhead, its white tail flecked with soot, something burnt in its yellow beak.

The stranger smelled the town before she saw it. She sat up in a wagon. Beyond the rises and hedges of the countryside, black pillars of smoke rose from over the next hill. The stink of burning buildings suffocated the air.

"What the hell…"

"I told ya!" said the farmer. "The Terror attacked. Brightfall is in ruins. You still sure you want to go there?"

The stranger wasn't sure. At all. "The what?"

◆

Brightfall was worse than the stranger could have imagined. She didn't know what it had once been, only what it was now.

The streams of black smoke were concentrated at the harbour. The farmer hiked his scarf over his nose and the stranger did the same with her bandana, but it didn't help to block out the reek of destruction.

Brightfall was a simple enclave under the Warwich King, but more likely a direct vassal to Grandton. It was safe from raids and other dangers that Appalachian towns faced. It lacked a wall or a standing militia like other places, and it was almost modern. Almost.

The outlying suburbs had absorbed the survivors of the attack. People crammed tents in patchy lawns. They gathered on stoops, in lawn chairs, on benches and on blankets, their faces hollow and haunted. The eyes of all of them—adults, elders, and children—were vacant. Begging for the nightmare to be over. A makeshift clinic filled one yard. The stranger could only assume the actual local clinic had been destroyed.

The simple houses were already decaying, wooden walls peeling with paint, asphalts shingles irregularly patched, wind-eroded plaster now stained with soot. The town was already struggling. This attack was just the latest in a long line of indignities and tragedies. It was the biggest and most dramatic, but they had already struggled through bad season after bad season.

The farmer pulled up to a soup tent. The smell of bubbling vegetables, potatoes, and onions was not enough to overcome the rank of the smoke. He hopped off the wagon and began unloading. The stranger nodded, sliding onto the ground due to the pain in her leg. "Thanks."

"Don't mention it," he said with a smile, though this one was more forced. "You take care now, miss—?"

"Ellis," said the stranger, it was the first name that popped into her head. "Ellis—Ekko Ellis."

The stranger—now Ekko Ellis—walked along the road. The buildings grew into concrete businesses, some boarded up, some in the throes of bankruptcy, and now some blackened and destroyed. The four-storey cement motel was bisected down the middle, still smouldering, the path of destruction clear through to the harbour.

Automobiles and carry-alls had been destroyed or flattened. Stores shattered, reduced to rubble and galvanized metal. Occasionally, Ellis saw a figure digging through the rubble. Her stomach twisted when she realized one of them was a child. She looked away, but was met with a perfect set of claw marks shorn through the concrete corner of the motel.

Ellis found a mother sitting on a stoop, clutching a crying baby, a dirty-faced toddler next to her.

Ellis knelt, holding out her canteen. "What happened?"

The toddler reached up, but the mother hissed. "It came," she said, with a hollow voice. "It just came. Walked in." The baby howled. "Shhhh, sweetie. Hush. We'll be with daddy soon."

The stranger walked away, horrified, helpless. She passed by destroyed parents and crying children. A pair of adult brothers argued, a mother clutched a rolled-up bundle to her face, an elderly woman just sat quietly.

One girl sat sitting against the bottom of an upturned truck. Her dark hair was a mess and her light brown face streaked with tears. Another ghost. A young man walked up to her, put blanket over her shoulders and gingerly helped walk her away.

God help them.

Shouts echoed nearby and people rushed towards the waterfront. Ellis followed the activity through the streets. She stepped in a puddle, then realized it was a huge four-toed footprint that tore into the ground.

"God," she said. The foot was a meter wide and nearly four feet long, with long marks that could only have been caused by claws. A man bumped her as he hurried to follow the crowd.

Adjacent to the harbour was a plaza that would have housed the market. Along the cobblestone path were old brick buildings from the first permanent settlers. A small meeting hall was filling up with people.

As people brushed passed the stranger, she looked down the shoreline, up the beach, to the destroyed boardwalk—the worst of the devastation. A scorched heap of wood and plaster, the shops reduced to pyres, the wooden struts collapsed into the sand. In the deformed rubble were more huge footprints.

Shouts and discussions echoed from the hall, and Ellis dragged herself away from the destruction.

She pulled down her bandana and stood on her toes to get a view. The town was predominantly Anglo, with a few smatterings of Latins and Celts, and even some dwarves, abhumans, and faefolk.

At the back of the hall was a long table covered in papers. In the centre was a blueberry shaped man with spectacles and a family emblem on his lapel. The local townlord. Ellis circled around the back of the crowd for a better look.

"Good people of Brightfall," began the lord, speaking out to the crowd. "As soon as this disaster befell our fair town, I sent the word to our king and any of his vassals with the capacity to aid us. It is with most gracious appreciation that—"

"Oh, just fucking tell us!" shouted a fisherman.

The lordling huffed. At his side were aides and several house guards, forming a wall around their lord. One handed him a fax. Ellis eyed the crowd; their anxiety filled the air.

"Dunwich," announced the town lord. "Has headed our call and is sending an expert from Miskatonic University, from the Oceanographic Institute—" Someone in the crowd screamed "Fascists!" but the lordling continued. "—to assess the situation and advise on the proceedings. Someone familiar with beasts of this nature. They will arrive today."

A shudder of confusion, disappointment, and frustration rippled through the hall. They were angry, forgotten, and now, in their moment of greatest need, the royal government was only sending an official. Not a ship of mariners, no supplies, no aide, or relief. An assessment to advise. It was like an aspirin for a broken leg.

A huge man stood at the front of the crowd. Heavy shoulders sunk, a grizzled face framed with grey mutton chops and a beaker hat in his hands.

The town lord looked at the fisherman. "Something you'd like to say O'Malley?"

"You want us to wait with that beast lingering off our coastline?"

"I do as our king bids."

"What about us?" said the fisherman called O'Malley.

"When the expert—"

"No, *my Lord Joyce,*" hissed O'Malley, venom in his voice. "We will not wait. We're the ones the world forgot about! We've called for assistance the last three winters and nothing! We've lost everything! Our families, our homes, our lives! And you're just as much to blame as the king!"

The murmurs grew into shouts of agreement. The house guards growled, keeping the people back and away from the townlord.

"The Terror is ours to kill, and we will not wait! We will not wait for some official, some proclamation, some useless duke or earl!"

Shouts of agreement rippled through the crowd.

"I launch as soon as the tides allow! Who's with me? I say we hunt down this bitch of a beast. Dunwich has forgotten us, and we will solve this ourselves. The next time their officials come they can see what we did without 'em!"

More people burst into whoops and cheers. The lord blubbered for words, aghast at the treason of his own people.

"The next time they come they can shove their taxes up the king's arse! They can see what honest Anglo folk can do without 'em!"

A single piercing sound cut through the noise. Nails against a chalkboard. The crowd hushed and winced at the sound. Ellis arched her head to see a woman seated against the far wall.

"You're all damn fools," she said, wiping the chalk from her nails before reaching into a bag of potato chips. "You'll all die if you run out like blood-hungry idiots."

O'Malley glared. "You think so, Regina?"

The woman was middle-aged, short, a solid sailor wearing a trench coat. On her hip was a sickle-sabre. Her short grey hair hung around her face in a mess of daggers. Her jaw set on edge, hard as rough granite.

"If you damn idiots think swarming the Terror will bring it down, think again. Bunch up your tackles, tangle your nets. You'll be running into each other. You don't send a school of fish after a shark. You send another hunter. A single precise hunter."

"And that'd be you, Regina?"

She shrugged.

"No, Claiborne, tonight I get to kill the beast," O'Malley said.

"You can try," she looked through the crowd to Lord Joyce. "For three thousand dollars I'll kill this Terror. Let an *expert* handle it."

Ekko's eyes glanced from the woman to the townlord. A low tension hovered over her words. The insult to the fisherman's capacity stung the man, but Regina's arrogance turned the entire crowd against her. Whoever she was, her seat in the local community was not a popular one.

The fisherman scoffed and left the hall, shoving past bodies with a handful of lackeys at his side. Shouts and arguments swelled through the townsfolk. Insults snapped at their lord, the incoming expert, and the king himself. They were frustrated beyond words, ready for action. Lord Joyce tried to get them in control, but he had lost them entirely.

As quickly as O'Malley left, dozens of men scattered to join the expedition. Anarchy rippled out from the hall as the survivors prepared for revenge.

Ekko stood outside of it, taking the weight off her leg, watching this town attempt its revenge against the monster. She saw the woman, Regina, walk away after smirking at the townlord. As she munched on her bag of crisps, she disappeared through the destroyed fish market.

The stranger looked out towards the wharf. *Guess I need to start asking if any are heading south after this.*

◆

The makeshift fleet took form within hours.

Every captain with a seaworthy vessel prepared to launch. Hunters gathered their vests, rifles, and ammunition. Fisherman in overalls and boots ran with ropes and equipment. A dwarf smith hammered out machetes, axes, and pikes in a makeshift workshop. Goatmen and wyrpigs hurried about their tasks. Even a pack of orcs carried huge bundles of fresh canvas and Jerry cans by the dozen.

Many volunteers weren't even fishermen, but still had a score to settle with the monster. They gathered chains, nets, saw-blades, shotguns, and everything in between. It was pandemonium as these people attempted to go to war without a plan.

Ellis's queries for passage were met with curses and annoyance. "Fuck off girl! Can't you see we're busy!"—"No passage until the Terror is dead. You blind?" Even her offers of assistance weren't met kindly.

"Hey, can I—"

"Don't you see we have a monster to hunt!" shouted the sixth captain she had asked, a bulldog of a man carrying a harpoon over his shoulder as he climbed the ramp onto his sloop.

She stared flatly. "Does it look like I give a shit? I can fight monsters. Give me passage, and I'll help you." She stood on the dock, glaring at the captain. The crew stopped, watching to see what the captain would do.

He glanced at her injuries before deciding. "You're a stranger. This is our fight," he glowered, fist on his hip. "Get outta here!"

Ellis growled and limped away; she'd find no help here. Several ships already floated out into the bay, passing the lighthouse and waterbreak.

Survivors in town waved their avengers goodbye. Women kissed their men goodbye, old men gave swords and harpoons to their sons and nephews, girlfriends tied favours to their boyfriends' arms. It would have been a beautiful moment, tragic and romantic. Ellis watched, the sun high in the sky. *No clouds here.* Her cloak stuck to her back. She knew the woman, Regina, was correct. This fleet was going on a fool's errand. It was exactly the kind of battle a big monster could win.

Someone on the docks screamed. "Fuck off, girl!"

This time it wasn't directed at Ellis.

A motorboat had just arrived and was arguing with the captain of the sloop. The motorboat was a slick white, black and green vessel with an emblem on its side.

An emblem the stranger recognized: *the Oceanographic Institute of Dunwich.* A research vessel from Miskatonic University.

In it was a woman shouting at the captain to let her dock. They argued back and forth until the harbourmaster—who had been drinking silently as he watched the fleet prepare—got involved and helped the girl reel herself in. She knew what she was doing, but the harbourmaster kept correcting her with slurred words.

The woman tossed a huge hiking backpack onto the dock before climbing up. She wore khakis pants and shirt with a dark grey Miskatonic University jacket. Her arm was covered in a sleeve of bright tattoos. Her face immediately attracted Ellis: round sunburned cheeks surrounded by thick brown hair pulled into a tail. Her sea-green eyes circled with thick horn-rimmed glasses. She must have been late-twenties or early-thirties. *Pretty, in that quirky girl next door kind of way.*

"Thank you, sir, name's Maddie Hooper," she said to the harbourmaster. "Would you tell me where I can find Lord Joyce?"

He ignored her question. "A guinee to house the boat." She nodded and handed him the money without even haggling. *Either she has money or she's just stupid*, thought Ellis. He walked away, buzzed, and returned to his office by the waterfront. The woman stood alone among the chaos of the fleet's preparation.

Ellis's eyes landed on the sailors who watched the woman hungrily. She asked around for directions, but they were as amiable to her as they were to the stranger. Then she made the mistake of saying that a pistol on the captain's belt wouldn't do him any good.

"What the hell do you know!?" barked a disgruntled sailor.

The woman's lips went thin. "Would you take it to hunt krakens? I don't think so. This is much worse. This is the Terror's territory now."

He ran off in a huff. The other sailor spat at her feet. "Dunwich bitch." They walked off back to their boats.

The woman laughed to herself. "They're all gonna die." She walked down the jetty towards the streets where Ekko was watching.

That was, until a young sailor walked up to her. He was tall and ruggedly handsome the way you imagined sailors to be. His hands in his pockets, he swaggered between the men, his rolled-up sleeves revealing anchor tattoos.

"Looking fa' Lord Joyce?" he asked.

"Yes," said the woman. "It's very important I find him. Can you take me to him?"

"This way, miss," he smiled and guided her off the wharf and towards the waterfronts.

Ekko watched, then she saw a pair of rough looking teenagers following loosely behind. She couldn't see any weapons, but she knew they'd have knives hidden under their coats.

Ah fuck. Ekko followed further behind, using the activity of the docks to cover her approach.

The sailor led the woman from Dunwich around the destroyed fish market and passed the hall where Lord Joyce had held the town meeting. She gawked endlessly at the destruction. The horror and sadness plain on her face. She followed the sailor down a turn in the alleys between the destroyed motel and other buildings.

The other two followed. There was a shout and a scuffle. The thugs rushed in. *Fuck*, hissed Ellis, and she ran into the alleyway. The thugs had the woman pinned against the wall; the handsome sailor had a revolver in hand.

"We just want the money, girl," he hissed. "Just the money. Give it!"

"Take it!" she screamed. "I'm just here to help!"

"Hey, dickheads!" said Ellis.

They all froze and turned to the stranger. She moved forward, nearly within sword range. The hilt and holster visible. The sailor eyed the weaponry cautiously. She wanted to avoid a shootout if she could. The sailor raised the revolver, "Mind your business, stranger. You could get hurt."

She glanced at the two thugs. They were young, too

young, scarred, scared, and traumatized by the monster attack. "Recruiting orphans from the attack for petty crime?"

The sailor glared, thumbing the hammer. "This is our town and we got to survive. Give us your money and you can survive too. Give me the sword, the gun, your money."

"I think—" Her hand trailed to her holster.

"Don't move!" he shouted, aiming the gun. An amateur criminal trying to make the most of a disaster. It would be infuriating if it wasn't just so pathetic.

"Alright," said Ekko, her eyes met the woman, this Maddie Hooper. She glanced from the stranger to the thugs then back again. *Don't do anything. I have this.* The woman seemed to understand.

The sailor stepped forward and reached to unbuckle Ekko's holster. He wrenched it away, holding his new trophy to sell and barter. "Now be a good girl and hand over the money."

"The thing is…" said Ellis. "I don't have much money." She looked at the woman, who struggled against the arm around her neck. "And I'm definitely not a good girl." Her raised arms reached for the sai hidden in folds of the cloak against her back, pinned in the fabric for easy access.

She snapped the sai in a blur of motion. The gun went off, but Ekko was already out of the way. The sailor screamed, the prongs of the knife dug into his fingers, the needle point through the finger loop. She wrenched the weapon away, shearing through flesh; the gun clattered on the ground.

Shouts from the waterfront told Ekko that the town guard would be here soon.

The sailor held up his bloodied hand. Before the thugs

could react, Ekko socked him in the face and kicked his legs out from under him. A swift jab knocked him unconscious.

One thug went for her with a knife. She easily wove around the attack and slammed him into the wall. She slammed the knife in her hand into the plaster next to his ear. He yelped, sweat glazed his face. The second one was still frozen with shock.

"You two gonna go and make better choices?" she threw the thug on the ground. "Lot of people need help, go do something with your lives."

The boys bolted.

The sailor groaned. "Fucking bi'th." Ellis slammed a boot into his sternum and looked at the woman from Dunwich.

"You alright?"

She nodded. "Thank you."

Boots splashed in the puddles. Two men appeared with truncheons in their hands, what little remained of the town guard. Their haggard faces and ragged uniforms made Ekko wonder if they had been able to rest or bathe since the attack.

"Nice town you got here," said Ellis.

They stopped, eyeing the unconscious sailor. They must have recognized him as a known troublemaker.

Before they could say anything, the woman, Maddie Hooper, marched up to the guards. "Take me to Lord Joyce immediately, otherwise Dunwich will assume that this place is not worth sending aide. Is that understood?" She commanded them like she was born into authority. They glanced at each other before nodding.

She picked her bag off the ground before looking at

Ellis. Her eyes seemed huge behind the glasses. "Thanks again. What's your name?"

The stranger blinked. "Ekko Ellis."

"Well, you're coming, right?"

"Why?"

She glanced at the sailor. "I could use someone of your talents. I'm Madison Hooper."

She raised an eyebrow, studying the woman from Dunwich. *She can probably get me a way south.* The sailor groaned. Ekko slammed her boot on his chest. "Okay, fair."

The guards took them to Lord Joyce immediately.

♦

They waited in the drawing room on the main floor of Lord Joyce's manor. A brick Georgian house just outside of town, in poor condition with ivy and stained fixtures, but still grander than anything in town. The yard of the estate was clean and crisp. None of the survivors were sheltered here. A few servants carried on with their duties through clenched jaws and barely-withheld tears.

Ekko sat on a cushioned chair, leaning her elbows on her knees. The white walls and stained oak furniture seemed a century out of place. House Joyce had enjoyed a long and illustrious station as the lords of Brightfall. Another forgotten corner of NeoAnglia, safe from the dangers of the Wrong Side, left to the plight of irreverence and stagnation.

Madison Hooper paced back and forth, constantly checking her phone. A genuine cellular device. The stranger hadn't held a phone in years. It felt so alien where once she couldn't imagine life without it.

"So, you're from Dunwich?"

"Mhmm," said Madison. "You have blood on your face."

Ekko dabbed at her cheek. "How about that. Assholes."

"You know anything about the attack?"

"I just arrived this morning."

"And...?" she asked, circling around, and taking a seat.

"I know what I can see. The town was already in bad shape when this happened. Everyone is pissed off. They're either looking for someone to blame or someone to take it out on. They sound like secessionists."

She stood up again, circling the room. "Common reaction to tragedy. Place trauma on an appropriate agent. The Royal Government has often forgotten these outlying settlements. Their quotas and zoning limits are extremely unpopular."

"You're from Miskatonic? From Dunwich?"

That's when Madison stopped. Eyes narrowed behind those big glasses, studying the stranger like a specimen. "And you're Exposed."

"Is it that obvious?"

"It's your humour, your cadence, mostly how you've been glancing at my phone each time I take it out, almost like a recovering alcoholic and someone else's drink."

"I thought that was just a nervous tick."

"It is," said Madison. "But you don't get far at Miskatonic without being perceptive. And yes, I am from Dunwich. I finished my doctoral dissertation this winter. It was lucky I was available.

Exams had just finished, my first term as a professor, and then I get called down here."

"Why is that?"

The doors swung open and Lord Joyce entered, an aide at his side. Ekko and Madison stood up. "Welcome, Miss Hooper, thank you for coming to us in our moment of need. I hope—"

"Yes, yes," said Madison. "How do you do? Now do you have what we requested? I was very clear on the phone."

Lord Joyce huffed at the lack of decorum. He snapped his fingers. His aide set a 2001 Microsoft laptop computer on the coffee table, thick as a book. Ellis smiled, reminded of her dad's old one. Lord Joyce snapped again, demanding tea.

Madison pulled up the laptop, booting it up immediately. Her fingers rattled against the keys.

"One of our young folks was able to capture some images," said Lord Joyce, sitting elegantly despite his roundness. One could not fault him for knowing his courtly manners. "Quite remarkable. I'm too old for such things—"

"Yes, yes, very good," said Madison, cutting the line of thought. Lord Joyce huffed again. Madison's typing stopped, leaving the room in silence. Her lips grew thinner.

Ellis circled behind Madison, who slowly tapped through several images. Out-of-focus photos of an immense dark form lumbering through the boardwalk. Flame blind images in between. One showed a ripple of water, like a surging tide, cracked a section of the wharf in half. Then something huge rose out of the waters. Big as a house. Bigger than any monster the stranger had seen.

The stranger felt like she had made a mistake coming here.

The screen flipped to an image from within a broken

shop. Columns of off-white flesh covered in blue-black markings in view, it was the monster's legs with each foot ending in splayed out webbed claws. Another image clipped sight of its crocodilian jaws and interlocking kitchen-knife teeth. Another image showed it next to a truck.

The long silence ended. "Miss Hooper?" asked Lord Joyce.

She flipped to the short video, only about ten seconds. From a distance and out of focus. The huge lumbering shadow charged through the boardwalk, its long snout brought up from out of frame. It turned at the flash of gunfire from the town's militia. It opened its jaws and a glow erupted from down its throat.

The video cut out.

Madison stood up, looking exceptionally pale. She pulled off her glasses and wiped them on her shirt. She looked at Lord Joyce. "Thank you, my lord. I'll confer with the Institute and have something for you by the evening."

"But the men are heading out within the hour!" he said. "Half of them are already out of the bay."

"And there isn't a thing I can do to stop them. You are their liege lord. If you can't command them, no one can." She glanced at the classy decor fit for a duke of higher standing. "One wonders if a lord unwilling to share his home with his people in their most dire times can hope to command at all?"

Lord Joyce went red, as if he'd been slapped. He looked down, his neck vanishing into so many chins. "Who do you think you—?" He saw the commanding look on her face and was quelled like a whipped dog. "I—I'll see what I can do."

Madison turned to Ellis. "You hungry?"

♦

The makeshift fleet was already well beyond the bay. Disappearing on the horizon to search for the monster.

They found a surviving pub along the waterfront—The White Anchor—the shattered windows replaced with sheets of plywood. Inside was warm, with old leather booths and deep green walls. Framed photos hung over the bar, pictures of fishermen, swimming meets, relays and other local events, many frames broken but still hanging. A fireplace at one end was surrounded by seven or so locals, some clutching their children and wrapped in blankets.

Despite the destruction, some managed to carry on and share what they had. Volunteers handed out chowder, bread, French fries, and fried fish.

Ellis followed Madison to an open booth. Their bags and the stranger's sword sat between them, as if the wolves on the sword's hilt were joining them for dinner.

A heavy woman in an apron stopped taking broken frames off a wall and went to their table. "We don't have a full menu right now," she said, dry and humourless. "You either get the chowda', the fries, or the fish. Pay what ya can."

"We'll take one of each," said Madison, fingering out a far larger wad of cash than Ellis had expected. "Thank you."

"And two whiskys," said Ellis.

"Make it the bottle. And sweet tea."

When the drink came, Madison drained and slammed her glass down before Ellis even had time to taste the smooth amber liquid. She shouldered off the Miskatonic jacket, revealing sunburned shoulders covered in more tattoos.

"You alright?"

She glanced at the redundant menu. "I hope the chowder is good. It's always good, but every town does it different."

"What is it?" asked Ellis.

"Oh, I just eat when I'm nervous, and I'm absolutely starving. It's my treat. Consider yourself employed if you'd like, I have the money."

"Tell me." Their eyes met. A long stare between the two women. Ekko noticed Madison's tattoos more clearly. Over her arm and shoulder were splashes of bright colour around a kawaii kraken and nautical images; through it was the remains of a Warwich Navy tattoo, same as several of the sailors from the docks. *Ain't that curious,* thought Ekko, her attraction to Madison twinging with an uneasy suspicion. *This girl is something else.* Madison rubbed her nose, nervousness showing through.

"It's big, one of the biggest I've seen," said Madison, as she poured another shot of whisky. "You know what a Kronosaurus or a Pliosaurus?"

"I assume a dinosaur?"

"Technically, no, but close. An extinct aquatic reptile in your world. Kronos's lizard. The Terror, the thing that attacked this town, is called a Kronotitanus Dracus. The evolutionary descendent of Kronosaurus. A Kronotitan."

"Dracus? You mean…?

"It's not an actual dragon, but close. Clade Draco is not Dracus. Dracus is often given to species with convergent dragon traits. Not the most elegant in describing evolutionary relationships, but very useful for explaining what the creature is." Ellis sipped her drink as Madison fell into what must have been her professor voice. "Kronotitanus, Kronos's Titan, is a genus of semi-aquatic predator from warmer Atlantic seas. Commonly found off the Yucatan coastline with various sub-species across the Caribbean gulf and Latin coastlines. As with Clade Draco, they evolved a gland which absorbs hydrogen-sulphide from their digestive track. Lighter than air and highly flammable. Most experts call it a Pecularus Abnoralus, which just means radiation of some kind, produced a fully formed mutation in a species past." Madison blinked. "I'm not boring you?"

"I've been Exposed for five years. I've never had an academic in this world explain things to me. Please go on."

"Magic makes weird mutations and sometimes it does it repeatedly, but, when an animal has a useful trait, it passes it on. Some modern scholars are trying to disprove it, but it's difficult to find evidence for when these organs showed up. It is likely convergent evolution, different species coming to the same solution for the same problem, filling the same niche. Birds, dragons, butterflies all have wings. Kronotitanus, the Terror, can breathe fire. Primarily, the glands it uses to fuel its fire-breath are used to control buoyancy, but it's an effective weapon. Just like dragons."

Madison sighed, looking out across the pub, her eyes heavy as she considered how her sterile understanding of the monster now had a human element. These people lost everything to a rogue predator. Ellis noticed one of the girls at the bar as one she saw among the destruction. The pretty Latin girl, now in fresh clothes and cleaned, her arms and legs covered in bandages. She stared at her bowl of chowder, unmoving.

Madison retreated into her lecture. "The longstanding theory in this world is that the Veil often makes evolution behave in new ways that wouldn't happen otherwise." Madison took another drink. "Charles Darwin never would have guessed the effect magic had on evolution. It's like a Galapagos Island under a kaleidoscope—things happen in our world that wouldn't otherwise. I don't know how true that is, but the existence of magic must have led to monsters somehow."

"You sound like you're Exposed too."

"No," she said. "Just very familiar with it. I've had a few colleagues who were born in your world. With their education and a stipend from the royal government, they can continue their studies. What were you do before you were Exposed?"

Ungrateful. Ellis took another sip, thinking about if her Arts Degree and teaching licence could have helped her. She could have made a real life in this world. Not this. *No,* she told herself. *I have something I need to do.* Her eyes glanced to her sword.

Their food finally came. The steaming bowl of chowder filled with clams, shrimp, scallops, corn, potatoes, and even bits of bacon. The fries and slab of fish crackled from the fryer. A pile of grease, more food than Ellis had seen in months. She gawked at it for a moment, the steam rising, as Madison already began shovelling chowder into her small mouth.

"Don't make me eat alone," said Madison. "Please."

"I don't want charity," said Ellis.

"You're *employed,*" said Madison. "I'll give you a hundred at the end of the week. I have the money."

"From the Institute?"

Madison ignored the question. "Eat."

Ellis pulled a basket of fried fish and fries towards her, drowning it in vinegar. The sweet tea might have been nectar, its herbal sweetness something Ellis had missed for years now.

"Then what are you going to do?" asked Ellis.

Madison looked up, face full of chowder and biscuits. "Me?" said Madison, she wiped her mouth with a napkin, almost daintily. "There's nothing I can do. Not right now. I'm going to contact the Institute in the morning. No one will pick up right now. A royal task force will come down and handle the situation. We'll probably bait the creature away or try to sedate it and ship it back south."

"Not kill it?"

"Not if we don't have to—"

"What a load of shit!" howled a voice.

The White Anchor was silent. Everyone turned to stare at their booth. Madison sat straight up, eyes wide behind her horn-rimmed glasses like a deer in headlights.

In the neighbouring booth, a woman turned to glare at Madison. It was the one from the town meeting, Regina. She rose from her booth, a beer in hand, and rested an elbow front of Madison, her crow's feet deepened as she glowered at Madison.

"You want to save that fucking thing? You some kind of idiot?"

Madison's mouth went very thin. "I don't *want* to save it. If we can, we will, but that will be determined by the Oceanographic Institute and what the navy is able to send."

"It's not Dunwich's job to decide what to do with the creature. They weren't attacked by it. We were. It's not for them to decide."

Madison blinked. "It *is* actually the Institute's job to determine the care, placement, and, in certain situations, extermination, of predatory megafauna in NeoAnglia. It's our job."

"And a poor job they do of it. I remember when they put quotas on my hunting and I had to fire three of my crew. You don't get it, Dunwich girl, it's our monster too."

Regina pointed to another, an older fisherman with a white moustache and his hands clasping a cup of tea. "Frank Mclode there, his son was in the militia. Was crushed under its feet trying to fight it." She pointed to pair of twenty-something girls further up the bar. "Both of them, their boyfriends just left on the *Saint George* to fight the Terror. You think they're coming back. *They* don't think so!"

She pointed to the Latin girl in the booth. "Isabel Romas, she lost her entire family to the Terror. She rammed a truck into it. Too bad it didn't do jack shit." Isabel glared. She pushed her meal aside and walked out, her eyes holding back tears as the door chimed shut.

Ekko leaned on her elbow. "Excuse me, Regina, right? Didn't you ask the town for money to track down the creature? If you were really so sore about what it did, why didn't you join the fleet?"

Madison blinked, looking from Regina to Ekko.

Regina sipped her beer. "It meant that only I'd be at risk. It meant that I'd be able to take some of the money from that useless Lord Joyce and give it back to everyone. It would have worked too if it wasn't for that idiot O'Malley." She glared back at Madison. "Answer me, princess, you really going to—"

"Don't call me that," snapped Madison.

"But that's what ya are, ain't ya?" Deafening silence took the entire pub, with only the crackle of the fireplace. Everyone was watching, even the cook who stepped out of the swinging doors, a few whispers and furious daggers shot at Madison.

Madison's face paled white, hands trembling on her knees. Regina smirked, seeing that her barbs had found their target. "Saw ya picture in the papers when I was in Dunwich three y'ars ago. First time you were with the whole royal family since that big scandal, eh? Princess *Madison Warwich*! granddaughter to the king? What are you, seventh in line for the throne?"

"Thirteenth... Please stop."

The sailor snatched Madison's hands out from her lap. "City hands. Royal hands. Like a baby's, soft from counting dollars, eating pheasant and caviar all your life."

Madison shoved off Regina. Her lips went so thin they almost vanished. "Say whatever you want about me. I don't care. I'm used to it. Why do you think I'm the disgraced royal granddaughter?" She sat back down. "The Terror will be removed from Brightfall's surrounding waters. I will personally ensure economic support is provided for the rebuilding process."

"Mmmm, taste that sweet government welfare. Lucky it takes a monster before they pay attention to us."

"What's your name?" asked Madison, she glanced at Regina's trench coat. "Captain?"

Regina finished her beer. "Regina Claiborne, of the *Tartarus*, at your service, *your grace*."

"Captain Claiborne, you strike me as the kind of person who'd be miserable if you were given the keys to the national bank. I will do what good I can, but I won't take insults to my face because you're using me to vent your pain. Goodday." Maddie gathered her bag, left a substantial tab of fifty Anglo guinee, which in NeoAnglia could go a long way, and went out the door. Several of the patrons at the bar spit in her direction as she passed.

Ekko sighed and felt compelled to follow. She offered a glare to Regina, picking up her scabbard and throwing it over her shoulder. "You interrupted my dinner." Now she was tied up with Madison Warwich. *She hid her name?* As she left, she saw the unrelenting hate in the eyes of the locals. Even the bartender huffed and turned into the kitchen.

I guess it was justified. She couldn't blame anyone for using an alias. The door chimed shut. *She's a princess...* Ekko Ellis, and her half-dozen other names, were wanted by authorities under the Warwich government. She licked her lips, trying to judge if she should run or not.

The night air was growing crisp. The salt wind from the ocean grew colder as the sky was cast in purple and orange. The brilliant sky promised a bad night. The smell of the storm coming off the horizon.

Ellis gulped, thinking about the fleet. They had left so quickly and without forethought. *They really are all gonna die.*

Madison stood by a bench near the wharf, looking out across the harbour. The darkness from the ocean was complete and suffocating.

"Come on," said Ekko. "Let's find a place to stay."

Madison blinked, looking at the cloaked warrior like she was surprised she stayed. "You... never mind. You're right. Let's go."

♦

Madison Warwich and Ekko were rejected at the first two surviving hotels. The third, the one that had been half-destroyed in the attack, was still renting out rooms and didn't refuse when Madison brought out that massive wad of cash.

They were given a small suite. Most of the other rooms had been filled, neighbourly favours to the other victims. Both windows were destroyed and replaced with plywood. The room reeked of smoke. The debris had been cleared away and the sheets changed, but the plumbing didn't work. The survivors carried on as best they could. It was the best place Ellis had stayed since Penn Valley.

"Well," said Madison. "This is... uh... cozy."

Ellis pulled the bottle of whisky from within the folds of her. Madison her gave a look. "What? You *did* pay for it. Help me finish it?"

"Is that all you want...?" said Madison, she looked away, blushing. "Forget I said that." She dropped her bag and took the bottle. She threw back her mane of brown hair and took a long swig of the whisky. She needed the drink after the altercation with Regina.

Ekko felt her heartbeat elevate. She snatched back the bottle and took a swig. The burning amber liquid left the pain in her side a dull memory.

Madison took the bottle and sat on the bed. She felt so small to Ekko. She was trembling since the pub.

"You okay?" asked Ekko

"I will be," said Madison, looking up and taking another sip. "I'll call the Institute in the morning. No one will be answering right now." She'd already said that, but it seemed she needed to tell herself that.

Ekko nodded and took back the whisky. She glanced at the room. A simple suite with a single bed. "I can sleep on the floor, it's better than anything I've had in a while."

"Oh, don't be silly. You can sleep here."

"Are you sure?"

Madison looked up, her eyes very big behind her glasses.

She studied Ekko for about a minute. The two women stood silent. It might have been the whisky, it might have been the stressful day, and it might have even been the anonymity of it too.

Madison stood up and kissed Ekko lightly on the lips.

Ekko stood still for a second. Her heart racing in her chest.

Madison pulled back. "Sorry. I just— I can get a different room it's no trouble. Its—"

Ekko reached out and took off the princess's glasses. Her eyes were just as big. Bright sea green and sparkling. Intelligent and wild. Behind them was a pain, something Ekko recognized whenever she looked in the mirror. She leaned forward, slamming her whisky-glazed lips into Madison's.

Madison wrapped her arms around Ekko's neck. She smelled of salt and seawater. When their embrace broke, they traded the whisky bottle back and forth. Ekko ducked her head, digging under Madison's chin with gentle kisses and bites.

Madison undid Ekko's cloak and then her belt. It fell heavy against the rough carpet. Ekko undid Madison's jeans and pulled them down, revealing a pair of simple men's boxers.

Ekko let out a small laugh.

"Don't give me that look!" said Madison. "They're comfortable in the field."

Ekko kissed her hard. "I know, I'm wearing them too."

Madison laughed and shoved Ekko onto the bed before climbing on and straddling her. The pain in her side, her leg, her arms, all of it melted away. The only sound was their lips smacking together. The smell of destruction, the pain surrounding them both faded away. Ekko flipped Madison under, and they both laughed.

Ekko sat up and began unbuttoning her blood- and dirt-stained flannel. Madison drank the whisky again.

Ekko tossed her flannel and undershirt aside. Madison let out a choked gasp. The scars were there, the pale criss-crossing patchwork of lines, the purple and green bruises from the fight with the Ellis twins, the still fresh stitching and tape on her side. Soiled bandages wrapped around her forearm and thigh. Her necklace felt warm against her skin.

Madison looked up with those big eyes full of concern.

"Kiss me, princess," said Ekko.

"You're sure?"

Ekko dug her nails into Madison's khaki vest. "Yes."

They became lost in each other when the first thunderclap echoed across the town.

◆

When Ekko Ellis woke up, it was just before dawn. Light hadn't yet bled through the edges of the plywood window, but she felt wincing light jab into her brain. She rolled over, wrapped in her cloak she had drawn over herself in the night. Her brain drummed in her head. *Fuck… I didn't drink that much… or did I?* It had become a blur of sensation, lips, teeth, and sweat.

"What time is it?" she groaned, hair a tangled mess.

"Five-fifteen."

"How the fuck are you awake?"

"I couldn't sleep," said Madison's voice.

Ekko blinked several times before sitting up. Madison sat in a chair by a small desk. Open binders, papers and books surrounded her like the battlements of a castle. She wore only a wrinkled t-shirt. She had pulled back her thick brown hair with a bandana. Her eyes were back behind her glasses, scanning documents. The lamp on the desk stung Ekko's frontal lobe.

She rubbed her head. "What are you doing?"

"Reviewing. Notes. Data. My thesis."

And she's supposed to be a princess? Ekko groaned, sitting against the headboard with the cloak covering herself. She reached into her discarded jeans for a cigarette.

"Could you not? Please?"

"No problem." Ellis put it away. She winced when she got up. The gash in her thigh was healing, but now the pain was coming through clearly. She checked the old cut in her side. It hadn't opened, the edges beginning to peel back, revealing re-knit flesh. Soon it would just be another bad memory. Another scar.

Ekko Ellis stood behind Madison. Her rough fingers trailed around the princess's exposed collar. Madison leaned into it and Ekko pulled her into a hug, her eyes trailing over the documents. "Tell me about your thesis."

"It was right after my masters, which was on the pylons we use to keep krakens away from our shipping lanes and ports. It helped stabilize their population in the late eighties when we were on the edge of ecological collapse. I did the twenty-year recheck on the system arguing the need for an upgrade. After that, I wanted... I don't know... something exciting, something with field work. My doctorate was on Kronotitanus, two years in the lab and library, then a year in the field. Managed to join a research ship from Republic of Dominica who were studying off the Yucatan peninsula, working with their own Oceanographic Institute. Naval experience was the big selling point."

"Naval experience? You make it sound so easy."

"*You* make fighting off muggers easy. The Caribbean was beautiful, but being on the ocean and in the jungle had its own trials. Studying monsters is always difficult. Their bodies rarely wash up."

"Don't whales?"

"There's a lot more whales in this world than aquatic predators. We've never found a Kronotitan corpse." She flipped to a page of photos. Distant snapshots of huge crocodilian shadows in open water or titanic hunched monsters in tropical lagoons. "My original thesis idea turned out to be a fool's errand. I was trying to figure out where its hydrogen glands are located, where it gets buoyancy, and where it produces fuel for its fire."

"And nothing?"

"Couldn't find any physical evidence. Dragons have them above the kidneys, behind the stomach... couldn't find anything definitive. Its possible they're located elsewhere. After six months, I ended up writing about their ecology and parenting habits."

Ekko chuckled. "Their parenting habits?"

"Yeah, it's kind of spectacular. The females are very migratory, but return over and over again to the same lagoons and reefs to breed. The males are territorial and keep to their own strips of shoreline and lagoons. They're the ones who stay and guard the nests, rear the hatchlings, protect them until they get big enough. Which usually takes ten to fifteen years given their size and metabolism."

"I can't imagine the monster carrying its babies to the shore."

"Heh, they carry them in their jaws. I know in your world

it was never proven in all aquatic reptiles gave birth to live off-spring, but some continued crawling up on the beaches and—"

A scream howled from outside.

Wide eyes met each other's. They threw on whatever clothes they could find. Ekko strapped on her weapon belt, jumping to get the baldric and belt to sit right. As they ran down the flight of stairs, she checked her revolver.

"Do you think it's another attack?" she asked.

"It couldn't be," said Madison. "Unless the fleet did something really stupid…" She came to a halt, eyes distant as she thought. "I'd forgotten about them. This could be so much worse." They ran down the last hallway towards emergency entrance that now functioned as the front desk. A couple confused and tired heads poked out. Madison slammed into the door. The morning breeze sent chills through Ekko.

The screaming continued towards the beach. The pair ran towards the destroyed boardwalk and the still-smouldering remains of the shops. The white sand was a coarse grain and full of burnt woodchips and broken boards. The water lapped gently against the shore. The water beyond the bay was glass, the horizon invisible as the dawn light grew in the distance, chasing back the night.

"Oh God," said Madison.

A girl sat sobbing on the shore.

A body had washed up on the beach. Covered in sand and seaweed. A dead man, grey haired, maybe fifty years old. Tiny crabs crawled along the body, picking at the soft pieces. His eyes were missing. His open mouth full of sand. The stranger grimaced; this wasn't the first dead body she'd seen, not by a long shot, but this was made worse by the sea and the scavengers.

Her head spun. She saw another body half-buried in sand,

another caught between rocks. Everywhere she looked, more bodies appeared. Another scream echoed from the jetty. More bodies were caught between columns of the docks, sloshing in the waves. Others stuck on boat lines or bobbed in the water. The gulls shrieked, many pecking at the carnage.

Madison leaned by the ruins of the boardwalk, vomiting just out of sight.

Ellis's stomach churned, but she stepped further down the beach. They were from the fleet, but most were unrecognizable. Bodies everywhere, covered in sand, broken, scavenged, and bloated.

Ellis stopped and studied a body further up the shore. "There's someone alive!" she screamed. She knelt. The man blinked, sitting up. It was O'Malley. His clothes were shredded, face caked with sand and burned skin.

Madison recovered, stumbling and running to join Ellis, pulling O'Malley out of the surf.

He mumbled something. Then his eyes shot open. "The beast! The beast!" he screamed, throat hoarse. "It's the devil! The devil itself!" He screamed, a long-terrified howl. His eyes focused on the distance ocean.

"Oh God, help us," whispered Madison.

The stranger followed their eye line to the horizon.

A shudder climbed up her spine. She gasped.

A hulking shadow was visible on the surface of the water, the horizon invisible from the blinding sunlight in the east. Its shoulders and huge reptilian head visible only as a silhouette. It surveyed the town like a lion overseeing its pride lands. It had let the corpses return to the town. The predator marked its territory for future attacks. The stranger knew it would not stop until the town was gone and it had fed upon all it could.

More townsfolk came to the shore, screaming and crying. The bodies of their friends and family nearly unrecognizable. The horror too much to comprehend.

The Terror dove back into the water, returning to the depths in a ripple.

"I need to make a call," said Madison.

♦

"What the fuck is that supposed to mean?" shouted Madison into the phone.

Ekko sat in Lord Joyce's parlour, clutching a cup of coffee. Her cloak hung on a hook. She wore a fresh flannel shirt from the lord's closets under her baldric. They'd even allowed her to use the shower while Madison used their phone.

The muted voice on the line snapped back at Madison. There was a back and forth with Madison, who paced around the parlour with an old beige landline, the wire trailing behind her. It was apparently the more reliable communication with the capital.

Lord Joyce sat sipping his tea with a practiced elegance. His clothes were the same as the previous night, but noticeable wrinkled. His eyes heavy and tired. His coffers and larder had been opened in the morning. From the window a line of shelters and tents were being set up, including a refitted and upgraded medical pavilion and soup station. Madison's words had hit the little town-lord hard enough. When he heard of her royal standing, it likely changed his opinion of the young scientist.

He became insufferably reverent. "Anything you

need, Miss Madison?" "Yes, Miss Madison." "Perhaps tea, Miss Madison."

Madison had stared at him, looking very exhausted, and just said she needed use of his parlour and internet access. She was currently in contact with... someone important. *Maybe her dad?*

"I don't...!" Madison paused as the voice yelled back. "I understand that! These people have been through absolute hell. They're lives have been destroyed! I know! We can't—" The crackle of the voice was too low for Ekko to discern. "I've said it once and I'll say it again, grandma, you're a terrible queen, and grandpa is worse."

She slammed the phone down with an aggressive chime.

"Did you just...?" started Ekko.

"Tell the queen she's terrible at governing? Yes, as a matter of fact, I did. She was a sweet granny when I was little. Then I grew up and realized she's a terrible queen. She and grandpa are in their eighties and still holding political authority. It's lunacy."

Lord Joyce shuffled uncomfortably, probably too close to the reality of his king than he'd like to be.

"Miss Madison," gulped Lord Joyce. "What is the policy of his grace the king?"

"Policy? Ha! As it turns out, the Yarldoms are in the midst of a civil war, and Dunwich and Franco are both on high alert if things escalate. They are *too preoccupied* with a feudal war to concern themselves with one town's monster."

"And Miskatonic?"

"Has nothing to offer. Kraken activity to the northern counties and shipping lanes has diverted our only local Research Vessel..." she sat down with a huff. "Not that the Institute could

196

do much without navy help in this case. The Kronotitan is too big for our only research vessel... all our others are in foreign seas. We need the navy and they aren't budging..."

Lord Joyce paled; his teacup trembled in his hand spilling droplets onto his lapel. "Miss Madison," he steeled himself, setting the saucer and cup on the table. "We've now lost everything. Our businesses, our ships, our livelihoods, and our menfolk. I know you spoke the truth yesterday, and I've done what I can, but my personal reserves have been quite empty for some time. We've nothing left, Miss Madison."

"Not nothing," said Madison. She threw her bag over her shoulder. "Come on. I have one idea."

♦

The door of the White Anchor flew open. All eyes turned to see as Madison of House Warwich, progeny of the crown of NeoAnglia, storm into the pub and march straight up to Regina Claiborne, her steel-nail fingers wrapped around a beer as she ate her breakfast. Ekko watched from bar, hand resting on the hilt of her sword. The entire crowded pub watched.

Madison slid into the booth across from Regina. Their eyes met, intense and humourless. "My friend," said Madison. "Says you'll hunt down the Terror for three thousand dollars?"

"Yeah?" spat Regina.

"I'll pay you six. We leave as soon as you're ready."

Regina slowly sipped a beer. "Are you coming?"

"Absolutely," said Madison. "This isn't some shark or kraken. This is a Kronotitan. I am going with you."

Regina stared for a moment. "Ya ever sail, princess? This ain't—"

"Since I could hold the wheel," said Madison, cutting her off. "Not just pleasure schooners. Twice second, once first in the Moor Sailing Meet. Four years in the royal navy. Navigation officer on the RWS Kingston and RWS Nelson, retired Lieutenant. Two more years on research vessels RSS Searcher and IRV Antilles, plus six field assignments. Would you also like my sixty-plus dives in hours or depth? Anything else... peasant?"

A tense shudder when through the pub. Regina raised her eyebrows, humouring Madison's bite. The Kraken Hunter would not be cowed. She smiled, "Tomorrow, my lady princess."

"Good," said Madison.

"What about her?" said Regina, pointing across the pub at the stranger.

Shit... thought Ekko, realizing what was about to happen. "I have no ship experience."

"Ya got a sword and a gun. You'll be useful." Regina downed her beer and gathered herself up. "Pay the tab, Princess, I'll see ya tomorrow."

♦

With the remaining hours of the day, Madison and Lord Joyce made a dozen calls to anyone who would listen in neighbouring towns, in Grandton, naval outposts, noble houses, Miskatonic University, sailors, anyone who could spare supplies, tools, or information.

The stranger had helped set up tents on Lord Joyce's estate and kept watch with several of the town guard. Bandits were being drawn to the area by the disaster like vultures. The sheriff may have given her a second look, but none offered any threat or hint of familiarity to any bounty. They welcomed the extra hand.

After pitching more shelters, Ellis was offered a bowl of soup at the makeshift soup kitchen tent. Before she sat down, she felt eyes on her.

At a picnic table, that Latin girl who Regina had pointed out in the pub was staring at Madison, watching, studying. Ellis glared back, and the girl returned to pecking at her bowl of soup.

Later, when Ellis was getting Madison something from her boat, the girl was standing on the pier above, fists clenched at her side. Ellis was in the boat, struggling to keep balance as she set a crate on the boards of the dock.

"You and that princess are going after the Terror?" said the girl, eyes intense. Her mahogany hair in a messy tail. She wore second-hand clothes that didn't quite fit. She must have lost everything else in the attack.

"Uh… yeah?"

"I'm coming too."

"Yeah right."

"I'm serious! I'm coming. You can't stop me."

Ellis hauled the other plastic crate onto the dock. "Well for one, yes I can. Two, I don't make that decision. Three, you're an idiot if you think Madison will let you come."

The girl huffed and walked away. Ellis guessed this wouldn't be the end of it.

In the night, Ellis found Madison in Lord Joyce's study. Madison leaned over a desk illuminated by a lamp, pouring over documents and charts. Her phone pressed to her ear.

"Hi dad," said Madison. Ekko stopped in the doorway, listening. Madison rubbed her eyes. "I'm in Brightfall… It's bad here. Really bad. The Kronotitan wrecked everything and when no help came the locals went after it. One man came back... what can you do? Get mom on the horn, get Grandpa Edwin and Uncle Henry to send help. A ship, a crew, supplies anything... Yes. Yes, I know. I know they won't care... Yes, I know..." She grew more and more disappointed. "I know... I know... Can you try? Please. Just try." Her voice cracked. "Thank you, dad. Thank you. Yeah I'm okay. I'll be careful. This isn't my first monster hunt. Yes, I know." She almost laughed. "God, dad, I'm thirty-two...Yes, I'll wear the sunscreen... well I got that from you. Pasty ass..." The stranger stepped back; the floorboard creaked. "Hmm? Thanks, dad, I gotta go. We launch tomorrow. Thanks. I love you. Tell mom? Okay, thanks. Love you, bye."

The stranger didn't ask. She didn't need to know. She'd leave when this was resolved... She didn't need to get involved with Madison's no-doubt complicated life... and Madison didn't need to get involved in the stranger's life. They were worlds apart in so many ways. Ekko Ellis would disappear like a bad memory and only the stranger, lost in this world, would remain. She had her own path to make. *Madison would understand that, right?* With her life as complicated as it was, she didn't need a thrice-wanted wanderer with a big sword around for long.

In the end, a truck arrived with two graduate students off-semester in Grandton. They brought scuba gear and the specialized supplies Madison requested.

At dawn the next day, the light just peaked over the horizon in a strip of gold. The morning breeze played with the final embers of the ruined boardwalk. The sea sloshed against the wharf. The pair arrived at Regina's vessel, the *Tartarus*, at the far end of the jetty. According to the harbourmaster, Regina had been out hunting krakens on the night of the Terror's attack.

We're gonna need a bigger boat, thought Ellis.

It was an ugly little ship, bobbing against the dock with tires hanging off its side. A blue-hulled trawler with *Tartarus* painted in black along the side, its mast and crane swayed with the ebb of the tide. The main deck was clean and tidy, netting and ropes holding down equipment and supplies. Along the rear gunwale were three domed metal shields, covered in sucker marks and scratches.

The stranger stepped onto the vessel. She rubbed her nose at the smell of salt and blood. The deck was stained black from ichor and ink.

"What does she do…?" she asked, looking under her boot.

"She hunts krakens..." said Madison. "It was a proud profession for most of NeoAnglian history, until my Institute developed the E23 pylons in the late-eighties and then deployed them fully in the nineties. Kraken numbers had been falling and it threatened the balance of the entire ecosystem." She knocked on the cabin door. There was a crash and clatter of bottles.

They looked through the window. Laying in a hammock, amongst a disaster of a cabin, lay Regina in the same clothes they had always seen her in, her silver hair a tangled mess. She spooned an empty whisky bottle.

Madison sighed. "This will do."

Regina's eyes shot wide open, and she tumbled out of the hammock in a crash and clatter of bottles. "Alright, mainland bitches!" she shot up. "Let's get this mixed bullshit underway!"

Ekko received Regina's sailing crash course. "Rule number one: do exactly what I say. Rule number two: don't do *anything* unless I tell ya to. Rule number three: see rules one and two. Now get them Jerry cans loaded!"

Ekko sighed and followed the others. Madison and her friends loaded up several metal cases. Regina brushed her teeth with beer and got the engine roaring to life. She glared at the supplies Madison brought. "The fuck ya' bringing onto my boat?"

Madison tied down a chest along the gunwale. "Scuba equipment, weight vests. The works. Along with something else that should help."

"Good to see where my tax goes," called Regina from the bridge. "Fancy toys for noble houses."

Madison's lips went thin, and she ignored the comment.

After a long pause, a smile grew across Regina's face. She began singing to taunt Madison. "Farewell and adieu to you, Spanish ladies. Farewell and adieu, you ladies of Spain!"

They loaded up. Madison hugged the grad students goodbye. They launched out of the harbour. The small bucking vessel passed the lighthouse at the end of the breakwater. The breeze lashed at the flag at the top of the mast.

Regina cackled her shanty, which echoed over the harbour. "We'll rant and we'll roar like true British sailors! We'll rant and we'll roar all on the salt seas!"

◆

PART 2

Hours later, under the blazing sun of the Atlantic, Ekko Ellis leaned over the railing of the NAS *Tartarus*. She looked especially green and certainly felt worse. She brushed her slick black hair from her face. Her cloak was wrapped around her like a poncho. It kept the spray and sun off her, despite the heat.

The hours dragged on with nothing but sea sickness and the tension between Madison and Regina.

"Fucking hell," she groaned. "Why?"

"Nothing cures sick like work," called Regina, who reclined in a chair on the bridge with a half-bottle of whisky. "Give the engine an oil, there's a can below deck."

Ekko nodded and slunk to the cabin. They hadn't found anything yet. Madison circled around the stern with a radar device. Ekko crawled down the ladder into the low cramped hold. She found an oil can and began dabbing the humming gears of the engine. It clearly hadn't been tended to in a while.

The motion of the ship in the dark only made her stomach churn worse. She leaned over and steadied herself. After a moment, the nausea slammed her and she turned around to wrench behind a spare barrel. She held herself up as yellow bile splattered the bottom hull.

When she turned back she met a pair of huge brown eyes.

They both screamed. A wave slammed the boat and knocked Ekko off her feet and the girl from Brightfall from her hiding spot and onto the puddle of bile.

Ekko looked up. "What the are you doing here!"

"Fucking hell!" yelled the girl. "What's wrong with you!?"

Feet scrambled on the deck above. Madison and Regina appeared over the ladder.

"Well," said Regina. "Seems we have a stowaway." She reached down, lifting the girl out by her arm. "What you doing here, Romas? You're supposed to be in town."

"You know her?" said Madison.

"Yeah," said Regina. "Isabel Romas. The damn girl who drove a truck into the Terror."

Romas looked down and away. She must have been sixteen with a small, gorgeous face; her scratches and marks from the attack hadn't fully healed yet, her curly black hair hung around her ears, but her brown eyes blazed with a rage Ekko found very familiar.

"Do you have any idea how dangerous it is that you've done this?" Madison crossed her arms. "What will your parents—?"

"My family is dead," hissed Romas, glaring at Madison. "Don't even start, princess."

Madison's lips went very thin. "Be that as it may, you must have people who are very worried about you."

"There aren't," said Romas. Her words hammered her purpose for stowing away. She wanted revenge for her entire destroyed life. The girl had rammed a car into the monster, but it hadn't saved her family.

"Can we bring her back?" said Madison to Regina.

"We could," said Regina, chewing her toothpick. "But then we'll lose time. Another hand ain't bad."

"She's just a kid!"

"Aye? How old were you when you first sailed?"

"Sailing is not hunting a leviathan."

Madison looked at the girl. The hate from Isabel burned in her eyes. Ekko climbed up, hauling herself into the cabin. "You can always toss her overboard and make her swim back?"

Romas glared, and Madison didn't find it funny either.

"Wow," said Ekko, between unpleasant burps. "Tough crowd. Fact is we can't turn back. We need to keep going and find this thing. Time running back is time wasted."

"Agreed," said Regina.

They looked at Madison. It was her charter. She technically had authority over the decision, despite it being Regina's ship. Though they were sure that Regina would howl if she didn't get her way. "Fine! Fine! Not like we have a choice. What should we get her to do, Captain?"

Regina smiled.

During the following hours, the boat drifted with the current. Romas, in a fresh Hawaiian shirt from Regina's things, spooned chum behind the boat. The girl's burning glare didn't quit but, she threw fish heads and blood into the ocean without complaint. A trail of red followed the ship for several miles, like a winding ribbon of scarlet.

Madison sat in a corner by the cabin, checking equipment, cleaning O-rings and valves.

Regina lounged on the bridge, sharkskin boots resting on metal crate as she sipped her whisky, but remained deadly sober.

Ekko passed the time by cleaning her boot knife, her sword, and her revolver, sitting cross-legged with a tin of oil and a rag. The four women sat in silence as the boat gently swayed across the endless field of water. The only sound was the slap of waves against the hull and the gull that followed them from the harbour. The coast was a paper-thin green line along the western horizon.

Isabel dumped the remains of the bucket over the stern. She had brought a backpack of food, a knife, and binoculars. Regina made quite a joke about using those to kill a monster. She looked up at Regina, who loomed like the sea queen of misery on her throne.

"Can I go up the mast?" asked Isabel.

"Can you?"

The challenge was enough, and the girl climbed up the ladder. After a few moments, she was in the crow's nest. The sun shining off her sweaty face, she scanned the waters with her binoculars.

Ekko ran a whetstone over her sword, the blade scratching and ringing with satisfying rhythms. She eyed the edge. It was stronger and harder than steel, but she still felt it required some regular care to hold the edge.

CLANG!

Ekko almost jumped. Regina had tossed her cutlass onto the deck. It nearly bounced into her lap. "Jesus!" yelped Ekko. "What the fuck, Regina! Warn me next time!"

The captain just chuckled. "Give it some TLC."

Ekko held the sword. It was rusted and caked with ichor all the way to the brass hilt. "You hunt krakens with this?"

"Aye?"

"How the fuck you manage that?" she checked the edge. "I wouldn't use this to cut butter."

Regina leaned forward, looking down on the stranger from the bridge. "Krakens usually only come up at night. They like it where it's deep and dark. At night they come up ta' feed. On moonless nights you can get a lot of them. They'll be talking to each other, flashing red and orange, like a goddamn firework show just under the water." Regina picked at her teeth. "You hunt 'em by getting 'em fast. You hook a couple of barrels to slow 'em down and keep 'em from diving. They're smart, they can rip out the harpoons if ya' aren't fast."

Ekko ran her stone along the blade. The ring was rough and dirty. As much as she wanted to tell Regina to go fuck herself, the boredom was getting to be too much. "How long does that usually take? To catch one."

"My record in ten minutes, but usually about two hours."

"Then what's this for?" asked Ekko, holding up the blade.

"Oh! Sometimes they get handsy, ya' need a curved blade to slash through them effectively. Yours won't do."

"It'll do fine," said Ekko. "Trust me."

"Might be the only thing I trust on this boat," said Regina under her breath.

"Why hunt the krakens?" asked Ekko.

"You don't know much about NeoAnglia, do ya, girl?"

Ekko starred flatly. "They don't give out pamphlets after Exposure."

"Princess!" snapped Regina. "Enlighten our dear Exposed friend."

Madison fiddled with a scuba mask. "Traditionally, NeoAnglia is said to be founded on kraken attacks. Anglo colonists who came to the new world, and got Exposed en route, would arrive on the shores in a new world, but without the support or administration of the British. A lot of those Exposures were from kraken attacks. My ancestors were wrecked on the Isle of Moor. They survived and formed a kingdom with Dunwich as the capital."

Madison looked up at Regina, the tension like static in the hot summer air. "Krakens aren't the problem they used to be. They were attracted to ships thinking they were whales, and, when sailors defended themselves, they got aggressive. So, for three hundred years, we hunted krakens for status, security, and food. By the sixties, it got so bad their population was endangered and ecological collapse was a threat. Throughout the seventies and eighties, they did studies to try and prevent it. The Oceanographic Institute developed the E23 pylons to repel megafauna from major population centres and reserve certain areas as nature preserves. Fish stocks have recovered in part due to that. It made kraken hunters obsolete in Dunwich and Grandton."

"Oh? Well, I'm sorry our little town can't compete with the King's Capital! I think they forgot to add the beacons when they added the extra tax on fuel? Then that zoning crap! Telling me where I can and can't fish."

Madison stared flatly. "If only I had a shilling for every sailor who complained about the nurseries."

"No fisherman on his own trawler ever overfished his coast! It's the goddamn Noble Houses and their fleets of cargo cruisers that overfish! For such an educated princess, ya' sure are stupid. Must be from being stuck in the palace."

Madison's lips went so tight they were invisible. She didn't say another word and went into the cabin to check on some equipment, any argument wouldn't help much here. Regina chuckled before cracking open a fresh beer and mumbling another shanty. "The Dunwich boys, those sweet boys, they'll spread 'em, seed 'em, and forget your name!"

Nothing happened the first day. The sun crept down towards the horizon, turning the sky from orange to purple, the clouds seemed to be burning in the light. The gull nestled in the corner of the pulpit at the prow of the ship. They dropped anchor and ate supper in silence.

Regina cooked up slices of bacon and grilled up some sandwiches with cheese and ketchup. The food sat heavy in their stomachs. Regina gave Ekko a beer. "It ain't a fishing trip without beer."

Everyone was exhausted, but they agreed that a watch was essential. Ekko took the first watch, climbing up into the crow's nest with her cloak flapping around her. She wrapped herself in the black fabric and watched the moonlit horizon. The stars were a cascade of white and blue that went on forever. She'd never seen the Milky Way properly until she was Exposed. The waterfall of diamonds spread from the sky through the water, rippling along the surface.

She'd rather be curled up with Madison. Isabel's sour mood was no help either, and Regina searched for every moment to tease and torment the princess. Four women on one very small boat and they were all at each other's throats. Class, upbringing, house allegiance, and fucking revenge of all these, were driving them apart when they should be working together. There was a monster in these waters and they couldn't be fighting each other when it found them.

The terrifying sway of the mast was all that kept her awake.

The nightmare beneath the waves followed them warily.

♦

The morning came quickly. The eastern horizon blazed as if on fire, promising another scorching day. Regina took them father from the coast. Isabel restarted the chum line. Madison checked and rechecked her equipment in silence before taking piloting shifts with Regina. What little words were said were curt and sour.

Ekko knew she'd have to make the attempt to keep the peace on the ship. Otherwise, they'd kill each other before the Terror had its chance. She approached Isabel at the stern. "I can take a turn."

"I got it!" she snapped.

"Okay, okay," said Ekko. She sat against the gunwale,

fiddling with the shields set between slots. *Must be for kraken to get stuck to when they chop at the arms.* She wondered if kraken tentacles were barbed; the surface of the shields were scored with circular marks and scratches.

She looked back at the Latin girl. Everything Isabel did she did with a noxious fury. She slammed doors, tossed the chum like she was throwing a baseball. The girl was angry, and Ekko couldn't blame her.

"So, who's the ginger boy?" asked Ekko, remembering how she first saw Romas in the streets. How a young man helped her up and guided him away. "He's cute."

"Why do you care?"

"Christ, it's not going to hurt you."

Isabel stared at Ekko for a moment. Her big brown eyes so full of anger, but it barely hid the real pain beneath. "Colm."

"Who's Colm?"

"Why do you care?"

"It's either talk to you, or the two delightful others on this tub," said Ekko, earnestly. Regina lounged on the bridge and Madsion stood off the prow pulpit with a sonar device. "Humour me."

"It doesn't matter," said the girl, throwing another ladleful of chum.

"Why not?"

"What? You think we're actually coming back from this?"

The stranger studied this young girl. Her whole life ahead of her. Wallowing in so much pain and grief. "I think *you* don't want to come back. You think it'll be easier to die out here."

Isabel's full lips clammed shut. "Yeah, so what?"

"So what? You think you're the only person who's lost someone."

Isabel threw the spoon back into the bucket. "I didn't lose someone. I lost *everyone*." Her tears glistened. Her beautiful face twisted with pain. "I haven't even stepped into my parents' house…"

"Where have you been staying?"

"A friend's family let me stay. I would be there or at Colm's. I just couldn't stay." She got up and walked away. She'd had enough reliving her nightmares.

Ekko wanted to pursue. She could help her if she could get through to her. She'd been through it all. Exposure had been brutal for her. Becoming a new person in your loss was sometimes the only option for some, but it wasn't the only option out there. The stranger had been so painfully normal, ungratefully mediocre… now she was a completely different demon.

Ekko got up just as Madison twisted around in the pulpit. She screamed, terrified. "We got—"

The *Tartarus* bucked. Ekko was thrown against the gunwale. Regina fell off her chair. Isabel and Madison both lost their footing. The bucket of chum spilled its disgusting guts all over the deck.

Regina scrambled to her feet, peering into the water. A smile curled on her face. "Found you."

No. He found us.

Ekko recovered and rushed to the starboard side.

In the bright sunlight, the surface of the water shimmered.

They were over deep water, below the sparkling surface was dark blue infinity.

And circling the ship, was the Terror.

Clear just below the surface, the crocodilian monster was enormous, longer than the boat but not as big. The Kronotitan's back was midnight blue and covered in jagged volcanic scales. It swerved elegantly beneath the ship, almost curious. It twirled gracefully underwater. It's underside of dense off-white muscle was marked with stripe patterns. Its belly and chest criss-crossed with scars and the occasional barnacle. Its limbs were like long webbed flippers, but with defined fingers, ankles, and claws. There was no doubt this monster could ravage coastlines across the country.

Isabel pressed against the railing. "How big is that?" she squeaked.

"Nearly eighteen meters—sixty-foot beast," said Regina, dropping from the bridge.

Its elongated snout cut through the water, propelled by its tail and the occasional paddling of its webbed claws.

Madison leaned over the pulpit. She wasn't scared or angry, just in awe, her sea-green eyes wide with wonder. She followed the curve of the beast as it circled the vessel, scrabbling to follow its movement. The beast swam around the prow. Its rocky back breaking the surface. Madison reached out but pulled herself back.

"Alright!" roared Regina. "Time to work for a living, ladies! Princess, on the bridge. Follow my orders exactly! No bullshit! You, sword-lady—"

"Ekko."

"—Yeah—that, you're with me!"

"For what?"

She opened a panel along the cabin wall. She hefty a huge shoulder mounted harpoon-launcher. Not for little barbs, but for hooked spears a meter long. "Romas!" Isabel snapped to attention. "How's your knots?"

"Decent."

"Come on, we got a monster to poke."

There was an eager rush of activity. Madison climbed onto the bridge. The engine roared to life, propellers gurgling below the stern. Regina stood at the tip of the pulpit, holding the harpoon launcher in both hands while Ekko inserted the harpoon into the front. A line of rope ran to the line of barrels on the prow. Isabel tied off the rope and gave them the thumbs up.

Regina grunted, hefting the launcher onto her shoulder, aiming at the water. She primed the weapon, a pressure-gauge rising towards a red "fire ready" level.

The Terror circled the *Tartarus*, the edge of his striped off-white underside just barely visible. He past the boat on an angle. He seemed completely unaware of the danger. *Did he care? Was he certain in his power?* Or was he just an animal, curious why one single ship would come after him?

"Gotcha," hissed Regina.

The harpoon fired with a burst of air, the line twirled and the barbed metal rod struck the Terror in the side, just below the arm. A ribbon of dark blood clouded the water. Its jaws snapped up on the water, letting out a pained hiss. Its throat was a black and pink tunnel, barbs lining its tongue and pallet. A yellow barrel flew from its slot, slapped the surface of the water and skidding on six meters of rope behind the beast.

"Two-thirds, princess!" shouted Regina. "Come on, let's joust the fucker."

Madison followed the orders without a word. She threw the throttle forward. The *Tartarus* jerked into motion. Ekko held her balance against the pulpit rail. They flew past the monster before it could counterattack. They sped ahead as they reloaded.

"He's following us!" shouted Isabel, who leaned over the foredeck railing.

"We pissed him off!" cackled Regina.

They readied the next harpoon. The Terror sped after them, all four limbs and its tail driving it forward after the ship. It swam parallel to the starboard flank, matching the ship's speed.

"Angle port, ten degrees."

The Terror followed their change in direction, just along the ship, as if to bash it from the side. Regina aimed down into the water. The Terror's vivid red eyes visible below the surface. Criss-cross scars along its jaws lined long interlocking rows of teeth. Regina fired, and the harpoon pierced where the shoulder and neck met. It roared. Another barrel flew overboard, skidding next to the other.

"All-ahead full!" yelled Regina. "Port side, forty degrees!"

Isabel screamed. A glow grew in the monster's throat. The *Tartarus* bucked into full speed, the prow skidding against the waves, sending up spray over the pulpit. Ekko blinked away the tears. Heat spread across her face. The *Tartarus* swerved away from a pillar of flame unscathed. The monster roared, steam hissing from between its teeth. Another barrel loosed from the foredeck, trailing behind the monster.

They reloaded the harpoon gun as the Terror lagged behind. The *Tartarus* was small, but its speed is what they needed. This was a dance. A lethal one. One wrong move and they would be at the mercy of the thirty-ton monster.

"Turnabout, port side!" shouted Regina.

Madison stared like she misheard the captain.

"You heard me!"

The *Tartarus* made a full U-turn, lurching to the side so hard everyone had to hang on. They hurtled back towards the Terror. Its long snout sprayed foam as it breached the surface, its back an island of midnight-blue igneous rock. Ekko gripped the rail of the pulpit to stable herself. Her teeth clattered at each buck against the water. Wind and spray whipped her cloak and hair. "You're playing chicken with it?"

Regina ignored the question. Her coat flapped in the wind. Bloodshot eyes narrowed and focused. This was the most sober Ekko had ever seen the kraken hunter.

Isabel tied off the barrel. She looked up, eyes watering and terrified. They were hurtling straight towards the jaws of the monster. Back on the bridge, Madison gripped the wheel with white knuckles, holding course. It wasn't Regina's nerve against the monster. It was Madison's.

Regina leaned into the launcher, searching for her target, but there was nothing but blue scaly armour. The distance closed to a mere dozen meters.

The Terror's jaws opened, and its foreclaws raised out of the water. Webbed paws with knife-length claws reached out to catch the small ship, like a falcon reaching for a rabbit. It was going to catch the ship and break it.

"Got you," hissed Regina.

Anger shone in its eyes and a glow grew in its throat as it swam towards them.

"Shoot!" shouted Madison. She turned the wheel. They

strained to keep balance on the pulpit. Regina fired, but the harpoon bounced off the dark armour on the Terror's shoulder. The ship streamed past the Terror, dodging a fresh pillar of flame. The sea boiled. Ekko dove back, throwing herself over Isabel as the heat slammed into the side of the ship. The *Tartarus* escaped its claws and barrelled away from the monster.

It roared in protest, disappointed, and turned in the water to continue the pursuit. The *Tartarus* sped away until the creature was a mile behind, a dark spot on the sparkling Atlantic plains.

Regina roared, shoving the launcher into Ekko's hands. "I had him! Fucking breast out like a prized whore!"

"He would have scuttled us!" said Madison. "Weren't you watching?!"

"No," said Regina. "You're just a coward. Move over."

Regina turned the ship around, but the Terror was gone. She swore. "Princess! Get up in the crow's nest, maybe those bug eyes will be useful up there. No wonder you're a fucking disgrace. Too dumb for the royals, too yella' for the navy."

Madison muttered something before climbing the mast.

Regina patrolled the *Tartarus* around the area for hours. Another shanty slipped between her clenched teeth. They searched and waited for the monster to resurface. Ekko waited in the caged pulpit with the harpoon launcher, her legs pressed to her chest, alert and terrified at first. Her brain told her the monster would take her whole, but dangling her legs over the water didn't feel right.

Hours passed. The afternoon waned. The sky was an endless burnished orange. A gull sat on the mast, watching. Regina patrolled the ship in circles, endlessly searching for miles until she swore and dropped anchor. "That's enough for today."

The crew retired to another bland supper of cheese and

ham sandwiches. Ekko again drew first watch; she sat on the lip of the bridge over the deck. A cigarette hung between her teeth, the glow scattering shadows across her face. Regina passed out in her hammock; Isabel curled into a ball in the booth around the cabin table.

Madison stepped onto the deck. "If the Terror doesn't kill us, I will throw her overboard myself."

Ekko silently tapped the cigarette. Madison looked up as if she wanted to fight, her big glasses stained with salt. Then she saw Ekko's small smile. They both laughed. Madison looked out across the water. It's cresting waves going on in the distance, forever in the night. The princess stared at the sea longingly.

A question hung on Ekko's lips, and she finally had to ask. "Why does she call you disgraced?"

Madison looked up, eyes confused and hurt. Ekko regretted the question, or maybe just how she said it. It rolled off her tongue and now she couldn't take it back. "I'm sorry. I didn't—"

"No," said Madison. "You have a right to know and I've been dancing around it." She climbed up and sat next to Ekko. They were quiet for a spell, staring out at the glassy water beneath the endless black sky. The stars dazzled unlike anything Ekko had grown up seeing.

"I went into the navy after my bachelor's degree. It is expected of the men in my family, but the women join too. I was going to be the first one to captain a ship if I continued. My aunts and cousins constantly pushed marriage, but luckily my parents had known I was gay for a long time then. They supported me, but knew that if I was out publically… the gentry, the church, everyone would have a field day with me. NeoAnglia is mostly still trapped in regency days: court politics, loveless marriages, lies, and high expectations. I remember when we first got internet and now most children in the gentry have cell phones."

"What happened?"

"I did something stupid..." Ekko sucked on the cigarette, eyes unmoving from Madison. "At my promotion to lieutenant-commander... I gave a speech... that called out the entire admiralty for their complacency and indifference to the sexism and homophobia in the navy... I outed myself publicly... and I did it in front of my family."

"The royal family?"

"Yup," said Madison, almost laughing. "My grandpa, my uncles, everyone. I humiliated the royal family of a weak country. I humiliated the family and things got bad. I got death threats, media take downs, gossip. I found graffiti in my locker at my local gym. Everywhere I went I was slandered. The dyke princess, navy traitor... I quit the navy and... well after a bad time I eventually resumed by studies at Miskatonic. There I could disappear into the work and no one really cared. Miskatonic is like that."

"I'm sorry," said Ekko.

Their eyes met. "I'm not. I patched things with some of my family and my uncle pushed the reforms I argued for." She laughed. "I got to watch an admiral be put on trial for protecting sailors who assaulted one of my friends. I got to watch them all go to fucking Matslock to rot."

Ekko held her face still. She'd been taken to Matslock when she was captured by an earl's militia. She escaped... but only with a riot that levelled a section of the prison. She didn't need to bring her own troubles into this. *I just need to head south.* She reminded herself. *I can't get involved.* She put a hand on Madison's, unable to resist the comforting gesture.

Madison smiled. "So yeah, that's why half the country hates my guts. The other half hates my family for other political reasons. And they *all* hate me because a talkative gay woman shouldn't exist in this country… and Regina… she hates the gentry. It's obvious. I don't blame her. No one chooses where they are born, from fishermen to princesses. I do what little I can and I've destroyed my life once already doing the right thing. If Regina wants to hate me… I can't blame her."

"I don't hate you," said Ekko, kissing Madison, even as she cried at herself, *This is temporary! DON'T!* She couldn't get involved with a princess, especially not one as complicated as this one. *I can't.* She just tasted so good, felt so right.

They broke the embrace. Madison dropped to the deck. "I'm going to get—"

The entire ship lurched to the side. Madison lost her balance and caught herself on the railing.

The Terror's jaws burst out of the water, interlocking teeth spread wide. Ekko reached out, grabbed Madison, and wrenched her to the deck. The jaws snapped just where Madison's head had been, and monster slunk back into the abyss. The ship shuttered beneath their feet, the Terror's back scraping against the hull.

Regina and Isabel burst out of the cabin. Her trench coat was off. Her wiry muscled arms visible, a Royal Navy tattoo emblazoned on her shoulder.

"We're taking on water!" barked Regina. "Princess! Get on the helm and go! Romas! And—whatever the fuck your name is! Come on! We have ta' patch the hull. If the engine floods, we're sitting ducks!"

◆

The night seemed endless in the sweltering hull of the ship. Salt water sprayed them from a dozen leaks and ruptures. The reek of fuel and exhaust suffocated their lungs as the engine roared in their ears. Isabel holding an electric lantern was their only light as they slathered glue and matting down. Their muscles burned as they took turns using a hand pump to clear the water.

Madison drove the ship in a wide erratic patrol, never stopping. The Terror had made its mark on them. One more play in their game of cat-and-mouse across an endless oceanic game table.

At first light, Ekko pulled herself out of the hull, wincing at the sunrise, her face covered in salt, sweat, and grime. She was soaked head to toe and reeked of gasoline. She dropped her sopping wet cloak onto the deck. After helping Isabel out, they stumbled to the side of the boat without even thinking and scrubbed their faces with sea water. It stung a cut on Ekko's cheek. Isabel had become a black ball of messy hair and grime. Tar and strings of mesh stuck to her face. The hull would hold, but barely, like a patched together basket of wood and glue.

The horizon dazzled with gold and silver as the sun rose higher, casting the sky from purple to blue.

They drank greedily from bottles of water. Madison stood on the bridge, leaning forward on the wheel. Her face haggard with heavy bags under her eyes. She had kept watch the entire night, keeping them from danger, reading the sea like a book.

Regina followed, looking pretty much the same as she always had. The grime itself must be what was holding her together. The kraken hunter downed some water before looking up at the Princess. "How we looking?"

"Haven't seen him in three hours. We should be... oh fuck..."

They all turned. Two barrels bobbed up in the water a kilometre away. The land on the horizon just visible as the merest sliver of green. The barrels jerked into motion, trailing behind a shadow in the water.

Regina swore.

"We going to run?" asked Isabel.

The older woman looked at the incoming monster then at the three women aboard. Her eyes narrowed again on the incoming monster, crow's feet deepening. They were all exhausted, drained to the point of collapse. She gritted her teeth. "Fuck. Yeah, we run. We take shifts in partners—"

"No!" snapped Madison, dropping to the deck. "We can't. We can't afford to run and cost more fuel and time. It's called Persistence Hunting. We'll exhaust ourselves until we're dead in the water. Then he'll have us."

"Then what do you have in mind, princess?" said Regina.

Madison pulled one of the metal cases from the starboard gunwale. She popped the lid and spun it around. The broken-down pieces of a gas rifle, several narrow bolts with jagged hooks, a syringe, and a bottle of amber liquid.

"This might just be able to put him down," said Madison. "A neurotoxin, synthesized from Basiliscus Hellas. It can put down bull theropods."

"It won't get through his hide," said Regina.

"I won't be aiming for there."

◆

The *Tartarus* kept a regular pace, just out of distance. The engine sputtered at irregular intervals. Regina worked to keep the old girl going, but the engine would break before they ran out of gas. The Terror swam patiently behind, like a pursuing crocodile, long tail swaying behind the island of his rocky back.

Isabel held the gas rifle while Madison slowly took the syringe and pulled a full measurement of the amber liquid, before depositing it into the spout at the rear of the harpoon. Sweat dripped down her face. Her bandana around her forehead was well soaked. She took the rifle from Isabel and the harpoon clicked into the gun. Madison exhaled.

"How are we going to do this?" said Ekko. "We don't have a cage or anything."

Regina slapped a bolt-action rifle into the stranger's hands, a Lee Enfield, with another resting on her shoulder. "If we piss him off enough, he might open wide." She had her own rifle on her shoulder. "Romas! You're driving! You follow my instructions, exactly. Got it?"

Isabel nodded and scrambled up the ladder.

Madison cocked the harpoon gun. "I just need him to open wide."

"How the hell can we do this when the entire fleet couldn't?" said Isabel.

"Those damn fools wanted to swarm the Terror with numbers. Ram it, shoot it, net it. They wanted to kill the Terror the same way it destroyed the town, with raw rage," said Regina. "We're not playing that game. Warwich, you think this'll work?"

Madison nodded.

"Then let's kill this fucker."

With Isabel on the bridge following Regina's orders, the *Tartarus* made a starboard turn at a slower speed. The Terror angled its pursuit accordingly, which was their plan. Within minutes the Terror was parallel to the ship, the ocean slapped against the hull. Ekko aimed down the sights, blinking through the salt spray. Madison stood behind them, waiting for her chance.

The Terror hurried to close the distance, tail paddling, driving it closer. Its eyes visible just above the waves.

"One clip to the head should piss him off," said Regina. "On my mark."

"I get to sell the teeth, right?" said Ekko. Regina raised an eyebrow. "What? I need the money."

"I'll pay you a tip," said Maddie.

The distance narrowed as the Terror paddled along the *Tartarus*.

"On my mark!" shouted Regina. "Few degrees port side, Miss Romas."

The Terror's split red eyes stared at the women. His nostrils flared with steam. This wasn't a battle, not like what had killed the fleet. This was a duel, a dance between opponents. They were playing this game with the monster. A wave splashed across its armour, and its secondary eyelid blinked.

"Fire!"

The rifles bucked. The first shots missed in sprays of water. They worked the bolts, adjusted accordingly, and fired. Flecks of scale flew off the Terror's armour. They unloaded their magazines, scales flying from its back or biting into the armour. The Terror's jaws snapped open; a gurgling roar echoed across the ocean. Instead of diving, it just took the gunfire.

Ekko narrowed her eyes. She exhaled and fired the last round in her clip.

It slammed into the soft white skin just below its eye. The monster's body shuddered.

"Nice!" said Regina.

"Is this even going to work!?" said Ekko. "He can do this all day. He doesn't care. We're just keeping out of range from wrecking us!"

"Burst of speed for ten seconds, Romas!" shouted Regina. "Then turn starboard and cut the engine. That'll tempt him."

"You crazy?" howled Isabel.

"Yes! Just do it!"

The girl obeyed and they flew ahead, leaving the monster in their spray and the engine sputtered to silence. The Terror closed the distance, tail thrashing with excitement. It was nearly close enough to touch when it dove under, the barrels following. Ekko pushed a fresh clip of cartridges into the rifle.

"All ahead full..." Regina held up a hand. The engine sputtered back to life. Ekko glanced back, praying Regina's play would work. "Now!"

The *Tartarus* bucked forward. The water astern exploded in a geyser of white foam. The Terror's snout shout upwards, snapping where their rudder had been. It had been close. Ekko fired. Bullets chipped off the blue armour, but several made red puncture marks under its jaw. It roared as it sunk back into the water.

"Circle around him, Romas!" Regina reloaded. "Keep your distance. Watch him!"

The *Tartarus* circled, just keeping ahead of the Terror. He swam after, ducking under and trying to surprise them, but with the barrels they could always judge where he was, even if they couldn't keep him from diving. The frustrated monster hissed, steam rising from the water around his mouth. They just needed him to open his mouth wide enough. "Slow us down! On my mark! Punch it!" said Regina as she pulled bolt of her rifle back, dislodging a brass cartridge onto the deck. "Warwich, you better—SHIT."

The Terror dived beneath the water's surface, the two barrels bobbing behind him.

Through the gunfire and Regina's orders, neither had heard the splash of water. They'd been so focused on their dance, they didn't see that Madison wasn't on the deck. A rope hung over the railing, one of the metal cases opened with a small mask and air tank missing.

Madison's boots sat abandoned on the deck, her glasses stuffed into a sock.

"That fucking idiot," hissed Regina.

Ekko immediately kicked off her boots. "A complete idiot."

"You can't go down there!"

"Fuck off," said Ekko, she tightened her belt, baldric, and the holster clip that kept her revolver secured. She pulled one of the shields off the rear gunwale and strapped it to her left arm, leaving the hand free. Its surface scarred and marked from barbed kraken suckers.

Regina hooked a rope to her belt. "It's the best idea we've had. Punch it, Romas! Let's give them some space." The girl nodded and they jerked back into motion. The rope dragged behind them, implying that Madison still weighed it down. *She's not dead yet.* The speed gave them distance from the barrels.

Ekko took a tank and mask, pulling the goggles over her eyes and biting down on the rubber mouthpiece. Regina clipped the tank to her baldric. "The weight of the weapons should balance out the buoyancy. You a good swimmer?"

"No."

Ekko looked at Isabel and Regina. She didn't wait for any

words. She turned and vaulted over the railing and into the water. She slapped the surface and icy tingles went through her entire body. She forced herself to breathe the pressurized air, bubbles streaming past her face until the infinite blue void became clear.

Ekko twisted around, kicking to keep stable while the belt pulled her down.

A short distance away, Madison floated, her rope tail trailing upwards like an extra-long umbilical cord. The *Tartarus* was nothing more than an oblong shadow. They cut the engine and drifted, water slapping the hull was one of the few remaining sounds below the surface.

Bubbles expelled from the regulator. Madison searched in the distance, her legs kicking above bottomless darkness. Ekko's heart drummed in her ears.

In the distance, the Terror approached. An immense shadow in the infinite blue. Its huge body driving forward like a submarine. Its burning coal eyes pierced the darkness. Beams of light from above illuminated the monster, its immense bulk, striped markings, and volcanic scaly back. Its tail swayed from side to side, webbed claws paddling it closer.

Ekko gripped her revolver, drawing it from the holster with the shielded arm. It would be useless in the water unless she was extremely close. She glanced at Madison, her hair swaying in the water like a bundle of kelp. She kicked to balance herself with the harpoon gun in her hands.

The Terror circled them curiously. It was absolutely enormous underwater, a god, or rather a primordial demon. A leviathan predator of distant realms. Ekko forced herself to keep her breathing level even as her pulse raged in her ears. It was an armoured whale circling them, wide webbed limbs paddled with sword-like claws.

It passed under the *Tartarus*, now uninterested in the vessel with two humans treading in the abyss like baited lines.

Ekko raised her revolver and fired. A pop ruptured through the water. Billowing bubbles of gas extended from the long silver barrel; the bullet dropped off into the abyss below. The endless waters were nearly as terrifying as the monster.

The Terror's huge head turned towards the noise.

Come on, you big bastard. Ekko cocked the hammer and fired again. The collapsing air bubbles sent ripples through the water. A curious spark went through the Terror's predatory brain, and it began cruising towards the pair. The water seemed to groan from the titanic carnivore's movement.

Ekko swam awkwardly towards Madison. They floated a few meters from one another. Their eyes met; an entire electric conversation passed unspoken between the pair. They nodded. The Terror paddled towards them at increased speed, excitement visible in its motions.

The Terror hurtled towards them. Bubbles escaped between its interlocking teeth.

Ekko drew her sword. Rays of fractal light danced across it. She bit down on the rebreather and held onto her weapons as tight as she could, readying for impact.

The distance closed. The Terror's greedy eyes narrowed. Its jaws stretched open, revealing a dark tunnel lined with fleshy pink barbs and a flap to keep water from filling its throat.

Madison fired the harpoon-gun. The muted thunk sent the barb through the water and struck the monster on its inner cheek. Its eyes snapped wide as it barrelled towards them, carried by its momentum. Ekko kicked Madison out of the way and raised the shield.

The Terror slammed into Ekko. With the shield caught between its jaws, the rim crumpled. It couldn't close its jaws or rip out the poisoned needle. Its throat poured hot bubbles, roaring and thrashing in the water. Ekko held on so tight the tendons in her hands burned. It drove upwards, light and noise howling around her, and they breached the surface at incredible speeds. Ekko was flying through the air in the monster's jaws.

Below, the *Tartarus* sat. Regina and Isabel stood on the bridge, their mouths wide open.

In the moment of motionlessness Ekko didn't have time to consider her life choices. She reacted fast as they began to fall. The shield began to crumple like paper between the monster's teeth. With her sword she slashed herself free and kicked off the monster's chin. The Terror's jaws snapped shut, crushing the shield.

Fuck me. Ekko expected to be free but was only trapped.

Her line to the boat had been cut and was tangled in one of the harpoons in the monster's flank. She was jerked by her belt into the monster's motion. They crashed back into the water. The surface slapped Ekko's side with stinging pain. The regulator slipped from her mouth. With all her desperate strength, she managed to hang on to her sword and revolver. The cold void embraced the stranger as she was dragged behind the thrashing monster.

The Terror twisted, whipping its tail, and pawing at its snout. It shrieked a stream of super-heated bubbles as the poison began to web through its body. Ekko slashed at her side, cutting the line. The Terror swam off, leaving her behind. She dove downwards just in time to avoid its tail. Its titanic immensity flew past, thrashing its tail and arms as it struggled through the pain.

Ekko swam upwards for air, awkwardly paddling with her weapons. She broke the surface, gasping for air and blinking. She shoved the pistol back in its holster and clipped it shut, freeing her off-hand. There was shouting. Madison was back on the boat. They were screaming and pointing.

Ekko turned.

The Terror was swimming straight for her. Its tail dipped back under the surface, the barrels bobbed loosely in the water, having been cut in the chaos. *Not this time, you bastard.* She gulped a greedy breath of air before she dove back into the water, paddling one-armed with a sword in the other. Her legs burned with kicking.

She spun, searching for the monster in the void.

Then she looked down.

Its jaws wide—the poisoned harpoon still lodged in its cheek—it slammed into Ekko. She caught its mouth with the entire length of the sword. She screamed, driving the tip into the lower jaw and using the hilt to keep the upper jaw from closing. It thrashed in the water with her, blood clouding the water, everything was bubbles and noise.

Its movements became slower, sluggish, and clumsy. Its drunken attack slowed at the surface. Her face found air in the spray and caught a breath.

She put her bare foot on its bottom lip, narrowly avoiding puncturing her foot on the teeth, using the leverage she drove the blade further into its jaws. It roared. A glow began to grow in its cavernous throat. Ekko reacted fast. She took her knife from her belt and slammed it into the top of its head. The blade snapped, leaving a jagged hilt. Without hesitating, she leaped, releasing her sword as she clung to the top of the monster's head, like straddling an upturned canoe. Her face inches from its huge red eyes. *Hello, you fucker.* Super heated air blasted under her legs, but she'd managed to pull herself out of the way just in time. Her sword remained unmarked by the fire-breath.

"Fuck you! Fuck you! Fuck you!" she slammed the broken knife into its eye.

Its roar became a squeal of pain.

She saw the ship on her left through the spray. Then, without warning, the monster dived back into the water. She was weightless, hurtling through the water at a speed threatening to tear her from its face.

It breached up and down, trying to shake her off. It was the worst ride she could imagine, her fingers curled around its teeth as water slammed into her over and over again.

Another spout of flame escaped its jaws, burning Ekko's knuckles. They dove again and she reached for her sword, still lodged in its jaws, keeping its mouth pried open. Her teeth clattered as it breached the surface again. *Fuck me too.* She switched her position, like a wrestler maneuvering around an opponent, one hand always clutching a fang. She reached down into the toothy maw. She felt the hot grip of her sword, the leather on the handle burnt away. The silver and black metal remained unblemished by the monster's breath.

Then, all at once, she leaped from the monster, wrenching her sword from its jaws. She had a moment of perfect clarity as she clutched her sword, falling through the air. The hot metal of the grip burned her hand, but she couldn't let herself lose the sword to the depths. That sword was all she had in this world.

She slapped the surface of the water, cold embracing her. When she came up, a life preserver slapped the water next to her. She hooked her arm in the loop and felt herself dragged through the water.

She assumed the others hauled her exhausted body to the *Tartarus*. The adrenaline slammed in her chest and drummed in her ears, and she tingled with exhaustion. The sword clattered on the deck. Her chest heaved as she gasped for air, her body trembling, she spat out sea water.

Madison and Isabel stood over her, their faces relieved and terrified.

"It's coming back!" screamed Regina, harpoon in hand.

The ship jolted; Isabel screamed. The Terror's huge head smashed into the stern, smashing the gunwale and the shields. Its eye a blinded bloody mess. Regina threw the harpoon at the Terror, right through its lower jaw. It roared, firing a blind jet of flame into the air before sinking back into the water.

The four watched as it breached the water surrounding them, thrashing, and twisting in pain. It slowed, then eventually stopped coming to the surface, the activity forcing the poison through its body faster and faster.

Madison rushed for her sonar equipment. The others watched over her shoulder as the whirling electronic showed an oval mass near the vessel. It grew fainter and fainter until it vanished from range.

After a long moment's pause, they all began laughing. Cathartic, hysteric laughs. The stranger's entire body vibrated from the adrenaline. Laughing was the only response to almost dying. The Terror was no more and all they could do was laugh. Isabel was laughing tears and collapsed next to the gunwale. Regina braced herself against the cabin door, cackling laughter like a wild animal.

Ekko and Madison collapsed on the deck, howling with exhausted laughter.

♦

They anchored in the shallows once it got dark. Regina didn't want to pull in a rush, despite all they'd been through. They were forced to stay one more night out at sea. The four women sat around the booth in the cabin, Ekko with bandages over her burnt knuckles and a dozen other fresh cuts.

Regina pulled several fresh lobsters out of a nearby trap, melted down butter, and brought out two bottles of chardonnay.

"Oh, real fucking funny," hissed Madison.

Regina popped the cork. "This is a celebration, don't get your lace knickers in the twist."

"They ain't lace," said Ekko with a sly smile, pouring a glass of wine. They all laughed, except Madison.

"Why so sour, Warwich?" said Regina.

"Why do you hate me?" said the princess, flatly.

"Oh please. You're—"

"It's not just that I'm wealthy or that I'm a royal. You have a special hate for me." Madison stood up. "We were both in the Royal Navy. Have *that* common respect and tell me why."

A long silence hung between the two women. Isabel and Ekko were hostages to their conversation. Both stared at the steaming lobsters with mouth-watering anticipation and growling stomachs. Then looked back up at the electric tension between the scientist-princess and the kraken-hunter.

Regina sighed. "Fine." She sat down and combed her silver hair with her fingers. "When I did my two tours with the King's Navy, I was a good king's girl. I fought for the Warwichs. I fought Franco, I fought pirates, I fought monsters, I fought rebels. I believed in my country and my king. I thought the world would be better if this country could unite properly. I still do after a fashion."

"And what? Did your officers leave you behind? King

abandoned you?" said Madison. She was speaking from her own experience, her own betrayal by the navy and her family.

"Let me speak, princess. After my two tours, I retired on my pension. I needed to start my life. I used what I knew and began hunting krakens, Jesus, this must have been the seventies at that point, right before when the coastal stocks got bad. I got married, had a son." She reached into her pocket and placed a crumpled photograph on the table.

It was of a much younger Regina, her skin smooth and tanned, and chestnut hair around her shoulders. Her arms wrapped around a Black man with salt and pepper hair. Between them was a baby in blue blankets.

"By the time my boy was three," said Regina, her voice flat. "We needed the vaccines. The king promised us vaccines. Our doctor wrote, our lord wrote, I wrote! I wrote to the admiral! Then year by year, no shipment came. A lot like when that tit Lord Joyce called for aid after the attack... Just like everything else, we were forgotten by Dunwich and the Royal Warwichs."

Regina sipped the wine. After a long pause she finally said, "Eventually, the measles got him, along with six other tykes in town. My husband left shortly after. Said there were too many memories and all I wanted to do was hide out at sea. Which I guess was true." She slipped the photograph back in her pocket. "And you know what I saw a week after he left?" she said, "This was over twenty years ago, probably closer to thirty actually." Madison gasped and Regina continued. "Christ, does time fly. My boy would be grown by now, maybe even married. I might have been a grandma by now."

Madison was shaking. Her face was red, lips thin as paper, her hands hidden under the table. Ekko wanted to hold Madison's hand, but couldn't. She couldn't get involved. She would be leaving after this. *I can't keep getting close.*

"A ship came into the harbour," said Regina. "A nice sailing vessel. You know who was on that boat?"

Madison looked up, her eyes on the verge of tears. "Me."

"Aye, the king's sons were on a day trip. With the grandchildren of the king in attendance. They looked so fine in their summer clothes." Regina poured wine into a tin cup. "You looked like a perfect little doll in that little white dress. What were you? Six at the time. Same age as my boy ought to have been."

Silence hung in the air.

"But today…" said Regina, pouring everyone a cup of wine, even Isabel. "I saw you jump straight into open water with only a leviathan for company. I can't forgive the Warwichs or any of the fucking gentry. They can all rot and the country would be better for it. But, for tonight, I think I can get drunk with a princess."

"FINALLY!" said Isabel, taking the cup and gulping the wine. From within her bag, she pulled out a baggy of paper rolled joints and a lighter. The older women gave her a look. "What? Just because you're all old. I've earned it."

"Someone's optimistic," said Ekko.

"You know," said Isabel, holding the blunt between her teeth. "I saw both of you jump into that water. You looked scared and you did it anyways. Maybe I've been scared too. Maybe you were right. If you could be that brave, I can be brave enough to keep living."

They then proceeded to get very drunk.

Regina started the songs. "We'll roll the old chariot along—" and Madison joined in, her cheeks red.

♦

And when they were very drunk, Isabel, despite herself, passed out. After a full meal of lobster meat and wine, coupled with the exhaustion and adrenaline, she fell asleep in the booth. The others moved onto the prow.

Madison threw back her head, finishing her wine, her cheeks hot and red. The moon hung in the sky; the stars cascaded across the black infinity. Ekko blinked through her buzz. *Finally,* she thought, a *moment to breathe.* She hadn't felt a calm like this since her few weeks scavenging for the gremlin in Penn Valley.

Regina leaned in the pulpit, a beer in hand.

"Where are you headed after this?" asked Madison, her face very flushed.

"I—" said Ekko. "I need to head south."

"What for?"

Ekko avoided the topic by snatching the wine.

"Come on," cooed Madison. "Where are you going?"

This was not a conversation to have drunk. Ekko needed to continue south. She had played this conversation a million times in her head. She wasn't Ekko Ellis, she was just another lost Exposed stranger, a wanderer. She had lost her home, her identity, everything. She had to find the men who did this. She needed to find the men who carried the black-bladed swords. But she kept moving her fucking mouth.

"You could come north," cooed Madison. "I can help—"

"Madison, stop," said Ekko. "You don't know a thing about me. You don't know what I've done or where I'm going."

"Then tell me!" She saw the hurt on Madison's face and stopped. Her big green eyes confused and very drunk.

"No! I... for the love of... I can't get involved with someone like you," her words spilled out like an open faucet. "You don't understand." It was Ekko's poor attempt to cut her off.

"How can I understand if you don't tell me," said Madison. "If it was just a fling, then fine, that's alright, but don't say you're done with me because we live in different worlds." Madison's eyes pleaded.

The poor brilliant beloved girl. Madison Warwich. This beautiful disgraced princess. She didn't know about the bounty put on Ekko's head by her family's government, the things she'd done to escape, to survive. She'd hurt people, she'd killed people, and they deserved it, or at least they put the stranger in a position where she had to. Ekko saw that personal familiarity, and worse, attachment. She should never have gotten involved the way she did. It had felt good. Safe. And now she just wanted to run. *She can't know what I really am. A killer, a broken murderer.* She struggled for the words. *I'm just another monster she found fascinating.*

"I..." She met Regina's eyes. The captain stood awkwardly, the unsaid was understood.

Regina faked a yawn. "Well, would you look at the time—"

From beneath the pulpit burst a pair of huge, teethed jaws. Ivory spikes on both sides of metal railing. They snapped shut, crunching metal. Regina vanished in an instant. The Terror's single red eye stared at the pair of screaming women.

Ekko whipped out her revolver, hammering the full six chambers in a repeated flash of gunfire. It did nothing more than chip away some flakes of blue scales before the Terror sunk back into the waves. The water was pitch black.

"GO—!"

It was all too late. The *Tartarus* bucked, and the hull cracked and burst.

◆

PART 3

Ekko Ellis jolted awake. She rolled over and coughed up sea water. Pain webbed through her entire body, and she groaned, clawing at sharp gravely pebbles to pull herself out of the surf. She lay on the shore surrounded by debris from the destroyed *Tartarus*.

She coughed again, wiping sand from her face. Her breathing fell to a slow easy rhythm as she attempted to centre herself.

She reached down, searching for her weapons. Her belt was gone. Sword gone. Gun gone. She didn't have the time to mourn the loss of her only companions in this world. She sat up in the sand and tried to remember what had happened. There was a blur of roars, fire and screaming. Once Ekko hit the water, she lost track of everything. Her body fell into the instinctual motions of survival until she blacked out.

She looked around, trying to find any familiarity.

The sky was a carpet of low grey clouds. The beach was a calm archipelago, reaching out into the shallows from the ragged coastal cliffs. Along the pebbly beach were boulders, arches and mesas of eroded stone that must have once been a part of the cliffs, all slick with algae and reeking of low tide. Scattered across the beach was the debris and skeletons of wrecked ships. *The rest of the destroyed fleet.* It was a sad grey graveyard of a fisherman's fleet with the half shells of hulls, broken cabin windows, off-set masts, and shredded sails. Gulls squawked, searching the wreckage.

Ekko groaned as she climbed to her feet. She was missing her boots and her jeans were shredded. Everything hurt. She checked herself for major injuries. The bandages on her forearms had fallen away, and her cuts were exposed and dirty, but uninfected. She touched her side and thigh, both still closed. Somehow. Her muscles howled from whatever she had done to survive.

She looked around, the destruction of the ship lay about her.

"Hello!" she called. No one answered. "Hello?!"

She began walking towards the cliffs.

"Hello?!"

The mission to kill the Terror was over. Nothing could stop that creature. Brightfall was its new buffet. No one knew how long it would be until Dunwich was able to send help. A ship, a crew, a batch of monster killers. Would bandits fall on the town? Would mercenaries extort them when they had nothing left? Would they be left to suffer? To fall by the wayside and vanish like so many other forgotten places in this world?

Between sections of scorched wood, a leg stuck out. Pale bare foot and a calf emblazoned with a kawaii Great White Shark. Ekko rushed forward "Maddie? Maddie! C'mon, princess. Madison we got—!"

Ekko stopped. Revulsion filled her stomach.

It was just a leg.

She turned away, bracing herself against a rock.

She retched up stinging yellow bile.

Guilt crept into her bones. *She was just trying to help me. I spat in her face.* That brilliant, beautiful woman. Now just a leg, half-buried in the sand. Nothing above the knee, showing that beautiful artwork that showed just how much the princess loved the ocean and all its creatures. It didn't seem right. It wasn't fair that the things she loved killed her. *It's always the things we love.*

She moved to hurry down the beach. She needed to get help.

The waves exploded behind Ekko. Like a reverse avalanche, the Terror rose out of the sea, its huge head covered in scars and bloody gashes. It rose onto its rear legs like an angry god. Water spilled down its snout, shoulders, and back. The woman, the stranger, tiny in the face of the Kronotitan, starred up with unimaginable horror.

She forced movement into her legs and dashed for cover behind a boulder.

The Terror surveyed the archipelago with its one red eye. It lumbered forward, each step shaking the ground, and its webbed paws hung at its sides, heavy tail holding its balance. Ekko glanced up from her hiding spot, her heart pounding. The monster was just above her with flaring nostrils.

She dashed for the next boulder, gasping for air. She tried to get her breathing under control, but her body wouldn't answer.

The Terror's quaking roar echoed across the shoreline. Ekko clapped her hands over ears. It snapped its tail, sending a boulder flying into the water with a violent splash.

Breathe. Think. Plan. She told herself. She inched around the boulder as the Terror dropped onto all fours with an echoing crash, its boat-sized head about seven feet off the ground. Its snout peered around the boulder; Ekko slunk lower, trying to stay out of its half-blinded vision.

Across the beach, she saw a small figure waving at her. Isabel Romas leaned out from behind a pillar of stone.

Ekko licked her lips, looking for an avenue. The hot smell of blood raised her eyes to the shadow growing over her. The monster's snout was a meter above her. Its massive forelimbs gripped the boulder and blocked her direct route to Isabel.

She picked up a stone and lobbed it away. The clatter echoed against a distant boulder.

The Terror's head snapped around and it lumbered away to investigate the sound. Each heavy footfall quaked the archipelago and threw up clouds of pebbly sand. Its tail slammed the boulder sideways, forcing Ekko to duck. She scrambled to her feet and bolted for Isabel. Her bare feet stung with pain from the sharp peddles.

She slid behind the pillar just as the Terror wheeled around to continue its search.

Ekko grabbed Isabel by the shoulders. The girl was alive, a cut on her forehead, her hair matted with sand, and her clothes shredded to rags, but alive. "You're okay?" She hugged the girl.

"I'm... okay?" she said it as a question, a surprise. "What are we going to do?"

"I don't know," said Ekko, peaking around the cover to make sure the monster was still elsewhere. "If we run, it'll get us. If we stay, it'll find us. I don't have my sword."

"Yes, you do," said Isabel, reaching behind her and holding up the tattered belt and baldric. "Found it in the sand."

"How did it not sink?"

"I don't know," said Isabel. "God gave us one thing? It'll help?"

Ekko nodded. Her scabbard was caked with salt and her revolver was full of sand. She grabbed the belt and snapped it on. The baldric was torn, and she broke it free and tossed it aside. She drew the sword; the unreflective black metal was the most calming thing in the world given the circumstances. It was completely un-harmed by the elements.

"It'll help," said the stranger. "Thank you." Crashes snapped her to attention and she whispered. "Go."

They rushed behind the metal prow of a broken trawler as the Terror's snout came into view. Its flaring top-facing nostrils smoked. The movement of tiny human creatures outside the water frustrated the massive predator. It roared, a pillar of flame erupting from its jaws, scalding the rock of its moisture and algae, leaving only steaming bare stone.

That's it, thought the stranger. Her mind rushed to every-thing Madison had said about the creature. She bit back the pain in her throat when she thought about the night together… and focused on what Madison had said about its biology. *It's a false dragon.* "We need to burst its glands."

"What?"

The pair hurried to a further rock, keeping low and mov-ing quick. Behind another pillar Ekko whispered. "Madison talked about how it has glands that fuel its fire. It uses it to breathe fire. If we can light it—"

"Boom," squeaked the girl. "I get it, how the hell can we—?"

Ekko glanced around the rocks. "Go go!" she hissed, and they dashed behind another rock. Where they had just been hiding was smashed into the beach, shattered by the frustrated monster. It reared up on its thick hind legs and let out an ear-shaking roar.

Both women clapped their hands over their ears. Ekko glanced around the corner of the rock, the Terror loomed overhead searching the garden of arches and mesas. Madison had said that she theorized that the glands were above the kidneys. That meant Ekko had to get behind the monster.

"Listen," whispered Ekko to Isabel as she checked the revolver, clearing the grit with a few quick blows into the chamber. "I need you to distract it. Just run as hard as you can. Save your shots, you have four. Hide. I need to get around to its back. I'm gonna need your lighter."

She handed her revolver to the girl. Isabel held the heavy firearm like it was radioactive. "I— I—can't."

"Hey, hey," Ekko took the girl's face in her hands. "We won't be able to run. It'll catch us, then it'll raze Brightfall to the ground. We need to kill it, or at least wound it."

Isabel found her courage and nodded. She handed over the lighter.

"Now go," hissed the stranger, gripping the lighter, checking it twice to make sure it still ignited.

Isabel nodded and ran. Ekko breathed, forcing her heart rate down. *Like water*, she said to herself. *Relax.* She looked at her sword with its silver leaping wolves crossguard. The indestructible blade of mysterious black metal. *You'll be able to cut its armour. You always have.*

A minute later, a gunshot echoed. The Terror roared and began lumbering away.

Ekko dashed out from behind the mesa of rock. The Terror was facing away, reared up on its hind legs and stomping forward. Its huge heavy tail cutting a trench in the sand. Isabel was a tiny figure running towards the cliffs. She was fast and agile, able to gain distance between her and the monster. Isabel fired again; the report thundered across the beach.

Ekko, running, leaped over the end of the tail and past its

tree-trunk legs. The monster didn't see her with its missing eye and its rage focused on Romas. She scrambled up heaps of shipwreck debris, then on to a triangle-shaped boulder, sword in hand. The monsters huge volcanic backside rippled and undulated with each heavy step.

Like water. She flipped her sword into a reverse grip.

She launched herself at the monster, screaming as she flew with her weapon aimed for its lower back. She slammed into the monster, the blade puncturing through its armour. Dark blood seeped out of the gash and streamed down Ekko's arms. The Terror howled. Its back seizing, it twisted and spun, unable to reach with its claws. It must have been that spot on its back it could never scratch.

Using the sword like a gymnast bar she adjusted her position and braced her feet in the crags of its scales. Through the epidermal armour, the sword had punctured something. A hot sticky smell flooded her senses. *Please be whatever Madison was talking about.* The Terror thrashed and spun, trying to dislodge her. Her hair whipped in her face, but Ekko managed to hold on—compared to the ocean, this was nothing.

Using her braced legs, Ekko pried open the gash. Blood seeped out, but not as much as Ekko would have expected. With a foot braced on the opening of the gash, she dug into the monster's flesh. Hot and sticky, dark blood flooded the gash. She forced the sword in as she was nearly ripped off by hurricane forces. She felt the sword scrape bone and puncture something leathery. *Please be it. Please be it.*

She looked over her shoulder and screamed.

The monster crashed through an eroded arch, shattering it like a child stomping through a sandcastle.

Ekko held on, rubble rolling off her shoulders. The monster had missed the parasite on its back.

She wrenched open the gash, with her free hand she flicked the lighter on and plunged it into the gaping wound. In a brilliant motion, she kicked off the monster's back, loosening the sword from the armour and fell backwards towards the sand. She landed hard, her spine and lungs howled.

She didn't know what she was waiting for, but nothing happened. The Terror turned and roared at her. She scrambled to her feet and ran. It charged after her with lumbering steps and outstretched clawed hands.

Fuck. FUCK. The lighter wasn't strong enough.

She dove behind a rock just as a spout of flame erupted from the Terror's jaws. Heat blew past Ekko, her wet hair steamed from the heat, the oxygen in the air vanished. She cowered behind the rock, covering her face and struggling to breathe or see.

A gunshot echoed.

The flames died. The Terror turned and roared at Isabel. She fired again, her last round, striking the Terror in the chin, chipping off a piece of flesh from its already deeply scarred snout. Isabel bolted, running for cover.

When Ekko opened her eyes, she saw a ship's emergency kit amongst the graveyard of shipwrecks.

She dove for it and ripped open the red plastic case. There was medical equipment and, more importantly, a pair of flares. She stuffed both into her belt.

The monster continued towards the cliffs. Isabel was sprinting from cover to cover with the Terror lumbering after her until she dove through a hole in a rock and into a tide pool. The monster leaned down, trying to see where the little prey had gone.

A scream echoed back at Ekko.

She ran after the monster, feet slapping the sharp pebbly beach, blood seeping from cuts on the soles of her feet. There was no rock or wreckage to launch from; she was left with no alternative. She put a flare in her teeth and scrambled up its broad swaying tail, leaping up its thrashing tail and then grabbing onto the crags in its armoured back. Its huge claws dug at the rocks where Isabel hid, shearing off limestone in sheets. Isabel screamed. Ekko couldn't see her, but she must have been trapped. Ekko climbed up the rough outcroppings of the monster's back, rough as the face of a volcano. A trail of black blood led back to the seeping gash.

When Ekko reached the wound, its shuttering reek gushing out with yellowish liquid, she lit the flare on the monster's back. With its burning red light, she jammed it into the wound as far as she could reach. Blood streamed over her front and face.

Unable to reach further, she let go and dropped from the Terror. She rolled when she hit the beach; sand clung to her. Her eyes were tiny white circles in a face covered in dark blood.

Again, nothing happened. The Terror was completely unbothered by the flare in its back. It continued to claw at the honeycombed cenote, pulling up sheets of rock perfectly formed by centuries of erosion. It belched a tongue of flame into the pool. Isabel screamed, ducking into the water.

Madison's hypothesis was wrong.

Where could those glands be? This was not the time for scientific exploration, but she didn't have a choice.

Ekko brushed the blood and sand from her face. She narrowed her eyes, scanning the creature as it attacked. It breathed a fresh spout of fire... but as it did so she saw it flex down its ribs with each gust of flame, like it was squeezing its diaphragm or the equivalent. The hydrogen glands weren't on its back above the

245

kidneys. They were above its stomach closer to its sides. Just under the armpits.

Isabel was still trapped by the monster and Ekko had to save her.

Ekko grabbed a rock and lobbed it at the Terror's head. It struck just under its remaining eye. Its huge head winced, it turned and roared at the human.

Got your attention now, you bastard.

Ekko bolted and the Terror lumbered after her on its rear legs. It kicked up rocks and broke through pillars boulders and ship debris. Now she had its attention. *But how the hell am I going to dig into its armpit?* she thought as she dove behind a rock, feeling the jet of fire around her. She held her breath this time.

Along the beach, was the scattered carcasses of ships leading to a huge, eroded arc of rock. It was bigger than the Kronotitan and just beyond the opening was the broken half of the *Tartarus*. The tangles of rigging and ropes wrapped and criss-crossed around the mast with its damaged crow's nest. The bars of metal so warped and broken it was like a curled claw of steel.

Consider the weapons of others. Consider your environment. Consider your enemy. She followed the ropes to a harpoon lodged in the sand and found her plan.

The fires evaporated and the shadow of the Terror loomed over Ekko. She dove forward, avoiding its claws, which threw up a cloud of pebbly sand. She bolted, pushing her legs against the sand, the soles of her feet stinging. Over her shoulder she saw the monster barrelling towards her, quaking the ground with heavy ponderous steps. The Kronotitan was not meant to walk on its hind legs. It did it so as a bear did: to reach, to look, and to intimidate. It threw itself forward, carried by its weight and momentum with only its heavy tail keeping it upright.

Ekko flew towards the arch, picking up the harpoon mid-step. The titan closed the distance as it gained momentum, shouldering through a rocky mesa and leaving it a mess of rubble.

Come on. Come on. She forced her legs to move faster over the unreliable ground, each step either sinking into the pebbles or finding the sharp edge of a broken shell. She flew under the arch and towards the wreckage, the harpoon in hand. Instinct took over her actions, the clarity of such intense focus that she found in her darkest moments. She found a cord she needed, wrenched it three times to get the appropriate slack and tied it to the harpoon with one of the knots Regina had shown her.

The Terror roared, closing the distance between it and the arch.

"Come here, you bastard," said Ekko. She raised the harpoon, her muscles winding up with energy like a coiled spring. She narrowed her eyes, focused on the monster, on its open jaws set with interlocking teeth meant for capturing prey in the ocean, its awkward webbed claws outstretched, and its hobbling bear-like gate.

She hurled the harpoon overhead, muscles exploding with the force.

The harpoon sailed over the arch and slammed into the monster's breast, the blubbery white underbelly striped with dark blue markings. Blood leaked down its chest, but the harpoon held.

The plan worked.

As the monster stomped through the arch, the lines snapped tight. Ekko jumped back as the debris and ropes flew out around the mast. Cords twanged and broke. The immense force of the monster's charge pulled the ropes tight, using the arch of water-slicked stone as a pulley-system. The Terror created its own impalement.

With a shudder and a groan, the rigging hoisted up the mast like a spear, flicking up sand and grit. The tip of the mast's broken crow's nest was a warped bundle of galvanized metal, like an immense harpoon stuck in the sand.

Got you.

The Terror couldn't even conceive of what had happened. Its weight carried it into the huge spear, sticking into its chest, metal and wood splintering in its off-white flesh with the echoing crash of a thunderclap. Ribbons of dark blood splattered its blue-black stripes.

The Terror could have died from the sheer shock of damage, but it was still alive and with plenty of fight left. It roared and thrashed, half-impaled by a ship's mast, burying the wreckage deeper into its front, tearing its belly through layers of blubber and flesh. Its scissoring jaws snapped, and its webbed claws pawed to free itself, but it only succeeded in tangling its paws in the rigging.

Down the beach, Isabel was visible, soaking head to toe; she must have ducked into a tide pool to stay alive. She looked aghast at what the stranger had pulled off.

Ekko drew her sword and slashed off a cord of the rigging that was still wrapped around the stone arch above. Her eyes met Isabel's as she laced the cord through her belt and over her shoulder, pulling a quick knot tight. She was scared, hell, they both were. *Run, girl. Just run.* Ekko breathed and let her world fall away. Her legs fired, feet numb with pain as they slapped the face of the mast, carrying her up with a sword in hand. The Terror, unable to retreat from its position with its big awkward frame, clawed at the mast, shearing off pieces of wood. It would break free if Ekko didn't finish this.

Ekko ran up the mast, facing the monster alone. It roared, a glow growing from within its throat. She knew what was coming. She exhaled and dove off the mast, the flames splattering where she's been, scorching the wood. Using the rope hanging over the arch, she flew under the monster's arms. She threw herself forward in an arc and slammed into its side, just below its armpit, her free hand digging her fingers into its scaly armour.

Before the Terror could react, she roared and drove her sword deep into its side. Blood covered her face. The sword edge scraped bone and punctured leathery organs, and there was an immediate thick smell of rotten eggs.

Again, using the sword as a handhold, she bit of the cap of the last flare and lit it on the edge of her sword. It burst into smoking red light.

Before she could plunge it into the open wound, the Terror's opposite arm reached around and grabbed her by the waist, webbed paw curled around her, gripping her with the force of an industrial claw. She tried to hang onto her sword, but the monster was too strong. Her blood-slicked fingers slipped from the grip and wrenched away.

"NO!" she screamed.

The Terror raised her up to its remaining eye, an orb like a glowing coal, full of soulless hate. The stranger had nothing, no weapon, no gun, and only the burning flare in her grip.

It raised Ekko towards its mouth. Lines of bloody saliva stretched between its jaws and Ekko faced down its throat lined with fleshy backwards facing barbs. Pressure ballooned in her ears as its grip tightened. She raised the flare and screamed, nothing more than defiance in the face of death. Screaming into the void was sometimes all you had in the end.

A gunshot fired, glancing the Terror on the soft flesh of its lower jaw. It raised its head.

Ekko looked back, expecting Isabel with a weapon—

Madison Warwich leaned against a rock, a bolt-action rifle in her hand. She cocked the mechanism, aimed down the sight, and fired. The bullet tore through the gash under its arm pit.

The Terror's remaining eye went wide.

An explosion burst out of the Terror's armpit. Blood and scorched flesh scattered across the wet sand. The Terror's right arm fell with a crash. Its rib cage was exposed, off-white belly burning at the edges, with half its throat open like dark red plumbing. Its single red eye rolled back into its skull.

Its claws went limp. Ekko fell, nearly weightless for a moment, and slammed into sand. Her lungs seized, and she gasped as she watched the Terror as it teetered backwards, groaning like a leaning building, before falling to the ground with a thunderous crash, water and sand spraying off the impact. Its entire body sagged, steam hissing from its wounds and smoke from its mouth.

The Terror was dead.

Ekko groaned, sitting up, rubbing her head. Her back ached; her lungs howled. Her eyes shot open. "Maddie!"

Isabel was running through the stone arch, avoiding hunks of burnt monster flesh. Madison collapsed against a hunk of debris, covered in scratches, her clothes torn. The biggest thing was her leg. Her left leg, slashed clean off below the knee, was wrapped in Madison's khaki vest and cinched with a crude tourniquet of fishing line.

Ekko scooped up the princess. Madison's sea-green eyes fluttered on the edge of unconsciousness. "That was a good shot."

"Yeah," said Ekko. "Best shot I've ever seen." When she looked beneath the crude tourniquet; she gasped. It was an ugly wound covered in sand and salt. There was risk of shock and infection. *By all the dumb gods of this world she is strong.* Madison needed medical attention or she would die out here. Ekko replaced the fabric with her own shirt and her belt. *I have nothing to clean it. God.* "Isabel! Get the medical kit!" The girl ran off to find the

"I guess my thesis was wrong," whispered Madison.

"Yup," said Ekko as her and Isabel picked Madison up. "Dead wrong. Keep talking!"

"Hydrogen-sulphide..." started Madison, voice hazy. "Produced from digestion and gathered into glands... weightless and explosive. Controls buoyancy, offers lift... breathes it out as fire..."

Isabel returned with a medical kit. They cleaned the wound as best they could, using iodine and fresh bandages. Madison winced. "I'm okay, really."

"Fuck you are," said the stranger. She and Isabel began to carry Madison. They would have to move quickly to get to Brightfall. Did they even know the way? Isabel would, she would have to.

"I guess I finally get that Kronotitan specimen..." Maddie's voice was slurred.

"Yup. Big nasty burnt to hell. Stay awake!

They hurried down the beach, leaving behind the titan's corpse. Its smouldering body was left to the crabs and scavengers.

"I..." blubbered Madison. "I actually—" Her voice petered off.

"Stay awake!" shouted Ekko. She threw Madison on her back and told Isabel to guide them towards town. They hurried, each step driven by desperation. "Stay awake! Just stay awake, Maddie! Keep talking!"

"You're so beautiful... you know that?—"

♦

Ekko stood in the entrance of the medical tent, half-naked, injured, and dirty. She looked like she had been through a hurricane. A local surgeon and a volunteer nurse knelt over Madison. They worked away trying to pump her system full of their remaining antibiotics. The infection was the real threat now. She had survived the shock. Now they needed to fight the infection and prevent sepsis. Isabel sat next to the princess, holding her hand. Madison was breathing—unconscious, but breathing.

Lord Joyce came down the estate grounds with an attendant. The blueberry-shaped man ran faster than expected; his face was red and sweaty. He was about to talk when his face went bone white at the sight of the princess.

"The Terror is dead," said Ekko, flatly.

"Oh my god, bless you, but the princess?" stuttered the little man. "Will she…?"

"I need the money I was promised," said Ekko, grabbing the lord's wrist. "Regina Claiborne is dead. I get one third now."

Lord Joyce froze, confused, eyes snapping back and forth between Madison and the stranger. He struggled for words.

"Now!" hissed the stranger.

He nodded; eyes wide. He held out a hand to his attended who handed over a few dozen large Anglo bills. The stranger just snatched them and began walking away. By the thickness, it wasn't the amount owed, but it was more than enough for what she needed. She began walking towards the harbour, her sword and gun on each hip, a shirt from a volunteer over her scarred body.

Isabel ran after her. "Where are you going?!" she shouted.

"I need to go."

"What—What about Madison!? Where are you going?!"

"I need to go."

Isabel looked so confused. Her small face covered in grime, hair a tangled mess. "You're just running! Leaving after everything?!"

"I need to go."

The stranger continued down the road, ignoring Isabel's protests. She had a pocket full of cash for fresh clothes and supplies. She could charter a ship southward and be done with this bloody country.

NeoAnglia could rot for all she cared.

As she hurried towards the harbour, trying to find a willing captain, she kept reliving the half-day march trying to keep Madison alive. The battle with the Terror had been horrible, brutal, and bloody. Her legs were still caked with darkened blood.

But none of it was half as terrifying as carrying the half-dead princess mile after mile. Every gasp and shudder of her small body was a terror the stranger hadn't asked for. She couldn't enter Madison's life like that. The stranger was wanted, a bounty on her head, a danger to everyone around her. The princess was better off without her. They all would be. This nightmare would pass from the town, and they would rebuild.

The stranger, nameless, vanished around a corner towards the harbour in search of her vessel southwards.

She continued her journey alone.

—The End—

WILD THINGS

Winter, 14,000 BCE—Northern Europe

The ancestors of the Dwyr spoke of the tall ones who drove them into the mountains. The elders said that was why they grew short, stocky, and hairy, like rocks and moss.

Noa followed her mate, Barr, through the snowy forest. There were eighteen of their clan, all short and covered in coarse brown hair. They were hardy enough to survive the winter age without fire or flint. The small creatures spread out amongst the trees, the old and young kept safe in the center of the group. The clan clung to the shores of the great ice mounts that made up the north of their world.

They were marching to the mountains where they would be safe for winter, after a summer foraging in the lowlands. As inhospitable as the mountains were, the Dwyr could survive better amongst the rocks than warring against the tall ones. They were safe in the mountains and caves, where they could hide from the tall ones and the mammoth-eaters. They only left in the summers to hunt game and meet with other Dwyr clans.

Noa clung to a bone-tipped spear. She had rabbit and bison furs wrapped around her shoulders and legs, and her face was covered in thick curly hair. Barr's face-fur reached to his chest and had started to whiten. He walked with a sharp spear and carried a flint chopper in his corded belt.

The Dwyr had so many enemies; The vermin-ones, the wakened dead, the tall ones, the mammoth-eaters, the will of the gods.

Ahead, Herka, snorted a command to halt.

The entire clan froze, the centre of young and old folded

in like wings of a bird. Noag, Kiab, and Lo, all hunters, closed in around their most vulnerable.

Noa and Barr crept forward to Herka's position. Their feet—wrapped in leather and laced cord—crunched softly in the snow. Herka pointed with his crooked arm. The Dwyr were strong and could live with injuries that killed tall ones, Herka survived, crooked and bent.

Through the trees, like black stalks in the snow, a shadow moved.

They stalked forward, two other hunters pushed forward with them, spreading out. Noa held out her spear, her hands trembling with fear. She looked over her shoulder, checking the clan and scanning for predators with her beetle-black eyes beneath her heavy brow. She and Barr had lost their young son the previous winter.

A jingle around her neck made Herka hiss a silencing command.

Noa nodded, slipping the shell necklace into her furs. The wind blew against her woolly face, the face-fur of the other hunters swayed. The females' thick sideburns and face-fur rarely grew so long.

Noa realized they were down wind as a thick musk filled her wide nose.

Whatever the shadow was, it hadn't noticed them.

They dropped to the ground as they reached the edge of the treeline that bordered the trail ahead. Noa felt snow seeping through the gaps of her furs. They crawled silently, pulling their small hairy forms towards the trail. Noa felt a hidden stick snap mutely in the snow. She froze, praying to the ancestors that nothing heard them. She looked towards Herka and saw him peer out from behind a tree.

All six hunters peered at the lumbering beast.

It was a huge horned rhino, nearly blind and up wind. The clan had managed to stumble nearly on top of it. It's hairy shoulders like mossy boulders shook to clear snow from its back. It drove its oak-like horn against a tree with the echoing crackle of breaking bark.

Herka waved the others over.

The beast would feed them for much of the winter. The gods and ancestors had been merciful to them. On their long march to their winter home, when birds, grubs, roots, and bark sustained them, they found a great prey.

Now they just needed to kill it.

Herka whistled a bird call and gestured for Noa, Barr, and another hunter to slip behind the beast. They nodded and got to their feet, they crept low and quick, their short legs making it difficult to clear the snow.

They encircled the rhino, but before they could make a signal to attack, a branch snapped. One of the children and ran up to see what was amiss.

The rhino looked up, eyes meeting Herka's. It only took a second before it charged.

Herka grunted and threw his spear, planting it in the rhino's shoulder. Herka leaped out of the way, but the other hunters weren't so fast. They were thrown sideways before they could thrust their spears.

Noa and Barr charged, jamming their bone-tipped spears into the rhino's hindquarters. It brayed, kicking its back legs and spinning. Before Barr could react, the rhino slammed its huge head into him, knocking him clear back into the trees. Noa fell backwards. She rolled away as the rhino swung its horn, bellowing at its attackers. Two hunters had recovered and rushed forward with their spears, planting them into the rhino's flank.

Noa looked back and saw Barr on the ground, covered in snow and pine needles. He clutched his chest, groaning. She ran to him to check his wounds and pulled up his face-fur and skins, seeing the already deep purple bruising across his chest.

He grunted, reaching for her.

The rhino, three spears hanging from its flesh and spilling blood onto the ground, charged towards the immobile pair.

Frosted fear shot up Noa's spine. She was stuck to the ground, her hands searching for her spear but unable to find it. The others screamed for her to move or run. Herka ran forward, driving another spear into the beast, but was thrown off. The rhino carried on by its momentum.

Noa's thick fingers wrapped around the haft of Barr's axe. Its wooden handle and flint-knapped head wrapped with leather and glued with resin.

She acted. She screamed and leaped forward with the axe, slamming it into the rhino's head. She felt the flint sink into the bone of its eye socket, cracking to pieces, but not before it pierced its brain. Brain dead but still carried on by its charge, the rhino threw Noa back. Her thick head cracked against a tree.

Dazed and dizzy, when she she looked up her mouth hung open.

The rhino had slumped onto its side, steam rising from its hulking frame. The frost on its fur glittered. Its hot blood pooled across the snow.

Noa got up and rushed over to Barr. The rhino had stopped barely a foot from him.

He groaned and tried to get up, wheezing from his cracked lips. She hooted and called over to the clan, and Old Mother, the elder, immediately knelt next to Barr. Her curt words did not give Noa any hope. She shoved herbs into Barr's mouth, but the pain was too much, and he spat it out. As Old Mother lifted his skins, they saw that the bruising had become far worse.. They rolled him over, despite his screams, and found that a branch had pierced his back and into his lung.

He wheezed, tears filling his eyes.

As hardy as they were, the Dwyr were not invincible.

◆

They butchered the rhino and carried it in pieces to a familiar cave. Barr died in the night clutching Noa's hand. She cried and clung to him as his body went cold.

Old Mother knelt next to Noa and pulled her away, whispering soft noises to calm her.

This cave was familiar to them. They'd used it for decades in their wanderings and had been forced to lay others there before.

They brought Barr's body to the deepest chambers. Noa was half-carried by Old Mother as Herka and Lo shouldered Barr's body. Weeping echoed through the halls as the rest of the clan mourned for their fallen kin. Torches flickered as they were led deeper into the mountainside.

They entered the chamber where two others were already preparing Barr's final resting place. They'd hacked off the spears of stone that grew in the caves like fungi and piled them in a ring.

The walls of the chamber were covered in drawings from their ancestors, which the elders added to every year.

They laid Barr in the ring of broken stone, setting a new axe, spear, and dagger with him. They left flowers and herbs to keep the worst of the rot away. He would be ready for the next world, armed and ready for whatever dangers the gods had in store for him.

Long songs were sung, deep and rumbling like the very roots of the mountains. Eventually the clan would need to move on; they were still so far away from their winter home.

Noa reached into her skins and, with a quick jerk, freed her shell and bone necklace. She looked at it for a long time, seeing the care that Barr had put into it. They lost their son and now Noa had lost Barr.

She felt the tears coming again and knelt to her mate. She kissed his head and laid the necklace in front of his face. She left him to his journey, praying the ancestors and the gods would keep him safe.

The last of the torch light vanished, leaving Barr's body to its solitary vigil. In the walls, gems began to shimmer. Without the light of torches to crowd out the light of the gems, they shimmered with the images of their ancestors. In their hidden light, they carried Barr to the next world.

Noa sat outside the cave, crying to herself alone. Herka grunted when others went to comfort her, saying she needed to work through it herself. They ate their fire-roasted meat in fatty chunks, tearing it from the bone with broad, hardened teeth.

Noa clung to herself, legs curled up to her chest. Her hairy cheeks covered in tears. A spear sat next to her, but she wouldn't have a chance to reach for it if she was ambushed. She didn't care. She'd scream to warn the others, but she just wanted to die. She wanted to be with Barr and their son. She just wanted to be free of the pain and the cold. She wanted the sweet sleep that Barr now had.

A branch crunched.

Noa looked up. Eyes ringed red and wet.

From the trees below the cave, she saw a shadow. It was a huge, tall one. Taller than a bear on its hind legs, long-limbed and thick-headed. In its fist it carried a club made from a tree trunk. Its huge hairy form was covered in entire mammoth skins. Its deep black eyes shimmered like rocks in a stream.

They stared at each other. She closed her eyes. She just wanted to sleep. She just wanted to be with Barr. Behind her the glow within the cave hinted at the clan within.

The tall one exhaled, breath pouring like a fog. It shook its head and wandered off.

Noa watched its huge form vanish into the trees.

Maybe the tall one knew what her pain was. Maybe it thought a clan was better left alone. It didn't matter. Noa lived a long life after.

1977 by Gregorian–Danish Coastline

Neanderthals never went extinct; many were absorbed into homo sapiens while many more were forced north into the glacial plains and steppes. There they split into Homo Veredus and Homo Maximums, Stocky Man and Biggest Man, Dwarves and Giants, wrote Gudfinna Noddottir.

Gudfinna sat at a varnished plywood table beneath a canvas pavilion. Around her were tables of equipment, plastic cabinets, and the general chaos of a dig site in full swing. She scribbled her notes as a stream of consciousness, not with the full scientific picture. They still had so much work to do.

She glanced at a book that had been translated from Jotunheim. There, Jotnar scientists were making progress unlocking their own history just as the dwarves were doing the same. The similarities between giant and dwarf skeletons had been known since the eighteenth century, despite the political and social pushback it caused.

She continued to scribble, only glancing out of the pavilion towards the slope of the mountain periodically. She imagined her short hairy ancestors climbing the mountain.

We will wait on genetic evidence to prove the hypothesis, but even preliminary examinations show the commonalities between ancient dwarven skeletons and ancient giants. She put down her pen and leaned back, stretching. She wore expedition clothes, a field vest and short denim slacks. She was four-nine and a hundred and eighty pounds on a good day. By human standards, that would be cause for concern, but, for a dwarven woman with only a thimble-full of human ancestry, she was almost underweight.

She got up and headed back to the site. The camp clung to the mountainside on a plain of rock and moss, trees below spreading out before becoming grassy fields, and then the shores of the Baltic.

She climbed through the cave, which was illuminated by a long cable of lights. Along the winding tunnel were dwarves, humans, and even an elf or two brushing away detritus and making records of everything they saw.

Neanderthals were traditionally thought to have gone extinct forty-thousand years ago, giving way to humans, dwarves, elves, and other hominids. This site, however, was dated to before the end of the last ice age when so much of northern Europe remained glacial plains.

She reached the rear cave where more students and researchers worked. In the centre of the cave were hundreds of stalagmites and stalactites broken off and scattered in concentric rings.

Dwarves could breed successfully with humans, once upon a time. Gudfinna was evidence of that, but there were still so many questions. How did elves fit into this? What about halflings and gnomes? When did giants split off from Neanderthals? Some fled into the mountains of Europe while others spread into the mammoth steppe.

So many questions.

In the middle of one ring, a skeleton lay curled up, blessed by the gods that they would one day be found by Prussian hikers.

The skeleton had yet to be sexed and examined properly. A camera flashed, casting stark shadows across the gravesite. A student from Albion, Cowyr Griffin, an elf with long blonde hair and exceptionally large, pointed ears, stood over the skeleton.

"Amazing," said Cowyr.

"They are," said Gudfinna.

"What do you think happened?"

"We still have a lot of research to do before we can even come close to theorizing."

"What do you hope happened to them?"

"I hope they were loved," said Gudfinna, kneeling just outside the tapped-off area. "I hope their hard life was made easier by the ones they held close at night. I hope there were some good days mixed amongst the harsh cold winters and dangerous hunts."

She smiled down at the body. Dwarves, historically, worshipped ancestors with a cultic ferocity, making them exceptionally conservative. She hoped that this one would approve of their work, and she hoped they would be proud that their story could be shared.

The skeleton lay on its side with its hands beneath its cheek, which could only be achieved by someone laying the body down intentionally. In that crook of the arms were a collection of shells and bones with telltale holes for a necklace.

And above the graves, across the domed roof of the cavern, were thousands of paintings. Ochre and soot images of mammoths, rhinos, wyrms, trolls, deer, bears, lions, and wolves.

Then, the most interesting of them all was a small drawing in a lower corner.

It featured the curled-up dwarf looking away, which was a strange image. There was no action, no hunting pose, no reference point. Next to the curled-up dwarf was a huge thick figure. It wasn't a stick figure like so many other hominid self-portraits. This was painted the way they painted the animals, with faded ochre and outlines of dark soot.

It was still early, but Gudfinna couldn't imagine anything else. A small interaction between dwarves and giants. No violence, no clan-against-clan images, no evidence of early warfare between the two lines of Neanderthals. Just two beings sharing a moment.

A moment frozen in time.

A moment of mutual recognition.

A moment of empathy.

That was her theory anyways.

—*The End*—

AFTERWORD

That was an adventure.

Since the beginning of the pandemic in 2020, I released four books in four years. Each built off each other and taught me a lot about writing, publishing, and myself. I learned how to scare myself and inspire others. We've all had to learn a new meaning for inner strength, for when things are hard in a big dramatic way, but also when things are hard in a slow, drawn-out "daily grind" way.

I write this after many months of struggle. I thought the pandemic had been hard, that was nothing compared to the last year of mental health struggle, economic uncertainty, strife, loss and pain amongst friends and family.

Fantasy offers us an escape that can often be disparaged as fleeing from reality, but I disagree. From Terry Pratchett arguing that fantasy is required in the fight for abstract concepts of justice and solidarity, to David Mamet and others believing humans tell stories as a matter of our fundamental humanity: we tell stories to give our minds a break from reality. We tell these dark stories, like horror stories, because it is freeing; it gives us space to process our reality and its darkness. What is weird is often what lets us process our pain.

I write these because this is how it can often feel in my brain — a mix of a screaming beast and snarling swordsman. The booming footfalls of a titan hits the same place in my heart as a deep echoing guitar rift. At no point, however, do I forget that there is still the fight for a better, more just and equal world.

How can I begin to express my appreciation to everyone who helped me along? Well, I should probably name them.

My family: Mom, Dad, Sarah, Josh, now added with Justin, Juli, Charlie and Claire.

My partner Rheann: my love, my silly, who found me halfway through this and is now my other half.

My friends and colleagues: Kellie Huynh, Sarah Doran, Quin Houdayer, Malak Abas, Jacob Davis, Ashley Kay, Anna Borren, Phillip Bollman and Shannon Penner.

All the local writers, artists and various scribblers who have contributed to these books or guided me through all these hurdles: Steven Kaul, Lyndon Radechenka, Angela C. Hebert, Gregory "GMB" Chomichuk, Adam Petrash, and Emma Maione. A special thanks to those who made this collection happen: Kyla Neufeld as editor, Nyco Rudolph for his art and once again, my long-suffering friend and graphic designer Chloe Brown.

For anyone who had to dig themselves out of a dark place and for everyone who helped me do so. For the dark places we hide in order to find the light. For the wild part in all of us, the beast, the monster, the barbarian.

To all the readers who have made it this far, I hope these have helped you as much as creating them helped me.

-Z. F. Sigurdson, October 2024

♦

BOOKS. CRAFTS. ODDITIES.

Z. F. Sigurdson is Winnipeg writer, creator and crafter of Icelandic, Russian, Ukrainian and Jewish heritage. He graduated University of Manitoba in 2017 where he studied Politics and History. A long time Viking-Age Reenactor with an immense passion for strategy games, medieval crafts and old movies. He lives with his partner and their dog and will be moving to Iceland for Fall 2025 to continue his education.